The Aristocracy Of Caddo County

Also by Keith Remer

Killing Bardoe, Book One of the Calamitous Breed Trilogy
Blood City, Book Two of the Calamitous Breed Trilogy
The Hiding Place of Thunder

The Aristocracy Of Caddo County

by

KEITH REMER

Honey Lee Press
Oklahoma City, OK

The Aristocracy of Caddo County
All Rights Reserved
Copyright © 2019 by Keith Remer

First Honey Lee Press trade paperback edition June 2019
Manufactured in the United States of America
10 9 8 7 6 5 4 3 2 1

Print ISBN 978-0-9998532-7-6
EBook ISBN 978-0-9998532-8-3
Library of Congress Control Number: 2019905472

For my long-time friend,

Dr. Bruce Stafford,

who believed in me during times

when others thought I'd lost my mind.

ANADARKO, OKLAHOMA

Self-named, "Indian Capital of the Nation," Anadarko is a rare town even in Oklahoma because the vast majority of its citizens are Native Americans. Comanche, Apache, Caddo, Wichita, Kiowa, and Delaware are the major Indian Nations that populate the area.

Some have assimilated fully to the white man's culture.

Some never will.

Prologue

ANADARKO
1980'S

Troy spotted Woop leaning against the bricked outer-wall of the gymnasium. He engaged his coolest walk to approach Woop, who was smoking a cigarette he'd no doubt stolen from his old man.

The much smaller of the two, Troy looked up at the dark-skinned classmate. "Seniors are going to be waiting for Red when he gets out of school today."

"Yeah? So what?" Woop exhaled along with a plume of smoke.

"Probably going to need our help."

"Of course he does, but why would we help?"

"He makes us laugh."

Woop turned his head to look off in the distance and seemed to consider the fact. After a few seconds he turned back to Troy. He took the last long drag off the cigarette and then flipped it away. "Yeah, guess we should go find those assholes Junior and Gabe."

* * *

Red swatted at the hand that suddenly gripped the nape of his neck. He struggled only a second before being swarmed by four other much larger boys. *Seniors.*

"Hey! What the hell, gentlemen?" he squealed.

"We're tired of your smart-assed mouth, boy. Gonna teach you some respect for your elders," the senior who had him by the neck hissed in his ear.

"Whoa, man, I'm just the joking type. It's what I do best."

"You can mouth your shit at other Freshman, but you won't be mouthing it at us anymore," growled a pimple-faced senior who moved to get in his face. "Let's take him over to the arena, Sam," pimple-face said to the guy holding Red by the neck.

"No, not the arena," Red pleaded. No true arena existed, but only a clearing in a wooded space just outside the school grounds. Kids called it the arena because it served as a place where those with differences met to slug them out. Red put up his most fierce resistance for about fifty-yards, but had simply given into his fate as they reached the edge of the woods. He knew three of his captors by their last names. Along the way he learned from Jackson, Wright, Boykin, and Sam, that the one with pimples was Tony.

It only took minutes for them to get Red to the clearing. He'd lowered his eyes to stare helplessly at his feet when Wright said, "Who are those guys?

"Just more punk-assed freshmen," Boykin replied.

Red raised his eyes, and pride suddenly swelled in his narrow chest. "Punk-assed freshmen my ass. That's the Four Horsemen, and you butt-wipes are in for one hell of a hurt."

"The four what?" Sam growled.

"Horsemen," Red grinned. "Like the Four Horsemen of the Apocalypse. Yup, and they are going to rain down destruction upon you pricks!"

"Why you call them that?" Tony-The-Pimpled snickered.

"I gave them the name. They all work together on a ranch in the afternoons. Not a horse born they can't ride, and they're four of the baddest dudes you'll ever encounter."

"Just more punk-assed freshmen," Boykin repeated, but this time with laughter. The other four laughed as well.

Red watched as his four classmates strode confidently up to within feet of the seniors. Red considered the four to be his friends, but had not yet fully convinced anyone of them of such. Still, here they were coming to his rescue.

"Best just let Red go," Gabe, the largest of the four, said in a relaxed manner.

"We're now so scared," Sam responded, "that we'll do just that. After we kick his ass."

"We won't let that happen," Junior snarled.

"You won't? How are you going to stop it from happening?" Boykin mocked.

Woop took a step up. "We're going to kick your ass."

"Really?" Sam asked. "Two Indians, a midget, and a hunk of fat are going to whip the five of us?"

Sam and his cohorts joined in another round of laughter, but cut it short when the one they obviously referred to as a midget, Troy, bolted in their direction.

Woop and Gabe grabbed the seemingly rabid Troy to hold him in place.

"Let me go, you bastards! I'll whip their five asses all by myself!"

Red glanced around at the faces of the seniors. They seemed more than mildly impressed that it seemed all Gabe and Woop could do to hold back the small but maniacal-acting Troy.

Junior jumped in front of the Gabe, Woop, and the nearly slobbering Troy. "Bullshit! Call me a hunk of fat? I'll be the one to whip their asses!"

Just as Junior stepped forward to launch his attack, Gabe freed an arm from Troy and grabbed Junior by his shirt collar.

What followed would have surprised just about anyone, except Red. He'd studied the four for some time now, and could have bet this would be the outcome. Junior wheeled about and slugged Gabe right in the forehead. Gabe stumbled backwards into Woop, who loosened his grip on Troy. Troy managed to swivel in Woop's arms enough to bring up a knee into Woop's balls. Gabe regained his footing and dove into Junior, and both went to the ground.

Troy's first knee had served to double Woop over. The smallest of the group planted his other knee square in Woop's face. Troy now in full frenzy, started stomping on Gabe and Junior as they grappled on the ground. Woop, bleeding from the nose and maybe even both lips, latched onto Troy, lifted him in the air and slammed him down on top of Junior and Gabe. In the next few seconds, all four of them were tangled on the ground in a flurry of punches, kicks, bites, and scratches while emitting foul language threatening to maim and murder. Red felt the hand on his neck fall away.

"These sons of bitches are crazy," one of the seniors gasped.

"More viscous than any animal I've ever encountered," said another.

One by one, the older boys slipped back into the woods leaving Red still standing. Knowing he could do no more, Red took a seat on the ground. Someday, he swore, he'd find a way to repay the Four

Horsemen for saving him from a beating. For now, he'd just sit and study them a little longer.

ANADARKO
Present Day

Chapter One

Tom Barnes held Betty in front of him with one hand gripping her right ear. He used his other hand to insert the barrel of a large revolver into her left ear. She tensed, but did not struggle.

"You two come any closer and I'll shoot this bitch right through the brain," Barnes bellowed.

Stub Mobley waved his one complete arm wildly in the air over his head and screamed at the top of his voice, "Sheriff Preston, stop him! Don't let him murder Betty!"

"Tom is not going to shoot Betty, Stub, so just settle down," Preston ordered. "And, Tom, what have I told you about standing in your front yard naked?"

"I ain't naked," Barnes objected, "Got my boots on."

"Yup, but all your ugly stuff is showing, Tom Barnes, and I'm taking you in this time for it. Toss down that gun, let Betty go, and get your bare ass in my car," Preston emphasized with a snarl.

"I'll go to jail, but I'm shooting this trouble making she devil," Barnes snarled back.

Preston noted that Betty seemed confused about the situation at hand.

"Oh, Lord Jesus! Shoot the stupid bastard before he shoots Betty," Stub screamed, bringing the stump of his other arm into the waiving frenzy.

Preston threw two good arms into the air. "Now, just settle down, boys. Tom, what did Betty do this time to get you so pissed off?"

"She shit in my yard again," Barnes huffed.

"Stub," Preston moaned, "I think I'll take you to jail with Tom, and put Betty in the pound. I'm tired of this bullshit."

"Oh, Sheriff, I can't control where my dog goes when she has to go. Besides, a couple of dog turds would only make this place look better."

Preston looked around the trash-strewn yard in front of Barnes' dilapidated shanty and could only nod to confirm the point. Still, the Sheriff of Caddo County had better things to do than referee yet another argument between Tom Barnes and Stub Mobley over the bitch Betty.

"Okay, Tom, here's what I'm going to do if you don't turn over the gun, let the dog go, and get in the back seat of my cruiser," Preston said with a grin. "I'm going to tell my Uncle Troy and my Uncle Gabe that you called them both a couple of sissy fags."

"But I didn't, and I'd never! I ain't no idiot," Barnes howled.

"They'd believe me over you, Tom."

Barnes evidently agreed because he tossed the gun aside, let go of Betty's ear, and started toward the Caddo county car wearing nothing but his pair of scuffed old boots.

"You don't have any other weapons in those boots or between the sagging cheeks of your ass do you, Tom?" Preston called to him.

"Want 'a frisk me, Sheriff?" Barnes hollered over his bare and bony shoulder.

"Last thing I want to do, Tom," Preston snickered.

Once Barnes shut himself into the back of the cruiser, Preston turned toward Stub. "Now what am I going to do with you?"

"Anything that don't involve your two uncles or the other two of the Four Horsemen," Stub said with utmost seriousness. "But, I'd rather not ride to the county jail sitting next to a naked man."

"All right, Stub, you take your dog and get the hell next door. If me or one of my deputies are called here one more time this month, you're going to jail."

"Yes, ma'am, Sheriff Preston. I'll do my best to keep Betty shitting in her own yard."

Melody Preston ran freshly manicured nails through her thick red hair and wondered if any job could fulfill her as much as putting smelly naked men in jail.

* * *

"Why don't you just pack up your belongings and get the hell out of my house?"

Sadie Saupitty held an index finger in the air and responded to the suggestion, "You hold that thought, and I'll be right back."

She tried to control her anger as she stomped into their master bedroom and straight to the closet. After retrieving what she wanted, Sadie stomped right back into the living room and leveled the double-barreled 12 gauge to point at her husband's broad chest.

"I'll tell you what, Saupitty, you son of a bitch, why don't you pack your belongings and get the hell out of *my house*." When angry, Sadie never addressed her husband by his first name.

"Don't threaten me, woman. You've pointed guns at me too many times in the past," Gabe Saupitty growled. "I might just take that away from you and beat your flat ass with it."

"Why don't you try it, big boy? And for the record, my ass ain't all that flat for a Cherokee, you Apache son of a bitch. "

Gabe's eyes narrowed to ugly slits beneath the brim of his work-stained and dusty black cowboy hat. "Mixed blood, that's the problem. I'd been better off marrying a white woman over a Cherokee."

"You should have thought about that nearly thirty-years ago, Saupitty. Besides, any white woman you'd gotten back then would have been fat and ugly like you are now," Sadie said, jabbing the shotgun at him for emphasis.

Gabe growled like a bear and pounded one beefy fist into the palm of his other hand. "Goddamn, I wish you could be a man for just two minutes. That's all it would take."

Sadie could not help but cackle. "How many times have you said that same shit over the years? And every time you say it, I see something in them mean eyes that tells me you really don't want those two minutes. 'Cause you know as tough as I am as a woman, I'd tear you apart as a man."

"Bullshit!"

"Better yet, Saupitty, remember that thing you did to me when we were young? I told you I didn't want you to, but you did it anyway? If I was a man, I'd bend you over our kitchen table and do the same to you."

Sadie noticed Gabe's shoulders slump just a tad, and he turned his gaze to the floor at his booted feet.

"That was a long, long time ago," he mumbled.

Sadie leaned over and tossed the shotgun on a nearby couch. "Yes, it was," she agreed.

Gabe took in a deep breath and exhaled it slowly before saying, "I need to feed the livestock."

"What do you want for dinner?" Sadie asked.

Gabe rubbed at the heavy calluses of his right hand with his left thumb. "I'll take you out for dinner."

He turned to lumber out the door when Sadie called out to him.

"Gabriel, do you even know what started this fight?"

Gabe removed his hat and scratched at the black hair pulled tight across his scalp ending in a single braid nearly two feet long. "Nope. Don't recall."

"And it don't even really matter," Sadie sighed.

She watched her man walk out of the door while wondering if the other three of the so-called "Four Horsemen" were mellowing with age as much as her Gabriel Saupitty.

* * *

Ryan Cornish shoveled furiously to remove the old shingles from the trailer, slinging them into the ditch beside the deserted country road. His brother-in-law, new to both the business of illegal dumping and Anadarko, Oklahoma, didn't share his sense of urgency.

"Best get a move-on, Marvin. We damn sure don't want to get caught doing this," Ryan said as he paused to wipe sweat from his brow.

"If you're so concerned about being caught, Ryan," Marvin Purdy grumbled, "why didn't we just take them to the landfill?"

"Told you why already, Marvin. We'd have to pay, and I'm betting these old shingles probably have asbestos in them. If so, we'd pay really big money, if the dump would even take them."

Marvin recently migrated to Oklahoma from California, and Ryan hired him at his wife's insistence. So far, her brother didn't prove handy or enthusiastic about the business of removing old roofs and replacing them with new ones. He seemed oblivious to the nuances of cost factors. Paying to dump, ate into profits. Any idiot should at least understand that much.

Another five minutes passed, and with the trailer almost emptied, Ryan looked up to find Marvin standing idle while staring off into a nearby clearing. "What are you doing?" Ryan huffed.

Marvin responded to the question with a question, "Who do you think that is?"

Ryan took a closer look and exhaled, "Oh, shit."

"You know him?" Marvin asked.

The lone man sat calmly on a big horse, staring in their direction. Ryan moved quickly into the ditch and started throwing the discarded debris back into the trailer.

"What the hell are you doing?" Marvin groaned.

"What you best get to helping me do. Hurry, let's get this shit back on the trailer."

"You know him?" Marvin asked again.

"Don't know him, but think I know who he is. Damn. Come on, Marvin, we got to bust ass here, man."

"Screw whoever he is," Marvin replied. "Let's just jump in the truck and leave. He's on a damned horse, Ryan. What can he do? Chase us down?"

Ryan did not pause in his hurried efforts to reload the trailer but spoke as he worked. "Look closely, Marvin. See that long thing hanging on his saddle? That's a rifle scabbard, and I'm betting it ain't holding a BB gun."

"No damn man is going to shoot us for dumping trash."

"Maybe not from where you came from in California, but this is Oklahoma," Ryan groaned as he heaved tiles. "You need to know that there are four ol' boys in this county that pretty much run it. Four dudes no one messes with. There's Junior Pernell, Johnny Conwoop, Gabe Saupitty, and Troy Rubottom. I'm thinking that's Troy on the horse. Don't bet your life that he won't shoot us for dumping trash. All of them are known to have done worse."

Marvin started to pitch in. "What are they? Some kind of gang?"

"Not exactly. I've always heard they can't stand each other, but together they own most of the county. They say if you cross one, you deal with all four of them. Hurry, Marvin. We don't want to deal with not a damned one of them."

Marvin grumbled, but picked up the pace. Ryan didn't look up until tossing the last heap of shingles on the trailer. The man on the horse looked to have not moved a muscle. As a gesture of good will, Ryan raised an arm overhead and waved apologetically. He started backing toward the driver's door when he saw the man retrieve a rifle from the scabbard.

"Damn! Run, Marvin. Get your ass in the truck."

Ryan placed his hand on the door handle as the back window of the truck disintegrated. Then he heard the sounds of repeated gunfire. "Hit the damn dirt, Marvin!"

The windshield shattered. Next, the driver and passenger windows seemed to implode. Two more shots obliterated both the right and left outside rearview mirrors. For the time it took, Ryan squirmed on his belly like a constipated snake. No more shots were fired, but Ryan dared not twitch.

"Marvin?" he barely whispered.

"I'm under the fucking truck!"

"What's he doing? Is he coming?"

"I ain't fucking looking!"

Ryan listened, but did not hear the clomping of hooves. Only after several long minutes did he convince his limbs to move. He carefully pulled himself up to peek over the bed of the truck. The man on the horse remained right where Ryan last saw him, but he'd tucked the rifle back into the scabbard. Ryan barely breathed until the man raised a hand and mimicked the wave Ryan offered earlier.

"Get in the truck, Marvin. Now!"

Marvin stared with a look of absolute horror out what had been the back glass as they pulled away with tires screeching.

"Welcome to Caddo County, Brother-in-law," Ryan said without even trying to calm the fear in his voice.

"Are we going to call the police?"

With hands helplessly glued to the wheel and eyes transfixed on the sweet road of escape, Ryan mumbled out the corner of his mouth, "Damn, boy, you best go back to fucking California."

* * *

Red Winfield swung into the booth opposite of a man who sported the build and facial characteristics of a bulldog. "Junior, I do swear you get uglier every day."

Junior Pernell stared at Red through the folds of flesh surrounding his cold piercing eyes. "Red, this might just be the day I grow tired of your insulting mouth."

Red laughed as he reached across the table and flicked the brim of Junior's cowboy hat, moving it to the rear part of his big head.

Junior calmly adjusted the hat back in place before growling, "That just cost you a whiskey and a beer, asshole."

"My pleasure, Junior," Red grinned broadly.

Red Winfield did not take his privileges to toy with Junior Pernell for granted. He did not know another man who could call Junior ugly or touch his grimy once-white cowboy hat without possibly losing the tongue that spoke and the finger that flicked. Red had, for many years, enjoyed a status that made others simply shake their heads in disbelief, while all along they envied both his privileges and status. For not only could Red get away with such with Junior, but practiced the same antics with Johnny Conwoop, Troy Rubottom, and Gabe Saupitty. All those who envied didn't understand that status and privileges with such men did not come without a heavy price. Since junior high school, Red worked feverishly as the "go-between" amongst four of the nastiest tempered souls God ever accidently dumped on the earth.

Few knew that without Red's efforts any one of the four would surely have long ago killed the other three. Only Red and the four women who long ago married the locally notorious men, could see in his life-long friends the deep-down, and almost hidden qualities, that others truly believed did not exist. Red could never go as far as to call these qualities morals, but all four men possessed a code they would not betray. They would not lie to a man. They would not cheat a man. They would not back down. Everything else proved fair game. As a boy, Red befriended the four ruffians by fulfilling his role as the class clown. Now, he maintained his relationship not only as their go-between, but also as their banker. Red liked to believe he'd played a key role in making each of them very wealthy men. He doubted that any one of them would disagree.

"The other three are ready to close the deal on that 3,000 acres, Junior. You're the only hold out," Red said before halting a waitress, "Beth, could you set us both up with a shot of Jack and two Buds?"

"Sure will, Mr. Winfield," the young woman responded with a smile.

Junior didn't respond until the girl walked away. "I told you, Red, I'm thinking we should pay cash for that land."

"I know what you told me, Junior, but right now, the smart move is to put down and pay out. In this economy, you need to hang on to cash money. Woop even says you're a dumb ass for not seeing that."

"Fuck that Comanche asshole," Junior growled. "Besides, I've said all along that I'm not in this deal until he sells me that new horse he has."

"Damn, Junior, you've offered him 3,000 more than that horse is worth, and our fine Mr. Conwoop is not going to sell him, and do you know why?"

"'Cause Woop is a Comanche asshole."

"Well, that he is," Red grinned. "Just like you're a plain white asshole, but that's not why he won't sell. He won't sell, because he knows you want it. Same damned games we've played for too many years to count, Junior."

"If you can't count that high, Mr. President of the Anadarko Bank and Trust," Junior hissed, "How can I trust you to keep count of my money?"

"Never said you could," Red replied with a wink.

Beth approached with the drinks, and conversation ceased until she left. Red hefted his shot of Jack Daniels toward Junior, "Here's to another 3,000 acres, Junior."

Junior studied his shot for a long minute before finally picking it up and bumping it against Red's.

"I still want that damned horse."

"You ain't getting the damned horse."

Both men chased their whiskey with a swig of beer. Junior wiped the suds from a bushy moustache before saying, "Another thing. You see Woop before I do, tell him to keep that worthless son of his away from my daughter."

Red let go with laughter. "Junior, that boy is nearly thirty, and your daughter is just a few years behind. Woop has no more control over him than you do her."

"That boy is a fucking thug," Junior replied.

"He learned from four of the best," Red winked again.

Neither man spoke another word until draining their beers. Red stood first. "If I don't see you sooner, I'll see you at the cabin Wednesday night."

"Same place; same time," Junior grumbled before adding, "Bring lots of money. I intend to win enough to offer Woop five thousand more than that damned horse is worth."

* * *

Rheta had dinner sitting on the table when she heard Johnny come in the front door. For reasons she could not explain, Rheta somewhat missed the days when they lived in a house so small she could see the front door from her kitchen. Her daddy told her many years earlier that Johnny Conwoop would never amount to a hill of beans. Just rodeo trash and, Indian, to boot. Back then respectable white girls seldom married Native Americans. But, in Anadarko, a town where near half the population registered as members of the

Caddo, Comanche, Apache, and Kiowa nations, just to mention a few of the tribes represented in the area, Rheta considered it a fifty percent chance that she'd marry right. All in all, she believed she had. She so wished her oil field working daddy lived long enough to see what she now called home.

"Howdy, Woop," she called out without seeing him. Decades ago she'd taken to calling her husband the shortening of his name that all others used.

"Hi," he responded from rooms away in his typical barking manner.

Rheta smiled at the sound of his voice. Over the years, she wondered about being with a kinder gentler type, but always figured she'd take advantage of a man like that. Woop was a rough fit, but still fit Rheta like a glove.

"Bo called my cell today," Woop said as he strode into the kitchen. "I didn't answer. Did he call you?"

"Yes, he did," Rheta said as she took her place at the table. "And, yes, he wanted money. And, yes, I told him he would have to talk to you."

Woop removed his cowboy hat and tossed it on a counter. He exhaled long and hard as he ran a hand through thick black hair stranded with gray. "The son of a bitch ain't getting another dime from me unless he wants to work for it."

"Woop, it does not speak well of me when you call our kid a son of a bitch," Rheta sighed.

"Well, it wouldn't work calling him a bastard either," he said as he plopped down at the table. "Or a motherfucker."

Rheta only shook her head before pushing a platter of fried chicken toward her husband. The torn and ragged relationship between father and son pained her deeply. Bo disappointed them both, but Woop proved less forgiving. Rheta deeply loved their only son. Woop harbored something closer to disgust. He certainly had his reasons. Bo seemed to do all he could to evoke the ugly feelings held by the father.

"Trash. Now, that will work. Bo is simply trash," Woop said as he piled chicken on his plate. "Any man that will not work for what he wants is trash. Pass those taters, Rheta."

"Let's not talk about Bo," Rheta said as she handed the bowl of mashed potatoes to Woop. "I worked too hard on this dinner to ruin it with foul conversation."

"And I worked hard on getting us another 3,000 acres. Only thing standing in the way is Junior Pernell. Now right there is a son of a bitch, a bastard, and a motherfucker."

"And that's more foul conversation, Woop," Rheta smiled.

"Damn sure is," Woop said as he began shoveling food into his mouth. "The man's name is Junior, but he's not a junior. His actual name is Junior. That's screwed up."

Rheta took her first bite of chicken. "Most things around these parts are, Woop."

* * *

"I don't normally beat a hand-cuffed man," Sheriff Melody Preston said as she worked the leather quirt in her right hand, popping the braided leather lash in the air.

"But I've been a bad boy," the confined man moaned.

"I think tonight I will call you Betty," Melody said. "I dealt earlier with a bitch named Betty."

"Call me what you want. I'll be your bitch, but just do what you know needs to be done."

Melody ran the fingers of her free hand between her bare legs and felt the sudden dampness. The naked man handcuffed face down to the bedposts of her bed squirmed in anticipation. The muscular cheeks of his ass twitched and begged to be lashed. Melody raised the small horsewhip high in the air and brought it down harshly on the exceptionally fine butt cheeks.

"Is that the best you got?" her man-bitch groaned.

"That's just a warm up," Melody snickered before unleashing a fury of lashings that raised angry red whelps and left "Betty" writhing in ecstasy.

"Enough," he finally panted. "Undo me."

Melody tossed the whip aside, grabbed up the key to the cuffs, and hurriedly worked to free the man's ankles and wrists. He rolled over, ferociously erect, and pulled her down on top of him.

"You were once a rodeo queen," he growled in her ear as he groped, found, and entered her.

"You bet I was."

"Ride me like one."

Later they snuggled in each other's arms.

"You ever going to let me spank you?" he asked.

"What kind of sick freak do you take me for?" Melody giggled.

Chapter Two

Sadie Saupitty stood beside her twin sister in front of a single tombstone bearing two names. Both women brought flowers to commemorate the anniversary of their mother's passing.

"Hard to believe she's been gone eleven years," Sadie said as she placed her flowers in front of the monument.

"Daddy's been dead nearly twenty," her twin commented.

"They had so very little. Just a trailer house, a couple of junk cars, and us three girls,"

Her twin sighed hard before saying, "That almost begs for the ending of, 'but they were happy.'"

"Yeah, but they weren't. He beat her up to the day before he died," Sadie said while shaking her head from bitter memories.

Several silent minutes passed before Sadie's sister asked, "Has Gabe ever laid a hand on you?"

Sadie looked hard at Kadie Rubottom. "Hell no. He knows what we went through and knows I would never put up with it. I damn sure hope you can say the same about Troy?" Sadie posed her last words as a blunt question.

Kadie paused a moment before responding. "Oh, no. He's never hit me. Has threatened to a thousand times. Has raised his fist at me.

Even shoved me once, but he's never hit me. From what I see on talk shows nowadays, I'd consider him verbally and emotionally abusive, but he don't hit on me."

"Well, I could say all the same about, Gabe, but he knows where to draw the line," Sadie said.

"Kind of surprising though, don't you think?"

"What?" Sadie questioned.

"That considering the types we married, that they don't beat on us."

"They were rough boys when we married them. They're rough men now, but no man should beat on his wife," Sadie declared.

"They're mean too," Kadie mumbled.

Sadie studied her twin for a few seconds before shrugging her shoulders. "We knew that when we married them." After a pause she could not help but ask, "Are you and Troy having problems?"

Kadie duplicated Sadie's shrug. "No more than we've ever had. Guess it was good to see how Mama and Daddy lived. I learned not to expect happiness."

Only then did Kadie place her flowers on the grave.

* * *

Jolene sat on the back patio mid-morning and sipped on her third cup of coffee. She reached for a cigarette on the glassed-top table when she caught sight of her husband stepping out of his large barn. She watched as he made his way to the house moving sluggishly. He looked tired again this morning and had reason to. Jolene lit her cigarette as he nearly fell into a chair across the table from her. She drew smoke deep into her lungs and exhaled it out the side of her mouth before addressing her husband.

"You're dragging ass again this morning, Junior."

"Yeah, I'm tired," Junior Pernell sighed.

"You want a cup of coffee?"

"No. Just want to sit here and rest."

"Guess you know why you're so tired again this morning," Jolene said before tapping ash into an ashtray on the table.

Junior reached for her pack of cigarettes and shook one out. "Oh, Jolene, you are so full of shit. Hand me your lighter."

Jolene skipped the lighter across the table before reaching into her jean's pocket and pulling out an iPhone. She laid the phone on the table and tapped it with her index finger.

"This time I have proof. I recorded it."

Junior lit the cigarette and blew smoke forcibly in her direction.

"Do you want to listen to it, Junior?"

Her husband just stared at her through his puffy eyelids. Jolene picked up the phone, thumbed an app and placed it back down. Junior dropped his eyes to look at the phone. In a second or two, the recorded sound of loud, deep, and mournful sobs erupted from the tiny speaker.

"That's you, honey," Jolene said, "and you are crying in your sleep."

"What the hell?" Junior mumbled.

"Don't know, but now you can't deny it. You've been waking me up about every other night now doing it."

"Turn the son of a bitch off," Junior barked.

Jolene thumbed the phone again and the pitiful wailing stopped. "Wish I could turn you off that easy at night."

"I wish you could turn me on at night."

"Funny," Jolene chuckled. "Now that you know you're doing it, what are you going to do about it?"

"Why, hell, I don't know. What can I do about it?"

"See a doctor. Or, considering all you have to cry about, maybe you need an exorcist," Jolene grinned. For a second, she thought Junior was going to grin back, but he fought it off.

"I'm not seeing a damned doctor."

"Then I'm going to start sleeping in another room,"

"Well," Junior almost grinned again, "Guess you can come back to my bed for our semi-annual sex."

Jolene laughed. "You know, you can be damned funny, but you never laugh. Maybe that's the reason you cry."

"I probably cry because you laugh so much."

Jolene laughed again.

* * *

Bob Nettle spit a strand of thick black goo onto the sidewalk from the bench he shared with Clint Avants beneath an awning in front of the Web Drugstore on Anadarko's Main Street. Bob used his tongue to adjust the ball of Beech-Nut filling his left cheek to the point of producing a facial protrusion that looked like a malignant tumor. Going on for nearly sixty years, Bob went through two packages of the chewing tobacco every day, dislodging the wad only to take his meals. At night, when he removed his dentures, the cheek sagged like the empty pouch of an elderly Jill kangaroo.

Bob watched as Clint rolled yet another cigarette with one hand using Prince Albert tobacco and a Bugler rolling paper. "That shit is going to kill you one day," Bob said.

"Not if a jealous husband gets me first," Clint chuckled before applying a match to the neatly rolled little cigarette.

"Had a jealous husband come at me once with a knife," Bob declared.

"I know. You've talked about it for fifty years now," Clint nodded while discharging a plume of gray smoke.

"I had to shoot the son of a bitch. Spent a year in the county jail. Then his widow expected me to marry her."

"I know. You done told me about a thousand times."

"Another man's wife will screw your legs off, but you end up marrying her, and she'll be screwing some other ol' boy's legs off."

"That's damn sure the way of it," Clint agreed.

Bob spit again before saying, "We ought to see if Woop or Troy would loan us a couple of horses today. It's a fine day for riding."

"My doc don't want me riding no more. Says my bones are too brittle."

"He also told you to give up that Prince Albert and whiskey," Bob added.

"Screw him."

"Nope. He ain't my type," Bob chuckled.

"Nancy is my type," Clint said as he flicked his ashes onto the sidewalk.

"Think she might be in the mood today?" Bob asked.

"Why don't we just go find out?" Clint asked.

"Hell, that would even beat riding a horse. Don't need no spurs with Nancy."

Bob helped Clint to his feet and both limped and hobbled their way up Main Street.

* * *

Only a day passed since Marvin Purdy experienced his brother-in-law's windows being shot to shit by a man on a horse. He'd damned sure never seen anything like that in California, and quite naturally, he could not help but obsess over it. Some other type of dude might want revenge for being put through such, but that's not what motivated Marvin's constant pondering of the incident.

All the thinking on the subject helped Marvin conclude that he did not move to Oklahoma to slay away at the shit job of crawling around on roofs sweating his ass off in the God forbidden humidity. Instead, he'd decided, what he wanted to do was hang out with men like the man who shot up other people's pick-ups. In less than twenty-four hours' time, Marvin made up his mind that he wanted to befriend the four men his sister, when told of the incident, referred to as the "Four Horsemen of Caddo County."

"They're all just a bunch of assholes with tons of money," his sister, Martha Cornish, had said.

In that Marvin seemed to have always surrounded himself with assholes with no money, why not get in good with these dudes? For most of the day, he'd been asking plenty of questions of anyone he could about the Four Horsemen. Seemed few knew a lot. Marvin learned of restaurants, and barbers, and feed stores they frequented. He learned that one of them, or maybe all four, could be found any given night drinking at a cowboy bar named "Spurs and Saddles."

For the moment, he toiled at the awful job of carrying bundles of shingles up a ladder. Tonight though, he planned on spending time at a cowboy bar, if his taskmaster of a brother-in-law would give him an advance on his salary.

* * *

Gabe Saupitty slammed on his brakes and pulled his truck to the curb before shouting into his cell phone.

"Are you messing with me, Red?"

"Not this time, Gabe. Passed them only moments ago, and they are headed in the direction of your mom's house," Red Winfield said. "You want me to go back?"

Gabe slammed his free hand twice on the steering wheel. "No. I'm not far off. Fucking bastards!"

"Might be best for me to deal with them, Gabe," Red offered.

"No. I'm tired of this shit. I'll handle it for damned sure."

"Now, Gabe, don't forget that those two old cowboys taught you practically all you know about horses as well as life in general. You'd not been worth shit without those two."

"Bullshit," Gabe bellowed before hanging up on the president of the Anadarko Bank and Trust.

* * *

"Oh hell! We are screwed, Clint," Bob Nettle exclaimed.

"Not yet we ain't," Clint Avants laughed. "But give us about another five minutes and we will be."

Bob grabbed one of Clint's bony arms and pointed up the street at the Ford truck speeding toward them. "That's Gabe's pick-up."

"Oh, hell, Bob. You are right. We are screwed before ever getting screwed."

Bob took a deep breath to clear his thinking. "Just let me do the talking, Clint."

"I'm considering running, Bob, but might break one of my brittle bones."

"He's most likely going to break every one of our brittle bones," Bob sighed.

The truck came to a skidding stop, and one big Indian with a long braid bailed out.

Bob choked out the only words that came to mind. "Howdy, Gabe."

"Howdy my ass, Bob Nettle," Gabe hollered as he stormed toward them. "I'm going to bury you two bastards in a shallow grave."

"Say something else, Bob," Clint begged.

Bob threw both hands up in the air in the universal language of surrender. "Gabe, we ain't done a damned thing."

"You are headed in the direction of my mama's house," Gabe thundered.

"But we weren't going to screw her," Clint nearly screamed.

Bob could not believe it, but those awful words brought big Gabe to a stop. Bob flinched as Gabe kicked and stomped at the ground before throwing his cowboy hat down and grabbing his head in both hands.

"Maybe that's what you should have said in the first place, Bob," Clint whispered.

"Shut the hell up, Clint," Bob whispered back.

Gabe continued to stomp and kick as he twirled in place, shouting stuff to the heavens that Bob did not understand.

"Is that Apache he's speaking?" Clint asked.

"Please shut the hell up, Clint." Bob replied.

Finally, Gabe seemed to exhaust himself. His big shoulders slumped. "I just don't get it," he groaned. "She's nearly eighty. Her mind is all but gone. Still, you two take advantage of her."

"She gives it willingly, Gabe," Clint chimed in.

"Oh, dear Jesus," Bob moaned.

For several tense seconds, Gabe just stared at first Clint and then Bob. "Get in my goddamned truck."

"Are you going to kill us, Gabe?" Clint babbled.

"Get in the fucking truck."

"Oh, God, Bob," Clint stammered. "What are we going to do?"

"We are going to get in the fucking truck, Clint."

* * *

Junior could not force it out of his mind. It plagued him. Even shopping for and buying a 1300-dollar pair of Lucchese full quill ostrich boots could not force the recorded sound of his wailing from his brain.

What the hell could make a man like me cry?

Junior could not remember the last time he shed tears. Surely, he'd bawled as a kid when his drunk of a father beat him relentlessly, but he'd never cried since manhood. It did not make sense, but bugged the shit out of him all the same. Junior didn't intend to see a doctor, but strangely felt a desire to discuss it with someone.

"Hey, Woop or Troy or Gabe, guess what? I've been crying in my sleep."

Like that would ever happen in a thousand years. Junior didn't talk about shit like that and didn't know another man who would either. This brought up the point that other men surely did not cry in their sleep. The thought left Junior feeling somewhat lonely, and lonely felt like a weakness, which made him feel inadequate. Junior had not felt inadequate since taking the beatings from his drunk of a father.

So, Junior made his way down the rural road back to his ranch feeling inadequate over the sounds of pitiful sobbing that would not leave him be. That's when he looked into his rearview mirror and realized another truck was right on his ass. A glance at the speedometer showed his speed at nearly ten miles over the posted limit. Inadequate or not, the tailgater offended Junior. He raised his head and mouthed into the mirror so his lips would show.

"Get off my ass, motherfucker!"

The driver in the too close pick-up responded by shooting Junior the bird. Junior responded in turn by slamming on his brakes. The truck behind him fishtailed to the right and then to the left before colliding into the rear bumper of Junior's GMC. The moment both trucks came to a stop, Junior bounded out of the cab.

The long-haired white man driving an already beat up old Ford evidently banged his head on the steering wheel upon collision and sat slouched and dazed in his driver's seat with his window down. Junior reached into the open window with both hands and filled them with the man's stringy long mane. He then applied a series of tugs to lift the man up in the seat and right out the window.

The man screamed, kicked, and clawed as Junior drug him to the side of the road and tossed him into the bar ditch.

"Tailgating is rude, motherfucker," Junior bellowed.

The man jumped to his feet and came up swinging.

"You just made my day, asshole," Junior grinned as he plowed in.

He hit the man with a series of lefts and rights as fast and hard as he could. The man quickly ended up on his ass, back in the bar ditch. From a sitting position, he buried his battered face in his hands and simply started to cry.

Junior started to say something ugly, but instead just stood and studied the weeping man. After several seconds of doing so, he stepped into the ditch and plopped down beside the man.

"Do you cry often?" Junior asked.

* * *

"You two stay in the truck, and don't mess with anything."

"Okay, Gabe," Bob and Clint said in unison.

Gabe started out of his truck, but then reached back in and grabbed the keys from the ignition.

"Hell, we wouldn't steal your truck, Gabe," Bob said from the back seat of the crew cab.

"Any two men that would screw my mama would screw me as well."

Clint started giggling, but cut it off after a sharp look from Bob.

Gabe walked toward the front door of the big house, thankful the place sat remote and far from public view. It would do him no good being seen here. He climbed the steps to the large covered porch that spanned the entire front of what people still called the Dampton Mansion. The outdoor furniture looked nicely arranged, and high-dollar, which did not surprise Gabe. He pushed the doorbell button and waited, but not long.

"Why, Saints preserve us, Gabriel Saupitty has come 'a calling!"

Gabe jerked his cowboy hat from his head. "Well, I ain't come 'a callin' for myself, Margaret Ann."

"I find that most disappointing, Gabe," Margaret Ann Blake said, flashing a coy smile that exposed a most lovely set of teeth.

Gabe felt his face flush. He never knew a Caddo woman more beautiful or beguiling as the one standing in the doorway.

"Gabe, is this simply a social call?"

"Uh, not really," Gabe stammered. "I have Bob Nettle and Clint Avants out in the truck."

Margaret Ann stretched and tip-toed to look around Gabe, exposing almost more breast in her low-cut blouse than Gabe could stand.

"I surely believed those two dead by now," she said.

"I wish they were," Gabe sighed.

Margaret Ann settled back into the doorway and simply stared curiously at Gabe, prompting him to continue.

"They been having sex with my mama."

"Both of them?"

"Yeah," Gabe said before clearing his throat, "both of them."

"My, my," Margaret Ann mused before saying, "So, I'm guessing you brought them here as a . . . diversion . . . of sorts?"

Gabe thought a second or two before responding, "Yeah, that's a nice way of putting it."

"Gabe, I guess you know that my girls are, well, high-dollar?"

"I've heard that," Gabe nodded before reaching back and pulling out his wallet. "I'll pay up to five-hundred bucks."

"Now, considering my special friend discount for the infamous Gabriel Saupitty, that'll work. Do you prefer anything in particular for the gentlemen?"

"I prefer anything that will take their minds and lust off my mama."

Margaret Ann rolled her eyes as if in deep thought. "What about something so kinky, that it might dissuade them from thinking about sex for a while?"

Gabe managed to smile for the first time in well over an hour. "I'd like that a whole lot."

He handed Margaret Ann the money, thanked her, and said his goodbye before trying to hurry away.

"Gabe?"

"Uh, yeah, Margaret Ann?"

"Remember the ninth grade?"

Gabe tried not to, but had to admit, "Yeah, I do."

"I'd still give it to you for free."

Gabe thrust his hat on his head and hurried off the porch to the sound of Margaret Ann's robust laughter.

CHAPTER THREE

"Do you cry often?" Junior asked again.

The longhaired man sitting beside him sniffed several times long and hard before responding, "Only when being beaten up by Junior Pernell . . . And only after finally giving into the truth that I'm a homosexual . . . And only after being caught by my wife in bed with another man not more than two hours in the past."

Junior shook his head and then turned it to stare at the young man next to him. It took several seconds but proper words finally came to mind. "So, you know who I am?"

"I do now. Everyone around here knows who you are. I didn't know it was you I was tailgating, or I wouldn't have done it in fear that you'd beat the shit out of me. Which you did."

Junior pulled off his hat, gave his head a good scratching, and then put it back on. "Oh, hell, I've given much worse beatings."

Both men sat silently for a few seconds before the one still sniffling asked, "Are you repulsed?"

Junior tried to avoid the true question. "Oh, I guess some men cry after getting in a wreck and getting punched around a little."

"About me being a homosexual," the man responded.

"Hell, I don't even know you."

The man extended his right hand. "I'm Craig Johns."

Junior stared hard at the hand before finally shrugging and grasping it. Johns applied a firm grip, which surprised Junior.

"Are you repulsed that I'm a queer?"

Junior emitted a series of stammered "I's" and "uhs" before finally having to admit, "Well, it just makes no sense to me. I can't understand it. Pussy is damned good."

"Guess I should use the word 'gay.' No sense in humiliating myself any more than I'm already humiliated. But I just feel so . . . inadequate."

Inadequate?

The word slapped at Junior. He considered just getting up and leaving, but what were the chances of ever meeting another man on a country road feeling inadequate?

"I'm not one to judge you, Johns. As a kid, I once tried to fuck a heifer."

Junior had heard Johns just take a deep trembling breath, but upon hearing the confession, Johns released it in a chuckle. "No shit?"

Junior drew in his own deep breath of air. "Yeah. No shit. It didn't go well. Don't know why I told you that. I've never told anyone else."

"Maybe when I bumped into you, you hit your head. Might have a concussion," Johns smiled, then said, "I don't like it that I'm a homosexual. I don't like it that I hurt my wife. But I guess there are things we just can't control."

"I've been crying at night in my sleep. I can't control that." Junior grumbled.

Johns looked at him for a few seconds before saying, "You want to talk about it?"

Junior stared back at Johns. "Not really. Don't know what to say. Don't know why I do it."

Johns nodded his head a couple of times before reaching into a shirt pocket and retrieving a card. He handed it to Junior. "If you ever want to talk about it, give me a call."

Junior read the card and stated, "You're a private investigator?"

"Yes, sir," Johns sighed. "Ironic, isn't it?"

"How's that?"

"I'm the one who's supposed to catch people fucking around on their spouses, not get caught by my spouse fucking some man."

Junior could only crinkle his face and shake his head.

* * *

Clint walked out of the Dampton Mansion's front door to find Bob already sitting on the porch in a wicker chair with a tall and wide back. Clint shuffled past him and took the seat furthest from Bob. Then he waited. Bob always spoke first. Been his way since their young days. Bob Nettle liked to always have both the first and last word in any setting. Now, Bob not only remained silent, but didn't even look at Clint. Instead he stared off into the wide expanse of the front yard.

"Uh, you okay, Bob?"

After a few seconds, Bob started to slowly nod his head, then he stopped, and started slowly shaking it. Then he stopped all head movements, but did turn to look at Clint.

"Can't say, Clint."

Clint Avants had never heard Bob not be able to say a damned word about any damned topic. It disturbed Clint, almost as much as what just happened to him upstairs. Clint guessed most would consider him the quietest of the duo, but at the moment, he felt a desperate need for conversation.

"Bob, you ever had a woman stick a string of beads up your ass?"

Bob jerked his head straightforward again to stare across the lawn. After long seconds of saying nothing, Bob finally asked, "How we gonna get home, Clint?"

"Don't know, Bob, but I don't feel like walking. My butthole hurts."

Bob started again to slowly nod his head.

* * *

Kadie Rubottom found her man standing outside a corral staring at his prized Quarter-Horse stud, Napoleon.

"He's a fine-looking animal, Troy," Kadie said as she stepped up beside him.

"Damn sure is," Troy agreed. "Much finer than that horse Junior is so hot to buy off Woop."

Kadie just didn't get it. She never had and doubted she ever would. The dynamics between her husband, Junior Pernell, Gabe Saupitty, and her brother-in- law Johnny Conwoop defied all logic. No four men could be more alike, or fight harder to deny it. She knew Troy would absolutely hate selling Napoleon to Junior, but would do so just to keep him from buying the horse Woop owned. With some twisted reasoning, he would do so to simply disrupt a perceived balance of power. But, Kadie didn't go looking for her husband to discuss horses.

"Troy?"

"What?" he grunted.

"Are you happy?"

He turned to look her straight in the eyes. She and Troy were the same height, making him by far the shortest of the so-called "Four Horsemen." But, no one denied, and Troy proved so many times over the years, to still be a match in strength, determination, and fighting ability with the other three. Now he gave her the look he so often employed of disgust, confusion, and deep thought.

Troy exhaled in a weary manner before asking, "What is happiness, Sadie? Define it for me."

"You don't know what happiness is, Troy?"

"Not really, and evidently, you don't either. You can't explain it."

"I know when I feel happy."

"Well," he snickered, "Good for you."

"Guess what I'm asking, Troy, is do you like our life together?"

"Ohhhh," Troy nodded, "So you're asking me if I'm happy with you?"

"Kind of."

Troy put a boot caked in mud and horse shit on the bottom rail of the corral. "Sadie, do you remember that Appaloosa mare I roped off of for God knows how many years?"

"Doll," Kadie answered.

"Yup, Doll. I was happy with that horse for many years, and then I sold her to a fellow down in Texas. You know why I sold her, Kadie?"

"Never asked. You don't involve me with your selling or buying."

"The truth is, Kadie, one day I just wasn't satisfied with her no more. Don't really know if satisfied and happy are the same thing."

"Yeah, okay, so what are you saying, Troy?"

"I'm saying, woman, that I've yet to get rid of you."

Sadie certainly didn't want to, but she could not help but smile. "Troy, let's go in and make love."

"Kadie, I'd be a fool to say no, but 'making love?' Well, that's as illusive a term as happiness is a word."

Kadie could take offense, but instead, she took her husband's hand and led him toward the house.

* * *

Anadarko Patrolman Jerry Eastridge called in the tag of the hopped-up red Chevy Camaro to dispatch before unfolding from beneath the wheel of his patrol car. He walked up to the car with his right hand resting casually on the grips of his holstered Glock.

"Whip out your license, Bo," he commanded to the well-known character occupying the driver's seat of the Chevy.

"Aw, fuck, Eastridge, you know I've got a driver's license," Bo Conwoop sneered out his window.

"Yeah, I do, and I want to see it, asshole," Eastridge grinned. He didn't like Bo Conwoop worth a shit, and didn't know an officer who did, but the other pussies he worked with handled him with kid gloves.

"And what if I'm not in a mood to whip it out today, Eastridge?" Bo grinned back with malice.

"Then, I'll just pull your ass out and beat you like your ol' daddy should have long ago."

As Eastridge knew he would, Bo pulled out his wallet and thumbed for his license. "Best be careful what you say about my 'daddy,' Eastridge. Could be detrimental to your career."

"Fuck you, Bo, and fuck your daddy too," Eastridge grinned again. He knew what Bo knew, and what Woop knew, and what the other three of Woop's accomplices knew: Patrolman Jerry Eastridge could and would take on any man in Anadarko, and beat them to a pulp. Eastridge relished being known as such a cop. Otherwise, he'd be at least a Captain by now.

"Oh, you're a big man," Bo said as he surrendered his driver's license.

"Huh-hu, six foot and six inches, Bo, and two-hundred and eighty pounds of fucking hard-assed muscle. You feel like taking it on today?"

"What did you stop me for this time, Eastridge?"

"Other than being a spoiled fucking asshole, Bo? Well, I stopped you for what I usually stop you for. Speeding. Now sit tight, and I'll be back with the ticket."

***

Bo Conwoop sat tight. And with Eastridge back in his patrol car writing up yet another ticket, he cursed the big cop. Bo didn't get along with his father, but because "Woop" was his father, no other cop in town dared treat him like Eastridge treated him. Bo often fantasized about getting the monster of a man fired, but knew the truth. Jerry Eastridge, other than being one bad son of a bitch, proved squeaky clean. He didn't steal, would not take a bribe, cherished the law, and sometimes dated the very well-connected county sheriff, Melody Preston.

Still, if and when the right opportunity came along, Bo intended to do Eastridge great harm. A physical kind of harm. The kind that ended up as a murder mystery. Bo now seethed as he watched the town cop approach in his rearview mirror.

"You know where to sign, pussy-boy," Eastridge said as he thrust the ticket book in Bo's face.

Bo grabbed the extended book and pen. "If I ever catch you out of uniform . . ." he started.

"Then you'll bleed from every orifice, Bo." Eastridge interrupted. "Your mama and daddy will have to identify what remains of you in the morgue. There won't be enough to bury. They'll flush you down a toilet. Your soul will burn in hell, and this town will throw one big fucking party because another tick on the dick of society will have been plucked and squished."

Eastridge took back the signed ticket and his pen before flicking Bo's license and bouncing it off his forehead. "I get off duty at four Monday through Friday. I'm off Saturdays and Sundays. I live at 317 South Will Rogers Avenue. Drop by when you choose to die."

Eastridge walked away laughing as Bo Conwoop fought back tears of rage.

* * *

Johnny Conwoop sat in a corner booth sipping coffee in Anadarko's Dixie Diner when he noticed Junior Pernell walk in the door. He hoped Junior wouldn't see him, but Junior did, and walked directly up and plopped down across the table from Woop.

"Have a seat, Junior. Make yourself right at home."

"Already have, Woop. Kind of late for coffee isn't it?"

"Too early for whiskey, Junior."

"Woop, I want to buy that damned horse."

"Have you seen that horse today, Junior?"

"Why, hell no."

"I have. And she ain't wearing no 'For Sale' sign."

Junior leaned over the table, getting as close to Woop as he could. "I'll tell you what, you son of a bitch, why don't we just step outside right now. Let's fight for that goddamned mare. If I win, you sell her to me. If you win, I won't bother you again about the damn thing."

Woop raised his cup and took a sip of coffee as he peered over the rim at Junior. He then calmly placed the cup back on the table and said, "The last time me and you fought was during our rodeo days. Somewhere up in Montana. I kicked your ass."

"Bullshit! I had you on the ground and I was on top. You picked up a rock and knocked me out with it," Junior replied.

"Old Apache tactic. Handed down from Geronimo," Woop grinned. "Besides, Junior," he said as he studied the other man's eyes that were surrounded by heavy folds of flesh, "You don't have the fighting look in your eyes." Woop pointed at Junior's hands on the table, "You don't even have your hands clinched into fists. I've seen you in the fighting mood too many times to know, you ain't in no fighting mood now."

Junior leaned back and relaxed in his seat. "Shit, we both just got too damned much money to fight for what we want nowadays. Instead of my fists, I'll just hit you with offers until you finally scream 'calf-rope' and sell the horse."

Woop chuckled at the comment, but continued to study the man sitting across from him. "You know, Junior, I believe something is eating on you, and it ain't that new horse."

"Hell, you're now sounding like that philosophizing Troy Rubottom. I ain't got a worry in the world."

"I can't help but hope it's cancer eating on you, Junior," Woop smiled. "With you gone, the remaining three of us would have more land and money to split between us."

"I ain't got no fucking cancer," Junior grunted, but then surprised Woop by changing the topic. "You know a private investigator here in town named Johns?"

"Nope," Woop shook his head, "but what the hell you need a private investigator for? Is Jolene stepping out on you? I mean, who could blame her if she was, but I can see how that would be eating on you."

"I don't need a goddamned private investigator, and watch your mouth about my wife. And the only damned thing 'eating on me,' as you keep putting it, you Apache son of a bitch, is that I want that damned horse."

"Well then, you bulldog looking white asshole, you can just want in one hand and shit in the other. Just see what you come up with first, a damned fine horse, or a handful of shit."

Woop called out a "So-long" as Junior stomped away from the booth. Junior only responded by displaying the middle finger of his right hand over the back of his meaty shoulders.

* * *

"It's just not good for your reputation. Not in a town this size."

Sheriff Melody Preston looked up at the ceiling and laughed at the comment made by the suited man sitting behind his desk.

"Oh, now that's exactly what I need, Brad Smith. Moral guidance from the sleaziest defense attorney in the county," Melody, still in uniform, said from her prone position on a leather couch a few feet from Smith's desk.

"Not to mention the damned best defense attorney in the county," Smith chuckled. "I'm just saying, Melody, you ought to be dating me exclusively. You have your career to think about. Carrying on with that Neanderthal cop, the dandy Doctor Morton, yours truly . . . and God only knows who else, is just inappropriate of an elected official."

Melody swung her legs off the couch to sit upright. "Okay, Brad, I came to see if you wanted to have dinner, not to be hounded, or get a lecture. If you've grown tired of sharing me with others, guess that means there's just more of me to go around for Jerry Eastridge, Robert Morton . . . and God only knows who else."

Smith stood up and reached to turn out the lamp on his desk. "Didn't say I'm tired of sharing you. Just said I wished I didn't have to. Guess I'll just have to settle for trying to outlast the others. Where are you buying me dinner?"

"Doc Morton never makes me pay for dinner," Melody smiled as she stood and started for the door.

"He's a rich gynecologist," Smith said as he turned from his desk to follow Melody. "Besides, he's a strange dude."

"If you haven't figured out by now, Brad," Melody giggled, "I do like my men strange. And you, my dearest sleazy lawyer, are a most excellent case in point."

* * *

"Hell, the name alone implies it should be filled with cowboys," Troy grumbled to Red Winfield.

"You'd think so," Red nodded as he sipped his Jack Daniels on the rocks.

"Spurs and Saddles they call the joint, and I'm the only man in here wearing a cowboy hat. There's something deeply wrong with that which speaks to the degradation of the cowboy way," Troy continued to rant as he picked up his glass of Jack without the rocks.

Red chuckled and shook his head. He'd always said that if you took the "Four Horseman" to a large body of water that Saupitty, Pernell, and Conwoop would only be interested in what floated in plain sight. Rubottom, on the other hand, would be more concerned with what dwelled beneath the surface. Not that Red would ever imply that the others were shallow, but Troy certainly had always been the deep thinker of the group. Being the only one of the four with any formal education, Troy spent two years at the Oklahoma State University pursuing a degree in general studies. Red always believed his efforts would have been better-spent studying philosophy.

After taking a stout swig of his straight whiskey, Troy said, "Kind of makes me want to just get up and start slugging every man in here without a western hat. I'd start with you, Red, but you've never worn a cowboy hat. Some in here once did, but don't anymore. And ball caps don't cut it. You'd never catch John Wayne wearing a ball cap. Even if it had John Deere on the front of it."

"John Wayne is dead, Troy," Red grinned.

"Fuck you, Red," Troy belched.

Red threw back his head and laughed. Deep thinker or not, Troy still possessed the base behaviors that connected him with the other three.

* * *

Marvin Purdy walked into the Spurs and Saddles bar wearing a cowboy hat he'd borrowed off his brother-in-law, Ryan Cornish. Being too big, the black hat rested a little heavy on his ears, but Marvin liked wearing it. He felt it made him stand out in the crowd of the fairly packed little bar. If he had to stay with roofing long enough to draw a full paycheck, Marvin intended to buy his very own hat and a pair of boots to go with it. Being raised on the west coast, he'd chosen a surfer's way of life and apparel, but now thought he'd take right to being a cowboy, or with any luck at all, a horseman.

Marvin made his way immediately to the bar and waited until one of the two bartenders worked him into his agenda. "I'd like a beer and some information," He said to the heavyset man who looked too old to be anything but the owner.

"You some kind of private investigator?" the bartender smirked.

"Hell, no. Nothing like that. Just need you to point out someone for me."

"No whores in here, cowboy. I don't allow them," the man grimaced.

Marvin smiled at being called a cowboy. It seemed to fit. "Not looking for a whore. I'm looking for any one or all of the Four Horsemen."

The bartender cocked his head and looked at Marvin with a wary eye. "Are you looking for trouble, young man?"

"No. Not a bit," Marvin said as he handed the man a twenty. "That's for one beer and you pointing them out to me."

The man snatched the twenty and said, "That's just for the information. You most likely won't be here long enough to drink a beer. Troy Rubottom is sitting way in the back with Red Winfield. Other than you, he's the only one in here wearing a cowboy hat. I figure if you're in here for trouble, Troy will deal with you easily enough."

Marvin thanked the man and started working his way through the bar's patrons until he spotted the other cowboy hat. He felt both surprised and relieved that the man wearing the hat looked rather small. He had looked bigger on a horse. Marvin didn't give it much thought, but considered the best way to make an introduction started with the truth. He walked right up to the table.

"Mr. Rubottom, my name is Marvin Purdy, and I'm hoping you don't immediately recognize me."

Rubottom held a glass of amber colored liquid to his lips. He took a gulp and sat the glass on the table before looking up. The man beside him, nicely dressed, slender, tall, and redheaded, noticeably stiffened in his chair.

"Am I supposed to know you, boy?" Rubottom asked in a low but deep growl.

What Marvin heard in the voice, and observed in the man's intense glare, seemed to overly exaggerate his diminished size.

"No, sir, not really, but I'm one of the two you shot at yesterday for dumping trash," Marvin somehow managed without stammering.

The man with Rubottom really stiffened at the proclamation and mumbled, "Oh, shit. Is there going to be bloodshed, Troy?"

Rubottom raised a palm at his friend to either keep him in place or comfort him before addressing Marvin. "Boy, you are either one stupid bastard, or have gonads the size of bowling balls."

Marvin had to clear his throat to jump-start his voice. "Neither one, sir. I'm just here to meet you, apologize, and buy you a drink. I'm thinking we ought to be friends."

Troy Rubottom turned his head to stare at the tall and slender man. "Red, do you know of any life-form more despicable than a son of a bitch with a funny accent who dumps trash on another son of a bitch's property?"

Red, as Troy aptly called him, looked up to study Marvin a second or two before responding, "Can't think of anything more despicable, Troy. Except maybe a son of a bitch who interrupts two other sons of a bitchs' whiskey drinking time."

Rubottom simply nodded his head before lowering it to a point where the brim of his hat concealed his eyes. "Trash dumping boy, I'm going to just stare at my whiskey a moment or two. When I do look up, you best be gone. I can buy my own whiskey, and I don't need any new friends. By the way, that hat is too big for you, and you look fucking ridiculous. Wearing it ridicules those who deserve to wear a cowboy hat. Are you still here?"

Marvin didn't bother giving an answer, and didn't run from the table, but he did move damned fast and didn't stop moving in such a manner until the door of the Spurs and Saddles slammed shut behind him.

Chapter Four

Gabe Saupitty sat at the kitchen table sipping coffee when Sadie walked past him without saying a word and retrieved a butcher knife from a kitchen drawer. Gabe considered mumbling a good morning, but figured Sadie to be in her typical early-morning funk. He assumed, and hoped, the knife would be used to slice off some ham for his breakfast. In the next instance though, Sadie held his braid in one hand and applied the big knife to it with the other.

"Move an inch, Saupitty, and I will cut the son of a bitch clean off," she hissed.

"What the hell, woman?" he bellowed, daring not to move even a half-inch.

"Susan Wittle saw you yesterday with two other men in your truck going toward the Dampton Mansion whorehouse, you Apache asshole. You think you can . . ."

"Hold on just a goddamned second, Sadie," Gabe shouted, "Do you think I'm stupid enough to go to a whorehouse in broad daylight in a countryside chalked full of blabbering old rumor spreading bitches like Susan Wittle?"

"So, you didn't go there?" Sadie shouted back as she used her grip on the braid to jerk Gabe's head backwards.

From this position Gabe stared up into a set of evilly angry brown eyes. "Now listen to me, Sadie. Just listen and don't do anything stupid, because I didn't do anything stupid, but I did go there."

Sadie gritted her teeth and hissed like a snake before pulling even harder on Gabe's braid.

"Goddamn it, Sadie, I took Bob Nettle and Clint Avants there because they was about to fuck Mama again!"

Sadie immediately released the grip she had on the braid and tossed the knife on the table in front of Gabe. "Well, you should have told me about that before it came to this," she said calmly.

Gabe grabbed the knife, jumped to his feet, and turned on his wife. "Did you cut any of my fucking hair?"

"Not a one," she grinned.

Gabe brought the knife up in as menacing fashion as he could produce. "Why, I ought to take this knife and . . ."

"And stick it up your ass for being a stupid son of a bitch," Sadie interrupted. Then she simply walked around him and sat down at the table to help herself to his cup of coffee. "You should have told me in the first place. You know how things get around here."

Gabe bellowed like a bull before spinning and throwing the knife at the wall opposite of where Sadie sat. His point would have been well made if the knife stuck instead of pinging against the wall and falling like a limp dick to the floor. Sadie chuckled.

"Some Apache you are. You can't even stick a knife in the wall."

"I could stick one in your throat," he growled.

"And I'd pull it out and cut your balls off with it," she said, imitating his growl.

Gabe wanted to just pop her right on the nose, but he'd never done so, and it felt too late to start doing so now. Instead, he stomped to the overhead cabinets and took down another coffee mug.

"Shit, if I'd known what I know now, I'd a' married a Comanche woman. They're said to be the meanest and nastiest you can marry, but you've proved that wrong, you Cherokee . . ."

"Don't call me a bitch, Gabe. Ain't in the mood for it."

"Asshole! Cherokee asshole is what I was going to call you!"

"Uh-huh," Sadie smirked before taking another sip of Gabe's first cup of coffee. "And by the way, what are you going to do about your mother fucking those two old bastards? That's very embarrassing. You know how things get spread in this town."

Gabe had nearly settled enough to pour a second cup of coffee and drink it at the table, but Sadie's last words just put him in an out the door kind of mood.

"I got fucking work to do," he said before stomping off toward the back door.

"Gabe!" Sadie called after him.

"What?" he thundered.

"Am I still prettier than that Caddo whore, Margaret Ann Blake?"

"Why don't you just go to the fucking Dampton Mansion and have a pretty contest with her," he thundered again before jerking the back door open.

"Pretty contest? You sure say some stupid shit, Gabriel."

Gabe stepped out and slammed the door so hard he hoped it jarred Sadie's teeth out, and then she could try to get some more as pretty as Margaret Ann's. Of course, he did not care to tell Sadie that.

* * *

Ryan Cornish just happened to be looking down from the roof when he noticed the red Camaro pull up and park behind his pick-up truck. He continued to watch as a man got out of the car, walked to Ryan's truck and started looking it over. The distance separating Ryan from the man below him made it impossible for him to identify the guy walking around his truck. Ryan decided it best to get down and see what the man wanted. He carefully made his way down the steep-pitched roof his crew was replacing and climbed down a ladder.

"Can I help you?" he called out to the man once he made it to the ground.

The man now leaned against the truck and didn't respond until Ryan walked up to him. By this point he recognized the man, and a knot formed in his guts. Ryan didn't know him personally, but knew Bo Conwoop on sight. Hell, who didn't?

"Is this your truck?" Bo asked.

"Sure is, Bo. What's up?"

"The sign on your door here says 'Cornish Roofing.' I guess you're Cornish?"

Ryan had no idea what Bo Conwoop wanted with him, but he would bet he didn't need a new roof. Ryan attempted to keep his newfound worry from sounding in his voice. "Yeah, I'm Ryan Cornish. Can I do something for you?"

"You can tell me what business you had with Troy Rubottom last night at the Spurs and Saddles," Bo said bluntly. "I pulled up just as you were tearing out in this truck. People inside told me what happened. You can't keep shit quiet in this town, dude."

Ryan threw his palms in the air and started shaking his head, "That wasn't me in this truck, Bo. It was my dumb-assed brother-in-law, Marvin Purdy."

"Is he working up on that roof?"

"Well, he's up there. I wouldn't bet he's working."

"Get his ass down here," Bo ordered.

"I'll go get him," Ryan immediately responded.

"Once you're back up there, you can stay. My business is with him."

Ryan nodded his understanding before hurrying back to the ladder.

* * *

Ryan wouldn't even tell him who the man was. When asked, Ryan responded, "You'll find out, dumb fuck. Just Don't track the shit you step in, into my house." Marvin really didn't know what that meant, but it couldn't be good. As he approached the tall and slender man leaning against Ryan's truck, Marvin grew even more apprehensive. The man looked to be around his age, mid to late twenty's, and carried a mean look on his face. He wore jeans and cowboy boots with a Harley-Davidson t-shirt. Marvin hoped he was no biker. Where he came, from bikers would fuck you up. But, what had he done to piss off a biker?

"You know who I am?" the man asked with a sneer.

"I have no idea," Marvin answered.

"I'm Bo Conwoop. Does that ring any bells?"

"I've heard of Johnny Conwoop, who they call Woop," Marvin confessed, having no idea where this might lead, but suddenly understood that somehow, he might have certainly stepped into shit.

"That's my old man. He's associated with Troy Rubottom. What business did you have with Rubottom last night in the Spurs and Saddles?"

It occurred to Marvin that what Bo asked did not concern him, but Bo looked to be the type who would not appreciate being told so. "You notice that truck you're leaning on don't have any windows in it?" Marvin replied with a smile he hoped Bo would consider friendly. "Well, Troy Rubottom shot them out the day before yesterday with a rifle."

Bo's chin dropped. "Jesus Christ, man, did you call him out?"

"Call him out?" Then the meaning dawned on Marvin. "Oh, fuck no!"

"Well, that's a good thing, because Rubottom would have torn your ass out and pulled it down over your head, suffocating you to death with your own asshole."

Marvin's head spun and no good words came to mind, "He's kind of a little guy," he mumbled.

"Fuck. Don't let that fool you, man. He's as mean and ugly as those other three assholes he does business with," Bo said.

"Assholes? But your dad is one of them, Bo," Marvin pointed out.

"He's the biggest asshole of the bunch."

"I, uh, well, thought it might be kind of cool, you know, being friends with the Four Horsemen."

"Four Horsemen?" Bo blurted, "That's so much shit. I get so tired of hearing that stupid fucking name. They ought to be called the four assholes, or four pricks, or four motherfuckers. And you want to be their friend? What kind of dumb fuck are you?"

"Well, I just . . . didn't know," Marvin all but whimpered.

"Shit, man . . . Uh, what's your name?"

"Marvin. Marvin Purdy."

"Shit, Marvin, those fucks ain't got no friends and don't want friends. You might as well try to find and give a blow job to Bigfoot."

Marvin chuckled at that, and then Bo did the same.

"Why would you want to be their friend?" Bo asked as the chuckle dwindled to a cocky grin.

Marvin exhaled heavily as he chose his words. "I'm new here in Oklahoma. I just, uh, thought if I could get in with them, I'd be off on a better start than working for my dick-head brother-in-law replacing roofs."

Bo seemed to chew on Marvin's words for a second or two before asking, "So you just kind of want to be somebody around here? A big man?"

"Well, yeah, somebody, sounds good, but not necessarily a big man."

"I can understand that," Bo nodded.

"You can?"

"Sure," Bo continued to nod, "I want the same. But let me tell you something, Marvin, all four of those fucks need to be taken down a notch or two. The man that does that, now he'll be the big man around these parts."

Marvin knew he was not the man for that job, and started thinking of ways to break off this conversation and get his ass back up on the roof.

"I'll tell you what, Marvin Purdy, I'm thinking you and I need to have a deep conversation on this very topic. Let's get in my car and go have some beer, maybe a joint or two. I have a good feeling about you."

Marvin could not return the compliment, but instinctively knew better than saying so. "Hell, Bo, I've got to get back to work."

"Fuck work, Marvin. If you can't be friends with the four horse turds, you know what the next best thing is?"

"Uh . . ."

"Being friends with me. I'm in line to take their place. I need a good man to join me. Have you ever considered being filthy rich?"

Marvin certainly had. All his entire life. He'd done so enough to know that neither here nor in California could opportunities like this fall in his lap every day.

"Yeah, Bo, fuck work. Let's go drink some beer."

Time existed for Marvin to make up a sufficient lie to convince Ryan that leaving could not have been prevented.

* * *

Junior sat at his desk in the office of his magnificent horse barn and stared at the business card in his hand.

"What the fuck have I come to?" he said aloud.

"I spent time on the side of the road with a queer and told him I once tried to fuck a heifer."

Junior tossed the card on his desk before opening a drawer and pulling out a bottle of Johnnie Walker Black.

"And I fucking cried again last night."

Junior uncorked the bottle and took a mighty swig.

"Now I'm drinking before ten in the morning. And I'm talking out loud to my stupid-assed self."

For the past twenty-four hours he'd searched his mind and memory for things that could bring a grown man to cry in his sleep. Tons of atrocities came to mind, and all wicked enough to have made him cry long ago. So, why now? He'd been a terrible father. Much more than once, but not in the past decade, he'd violated his wedding vows to Jolene. He'd been on the wrong side of the law, but never got caught. Never paid his debt to society. He'd beat and stomped and busted up so many men who probably didn't deserve as much pain as he'd . . .

And what about that family up in the Rocky Mountains?

"Oh, dear Lord," he mumbled out loud at the sudden resurrection of the deeply buried memory. Then Junior really got serious with the bottle of Scotch.

* * *

Bo climbed back in the Camaro with a case of cold beer that he handed over to Marvin in the passenger seat.

"Damn, this is a nice car," Marvin said as he ripped into the case and pulled out two beers.

"My mother bought it for me," Bo said as he started the engine and pulled out of the convenience store parking lot. "That was before my old man made her stop buying me things. The Comanche bastard."

"You don't look all that much Indian," Marvin said as he handed a beer to Bo.

"My mom's very white. Don't know what she ever saw in that son of a bitch. I've always dreamed that since I look more white than Indian, maybe's he's not my real father."

"I think it'd be cool being Indian," Marvin said as he slurped his beer.

"I think it'd be cool if I still got money from my mother," Bo said as he pointed the Chevy out of town.

"Where we going, Bo?"

"You'll see. Part of the story I'm going to tell you."

Since getting in his car back at the construction site, Marvin Purdy nearly bombarded Bo with questions about the four jack-offs.

Bo wanted beer in his veins before having to mention their names and tell their stories. He took several hardy swigs before starting to introduce Marvin to the four men he'd grown up knowing.

"All four of them grew up in Anadarko and went to school together from the first grade. All of them came from trash, but were damn good athletes . . . probably the only thing that got them through school. That, and they all ended up marrying good gals they went to school with. Two old cowboys who owned a ranch outside town took an interest in all four of them. God only knows why. Anyhow, because of the two cowboys, they all ended up being in the PRCA . . ."

"The PR what?" Marvin interrupted.

"The Professional Rodeo Cowboy Association, PRCA," Bo repeated. "To make a long story short, they all did really well, and made some pretty good money, which they brought back to Anadarko. That's when they fell in with Red Winfield and started buying up land, making more money with cattle and horses, and investing money. And that's how they all got so damned rich and powerful. Give me another beer."

Marvin popped the top and handed Bo a fresh one as Bo tossed the empty out his window.

"Hope that didn't land on any of their land," Marvin said with a serious shaking of his head. "I know enough about them to know they don't put up with that shit."

"You can't spit around here without hitting something they own," Bo nodded, "but that's what is going to make you and me rich men. And powerful ones too."

"I don't understand, Bo."

"Oh, you will, Marvin."

* * *

Gabe Saupitty stood on the front porch banging on his mother's front door. Her hearing seemed to be dwindling along with her mind. He didn't even try the doorbell knowing she couldn't hear it because it made too soft a noise. Gabe moved his mother into town and bought the nice two-bedroom home for her ten years ago. Prior to this she'd been accustomed to living in a near shack in which Gabe had been raised. It'd felt good buying his mother something fine, and until the last year or so, she'd cherished it. Now her cleaning skills and personal hygiene seemed to be following the path of her hearing and thinking. Therefore, he paid her more frequent visits nowadays. Sadie had been talking lately of putting her in a home, but Gabe couldn't bear the thought of doing such. His mother, he insisted, was not that bad off just yet.

Finally, the front door flew open, and there stood Nancy Saupitty without a stitch of clothing, but she wore make-up and had her hair done.

"What the hell, Mom?" Gabe exclaimed as he jerked open the glass storm door and stepped inside.

"Oh, it's you," Nancy said with a pout. "I thought it might be Bob and Clint."

Gabe averted his eyes and grasped at his chest, "Dear Jesus, Mom, so you came to the door naked? Oh, shit, go put on some clothes. Goddamn!"

"Don't take that tone with me, boy," Nancy said as she padded away toward her bedroom. "A woman has her needs. I might be old, but I have body parts that . . ."

Gabe slammed the door shut behind him and brought his hands up to cover his ears just before the doorbell started to chime.

"What the hell?" he gasped.

"Better yet who the hell?" Nancy responded as she turned and once again started in Gabe's direction. "It might be Bob and Clint!"

Gabe jabbed with a pointed finger and yelled, "Get the hell to the bedroom!"

To his surprise, Nancy turned like a robot and did as told. "I'll castrate the bastards. I swear to God I will," he hissed before turning to jerk the door open.

"Junior? What in the world do you . . ."

Junior Pernell raised his right arm to expose a very large Colt revolver. "You have ruined my life, Gabe Saupitty. Sadie said I'd find you here, and I'm going to leave you lying here."

Gabe stared down the barrel of the gun pointed at his face and shook his head for clarification. "Junior, have you lost your fucking mind?"

"I most certainly have, and it's all your fault."

He slurred the words and Gabe drew a conclusion. "You're drunk on your ass."

"That's the truth," Junior agreed.

"What the hell?" Gabe bellowed.

"It's come back to haunt my sleep, Saupitty," Junior followed with a burp.

"What has?"

"What you made happen north of Durango, Colorado, many years ago."

The memory came immediately to mind. "Best get that gun out of my face, Junior."

"Everyone in that car might have died," Junior hollered.

"And they might have lived through it," Gabe hollered back.

"I'm betting they died," Junior concluded before thumbing back the Colt's hammer.

All in the course of one morning, Gabe almost lost his braid to a jealous wife, encountered his elderly mother naked and wanting, and now this? It proved too much in too little time. Gabe released a vicious undercut with his left that connected squarely with Junior's chin. The gun went flying and so did Junior, right off the porch and flat on his back. Junior made a feeble attempt to get up, but collapsed and fell unconscious.

Gabe stepped out of the house, pulled the door closed behind him, and stepped over the downed man. "You just happened to fuck with the wrong man at the wrong time, Junior," Gabe said as he stomped toward his truck.

* * *

"It's a cabin," Marvin said as he looked around the small clearing surrounded by thick woods.

"It's their cabin," Bo nodded as he turned off the ignition and threw open his door.

"Should we be here?" Marvin asked, remaining in his seat with his door closed.

"Hell no we shouldn't be, but we are. Get out. Let's take a look around."

"What if one of them shows up?" Marvin had not budged, and didn't care to.

"We'll have to fuck him up."

"What if two of them shows up?"

"They'll fuck us up. But don't worry. They never come here in the daylight. Get the hell out and follow me."

Marvin took a deep breath and figured he best do as Bo commanded. He'd spent just enough time with his new acquaintance to feel barely comfortable in his presence. Bo acted friendly enough, and even bought beer, but Marvin sensed that the man had a short fuse. He got out of the car and followed Bo to the front door of the cabin.

"Are we going in, Bo?"

"Don't have a key. But nothing in there anyway but a round table and chairs."

"Why are we here then?"

Bo smiled broadly and clasped Marvin on the shoulder. "That's a great question. You're a thinking man, and I like that. The reason we're here is that this place could be the first place we start making money."

Marvin had no clue, but knew a thinking man would not readily admit such. So, he just nodded his head and did his best to look thoughtful.

"One night a month they all show up here along with Red Winfield. They bring great gobs of cash, Marvin, and they play poker. I've heard them comment that sometimes there's as much as fifty thousand dollars on that little table in there."

"Fifty thousand?" Marvin gasped.

"I'll bet there's times when there's more than that. I'd also bet there's never less than twenty."

"Twenty's a lot," Marvin nodded.

"Ten thousand a piece, my man," Bo grinned.

"Huh?"

"Sure. I wouldn't think twice about splitting fifty-fifty with a man like you, Marvin."

Marvin felt as if something suddenly hatched in his belly. Something with claws and fangs.

"Bo, are you talking about . . . robbing them?"

"The perfect crime, Marvin. Hell, they can't report it to the police. It's illegal to gamble without permits and that kind of shit. What could they do?"

They could kill us both right here.

They could hunt us down and kill us somewhere else.

This is fucked up.

"Huh, Marvin, what could they do?"

"Well, I, uh, you know, uh . . ."

"Are you in, Marvin? Want to do this with me?"

Marvin considered his right here and now options while surrounded by thick woods at the end of a long and deserted dirt road. What else could a thinking man do?

"Sure, Bo. I'm in. You can count on me."

* * *

"What are you going to call me tonight?"

"I don't know. What do you want me to call you?" Melody Preston said as she stared down at the back of the naked man handcuffed to her bed.

"Don't know. Don't care. Just make it nasty," her captive moaned.

"I think I'll just call you by your name," Melody said simply for a reaction, and got one. Back and ass muscles tensed before her eyes.

"Not when I'm like this."

"Yeah, that would be just too weird," Melody giggled.

"Unlock these cuffs."

"Fuck you," Melody growled as she raised the quirt up and brought it down viciously on the helpless ass.

Chapter Five

Marvin used the small blade of his pocketknife to remove several layers of paint and caulking from the window jamb. He thought he might work faster and more proficiently had he forgone the last ten or so beers. Too, it didn't help being damned dark outside at four in the morning. Eventually, he did manage to start inching the window upward without making a lot of noise. It did squeak, but probably not enough to wake those sleeping on the inside. Even with the window raised high enough for him to crawl through, it took Marvin several tries to make it through the opening. For some reason his arms and legs weren't working all that well.

Inside, Marvin crawled on hands and knees and dared not try to find the light switch. Within inches of his destination, the light on the ceiling suddenly came on with blinding effectiveness and an angry voice boomed.

"What the hell are you doing?"

Marvin fell back from the nearby bed and shielded his eyes from the bright light as he addressed his challenger while trying not to slur his words. "The door is locked and I didn't want to pound on it, Ryan. Didn't want to wake you and sis and the kids."

"So, you snuck in like a thief in the night?" His brother-in-law howled.

Marvin squinted to look at Ryan and recoiled at the sight of a pointed shotgun.

"Damn, Ryan, that thing might go off!"

"Yeah, it just might, you son of a bitch," Ryan agreed.

"I'm sorry, Ryan. I'm really . . ."

"Sorry? Yeah, you're sorry all right. You left the work site without permission. You didn't even call to tell us what was going on, and now you break into my house before sunup."

"I didn't want to go with him, Ryan. He forced me. Said he'd do things to . . ."

"And then he forced you to get drunk and stay out all night?" Ryan interrupted again.

Marvin searched for words, but Ryan found some first.

"You just crawl your ass back out that window. I'm finished with you. I don't want you around my family."

Marvin spoke without thinking, "I want to talk to my sister."

Ryan took an aggressive step in his direction and raised the shotgun like a club. "I won't shoot you, but I'll bash your head in."

"Okay! Okay! I'm going," Marvin squealed as he turned and crawled back toward the open window. "But where will I go?"

"No longer my problem. Guess you best go back to your buddy, Bo Conwoop."

Marvin considered thanking Ryan for the obvious solution, but concentrated instead on crawling back out the window with his head still in one aching piece.

* * *

"Thanks for meeting me here," Junior said.

"Hell, Mr. Pernell, just you, my wife, and that one dude knows I'm a closet gay guy. We could have met in public."

Junior almost chuckled, but, as usual, wasn't in a chuckling mood. "That's not the only reason I wanted to meet here," he admitted, "Most of all, I don't want anyone knowing that I'm talking to a private investigator."

Craig Johns laughed and shook his head, but it seemed to be a sad gesture.

"What's funny about that?" Junior grunted.

"I was just thinking while on the phone you made it clear you wanted my investigative services. Very clearly implying you didn't want to meet me in the middle of nowhere for, well, you know, things of a despicable nature."

It took a second, but Junior got his drift. "You want me to whip your ass and throw you in a ditch again?"

"No, sir!" Craig said as he exhibited the palms of both hands. "I don't mean to piss you off. Just getting that out of the way. I mean I would have never thought you wanted me out here to . . ."

"Would you just shut the fuck up about that?" Junior interrupted as rudely as possible. "All I need and *want* is a private investigator."

Craig nodded his understanding enthusiastically. "Okay. But may I just ask one more question?"

"You better make it a question different from what you were questioning," Junior emphasized.

"Oh, it is, Mr. Pernell. I just want to know why, when you can afford the best investigator money can buy, you'd call me?"

"That's simple. I don't know any other investigators."

"Okay. Makes sense to me. Looks like you got hit by a truck. Is that why we're here?"

Junior rubbed at his swollen and bruised chin and considered if Johns' blunt nature should offend him. A moment of doing so made him decide that bluntness could be counted as an asset for someone in the man's line of business. "It's related," Junior admitted.

"Okay, Mr. Pernell, I'm all ears. What can I do for you?"

"First, you can call me Junior. I have no use for the type of man that thinks mister is a title worth a shit. After that, I want you to find out if some people are dead or alive. Do you travel out of state?"

"I'll go where you pay me to go," Craig grinned. "But, Junior, what if I find out these people are dead. What's that going to mean for you?"

Junior didn't have to apply deep thought to provide an answer. "Most likely will mean I'll continue to cry in my sleep . . . even in prison."

* * *

Robert Morton walked out of one gynecology exam room and started for another before being hailed by his nurse.

"Doctor, the new patient in 5B is presenting somewhat of a challenge," Janet Bray informed him.

"What's her problem?" he questioned.

"Don't know what her medical problem is, or even if she has one. She refuses to say. She also refuses to put on a gown, and insists that she talk to you alone."

"Well, as long as she's fully dressed, don't guess that's a problem. What's her name?"

Janet handed the doctor a file. "Margaret Stinney."

The name did not ring any bells, nor did Morton expect it to. In a community where most citizens had lived their entire lives, Morton, after five years of calling it home, still considered himself a newcomer, as did most of the long-term residents of Anadarko. He took the scant file and knocked on the door of 5B before entering.

"Ms. Stinney, I'm Doctor Robert Morton," he said to the middle-aged lady clearly of American Indian descent.

"I know who you are, Doctor, and it's a pity you don't know who I am," Margaret Stinney replied sternly.

"Should I know who you are?" Morton asked as he moved to a chair opposite of where Stinney perched on an exam table.

"You certainly should. My sisters, a set of twins, are married to two of the county's most notorious characters, and on top of that, for the past six months, you've been screwing my daughter."

Robert Morton spent his entire days examining vaginas. Little surprised him, but this did. He lowered himself into the chair and cleared his throat before responding, "You're Melody's mother?"

"I am."

"And that's why you're here today?"

"Nothing wrong with my female parts," she declared.

Morton crossed one leg over the other. "I do see only a slight resemblance, but like your daughter, you don't mince words."

"I say what needs saying. And I came here today to say that you need to marry her."

Surprised yet again, Morton could not help but chuckle.

"It's not a funny matter. She's sexing you and at least two others that I know about. I'm surprised that as a gynecologist you're not in fear of catching some awful disease from her."

Morton uncrossed his legs and sat upright in the chair. "Well, Ms. Stinney, I don't consider that any of your business, and I don't believe Melody would either."

"I'm making it my business, Doctor. I'm Cherokee, and the reason she doesn't resemble me is because her father, a worthless bastard, was a redheaded Irishman with evidently more dominant genes. Melody is not worthless. She's the first female sheriff of this county. I think she could someday be the governor of this state . . . if well married. I don't want her marrying a sleazy-assed attorney or a small-town cop with no future. You are her best choice."

Morton seldom found himself lacking for words, but surprised once again, he could only manage, "I will take the matter up with Melody."

"I hope you do not intend to charge me for this visit."

"It's on the house, Ms. Stinney," Morton said as he stood and walked toward the door while looking warily back over his shoulder.

Margaret Stinney smiled for the first time. "You're a fine looking and fit man, Doc. Nice ass. You ought to throw some dandy pups."

Another damned surprise. Morton could not recall the last time he blushed. He'd thought studying vaginas robbed him of such reactions.

* * *

He considered Anadarko a small town, until he started searching for just one person while on foot and without benefit of a cell phone or a quarter to place a call from a phone booth. Even if he could make a call, he doubted he'd be able to find a number for Bo Conwoop. So, Marvin did the only thing he could think of to find Bo. He asked questions.

"Do you know Bo Conwoop?"

"Do you know where he lives?"

"Do you know where I might find him this time a day?"

So far, no single person seemed overly enthusiastic about Bo, or a stranger asking questions about Bo. A few simply ignored him, and more than one gave rude responses. All these uncooperative vibes didn't encourage Marvin's overall intent, but compounded his doubt and anxiety. For when and if he stumbled across Bo, what then?

Say, good buddy Bo, how about letting me live with you?

To say the least, Marvin already felt an overwhelming sense of doom as the Anadarko police car pulled to the curb in front of him. He already feared life, from this point, held nothing but a solid screwing for him even before the giant cop got out of the car and approached him.

"What's your name, boy?" the mound of uniformed muscle asked in a most unfriendly manner.

Marvin looked up at the nametag above the officer's right shirt pocket. "I'm Marvin Purdy, uh, Officer Eastridge . . . sir."

"Show me some identification proving that, Marvin Purdy," Eastridge demanded.

Marvin pulled out his wallet and fumbled nervously to find his driver's license. He handed it to the great big man with a trembling hand. Cops had always frightened Marvin. Just the sight of this one all but terrorized him.

"A fucking Californian? What the hell you doing in Anadarko, Purdy?"

It seemed a mouth full of peanut butter held his tongue hostage, and it took great effort for Marvin to move it. "I came here to work with my brother-in-law, Ryan Cornish, sir. Do you know him?"

"I'm the one asking questions, dumb ass. You got that?" Eastridge bellowed.

Marvin suddenly had to piss. He fought the urge to grab and hold his crotch. "Uh, yes, sir. I sure got it, sir. I also need to pee really bad."

"Don't you soil my sidewalk, boy," Eastridge smirked as he reached for a microphone attached to his shirt just above his badge.

Marvin didn't understand all the man barked into the microphone, but he did catch his full name and date of birth as Eastridge read it from his license. Damn sure not wanting to soil Eastridge's sidewalk, Marvin went ahead and grabbed his crotch, and could not help but dance in place.

"Stand still, fuck-face."

"I can't, sir, I'm just about to piss myself!"

Eastridge abruptly grabbed Marvin's left arm and nearly jerked him off his feet as he pulled him around a corner to shove him between two buildings, blocking the view of any passersby.

Marvin had heard of this sort of thing happening in small towns and his sudden fear could not be held within. "Oh, Jesus Christ! Please don't beat me, Officer! I haven't done anything . . ."

"Piss, fuck for brains," Eastridge thundered.

Marvin spun in place and fumbled with his zipper, "Don't know if I can with you watching," he groaned.

"Maybe a size fourteen boot up your ass might help," Eastridge offered.

"Don't think it would, sir," Marvin whimpered as he struggled to remove his fear-shriveled member. A voice came from the radio on Eastridge's gun belt and he grumbled something back as Marvin emptied his bladder in squirts and dribbles. Finally, Marvin felt relieved and zipped back up.

"You came back clear, Purdy. No warrants out on you," Eastridge said as Marvin turned to face him. "However, there is this matter of you pissing in public. That's illegal, Fuck nose."

Marvin's tongue suddenly stuck on one word. "But, but, but . . ."

"Another however," Eastridge interrupted, "we might be able to work this out between us, Fuck ears."

"How, sir?"

"You've been asking all over town about Bo Conwoop. Are you and Bo friends?"

A moment earlier, Marvin felt he might cry. Suddenly, it seemed God for once decided to smile down upon him. And he had Bo to thank. More accurately, he had the Four Horseman to thank. He'd heard it all his life, but only now witnessed the truth first hand. "It's not what you know; it's who you know." Obviously, no matter how gigantic of a man, this cop didn't want to mess with Bo Conwoop, his dad, and near uncles.

"We are the best of friends," Marvin announced. "Like brothers. As a matter of fact, I'm moving in with him today."

"No, shit," Eastridge grinned.

* * *

Bob Nettle and Clint Avants sat on their bench beneath the Web Drugstore awning and watched Eastridge harassing the kid across the street from them.

"That's one big damned cop," Bob said.

"A bad son of a bitch. Nobody messes with him," Clint agreed.

"Shit. Back in the day, I'd mess with him," Bob grumbled.

"Like you did with Officer Butch Cantrell? He wasn't near the size of that Eastridge, and he whipped your ass up and down Broadway that one Christmas. Remember that, Bob?"

"I held my own," Bob shot back.

"Yeah, all the way to the hospital," Clint chuckled.

"Well, asshole Cantrell's dead now, isn't he? And I'm still living, ain't I? Guess it means I won in the long run."

"Yup, cancer got him," Clint nodded.

"I wish cancer would get that Gabe Saupitty," Bob said before spitting a stream of processed chewing tobacco.

"Oh, bullshit, Bob. Him and the other three were like sons to us. Still are in ways."

"Ain't much of son that would keep his practically adopted daddies from his mother," Bob hissed.

"I don't even want to think about Nancy, Bob. Hell, I don't want to think about no woman just yet."

"Well, I want to think about her, Clint, and I've been thinking about her. Matter of fact, I've come up with a plan."

"I don't think I want to hear it," Clint said as he started to emphatically shake his head.

"I'm going to tell you anyway, Clint. I think we should go to her house and get her, and the three of us just hit the road. Get the hell out of this one-horse town."

"That's a dangerous plan, Bob. Besides, we gonna walk her out of town? We don't have a damn car."

"Not right now, but we will have. We're going to steal one."

"Oh, dear Jesus," Clint started to chant while Bob stuffed more tobacco in his face pouch.

* * *

"Why, hell, *Mr. Purdy*," Eastridge toyed, "That kind of makes you someone in this town."

"I was hoping you'd see it that way, Officer Eastridge," Purdy replied with just an edge of cockiness.

"It makes you damned important to me, too," Eastridge said as he moved up close to Purdy. The punk started nodding his head. Forcibly at first, but slowing it considerably as Eastridge moved even closer.

"Uh . . . how's that, Officer?" Purdy asked without a trace of cockiness.

"I'm going to let you be my snitch."

"Oh, shit, sir, I don't know about that. I don't think . . ."

"Don't give a fuck what you think, fuck turd," Eastridge interrupted. "See, I honestly hate Bo Conwoop. I know he does drugs. I think he even sells them. I wouldn't be surprised what all he's into illegally, but you are going to help me find out."

"I can't do that, Sir," Purdy moaned.

"Okay. Then I'll just take you to jail for pissing in public. And on the way to jail, I'll find and pick-up big Jake Wallace and put him in the back seat with you. Then I'll arrange for you and him to share a cell."

"I don't know that dude," Purdy groaned.

"Oh, you will. He's a giant of a butt-fucker. Likes them young like you," Eastridge said, struggling to keep a straight face.

"Jesus Christ, Officer Eastridge, I lied to you! I just met Bo yesterday. Hell, I don't even know where he lives. I was just trying to find him because I need a place to stay."

"I know where he lives," Eastridge said, allowing a smile. "Get in the back seat of my car."

"Shit, Officer, he might not even let me stay with him,"

"Big Jake will," Eastridge laughed.

Marvin started for the police unit, and Eastridge followed right behind him.

* * *

Marvin felt nauseous, and not because he hadn't eaten a bite in nearly twenty-four hours. Life simply had not been kind to him on this day. His luck plunged from bad to shit, and now he sat in the back of a patrol car being taken to beg a man for a place to stay so he could, in turn, report the man's dealings to the awful cop driving the patrol car.

Of course, Marvin didn't have to do that. He could just lie to the cop. Tell him he had nothing to tell him. How could he prove different? Marvin decided to find out.

"Uh, say, uh, Officer Eastridge, what if it turns out I don't have anything to tell you about Bo?"

Eastridge turned mean eyes up to the rearview mirror so Marvin could see them.

"Then I know you will be a lying motherfucker, Purdy, and I'll make your life a living hell."

Marvin moaned out loud. His stomach hurt and his mind spun like a carnival ride terribly out of control. His option box seemed as empty as his stomach, and his wallet, and his future.

A few minutes later, Eastridge pulled his car to the curb, and put it in park. "Conwoop's house is at the end of the next block on the left."

"What if he ain't there?" Marvin blurted.

"He's there. I can see his car parked in the drive."

Eastridge got out and opened the back door. Marvin didn't want to get out, but didn't want butt-fucked either. He stepped out of the car to stand wobbly on legs of gelatin. Eastridge handed him a card.

"My cell number is on there. I expect your first call no later than three days from now. If you don't call, I'll come looking for you. You don't want me to do that."

No, Marvin felt convinced, he did not want that. "I don't really know how I'm going to do this," he mumbled.

"Oh, you'll find a way," Eastridge grinned, "and it will come down to this, boy. You'll either fuck Bo Conwoop, or you'll *try* to fuck me."

Marvin stuck the card deep in a front pocket of his jeans and knew however it went down, he was already fucked.

* * *

Bo took a heavy pull off the joint and placed it in a nearby ashtray. He stood and looked at the front door as he hollered, "Who is it?"

"It's Marvin Purdy."

Bo picked the joint up before walking to the door and pulling it open.

"Hey, Marvin, how did you know I live here?" Bo didn't intend his question to be an assault, but it seemed Marvin took it as such. He looked uneasy as hell.

"I asked around, Bo. Sure hope you don't mind," Marvin practically stuttered.

"Hell no, I don't mind. I'm glad you did." Bo stepped aside and waved him in. Marvin hesitantly stepped past him. Bo thrust the joint in his face. "Want a hit?"

"Uh, well, no thanks. I ain't feeling all too good."

Bo pointed to the nearby couch. "Hell, I can tell. Have a seat, man. You look like shit."

Marvin all but fell on the couch. "I feel like shit."

"Damn, Marvin, what's going on, man?"

"My brother-in-law kicked me out. Dude, I ain't got no place to stay."

The joint had Bo feeling good, and he burst out in laughter. "Shit. If that's you're only problem, Marvin, you ain't got a problem. You can stay here with me, brother."

Marvin suddenly went from looking like shit to looking awfully surprised. "I didn't expect it to be that easy," he mumbled.

"Considering all we got planned, Marvin, this will work out great. Man, I ain't known you long, but I know you're the kind of man I can depend on."

Then Marvin went right back to looking like shit, and Bo knew why. Marvin Purdy, he'd bet, was not the type to take kindness for granted.

Chapter Six

As soon as Troy left for the morning, Kadie Rubottom crawled back in bed. She didn't feel tired. She just felt like being unconscious. But just like the three mornings previous, sleep refused to provide an escape. So Kadie just stared at the ceiling, and tried to wish she could be someplace else living another life. She might not be able to define happiness, but she certainly had her own definition of sadness. It was hating her life, but not being able to imagine another life any place that could bring happiness. Whatever that might be.

She tried so hard not to blame her sadness on Troy. He'd not changed. He was still simply the same man she'd married so many years ago. He'd not grown meaner, and he'd not grown kinder. He did not love her more, and he did not love her less. Kadie wished she could say the same about herself and her feelings toward him. Lately, she wondered if she might not be *happy* living her exact life, but only without Troy.

Divorce?

Oh, no. Troy would never agree to a divorce. He would see that as losing. Not just losing a wife. Not losing some of his land and property and money. Just losing. So far, Troy Rubottom had never lost at anything in his life. Kadie knew that only one thing would ever make that man accept loss.

Death.

* * *

"Sheriff, I'm sorry to call you out so early," Deputy Mike Young said as he met Melody Preston at the door of her cruiser. "But he said he won't talk to nobody but you."

Melody smiled and nodded her understanding at the youngest deputy on the department. "Mark is threatening to kill himself again," she replied.

"Yes, Ma'am. His wife says he has a gun to this head. I just spoke to him through the front door. She's sitting in my car."

"That's good, Mike. You just keep her calm and I'll talk to Mark. I've talked him down before."

"You're not going in there are you, Sheriff?" Mike asked as she started for the small house on the outskirts of the county.

"I'll play it by ear, Mike. You just keep Jessica in your car."

Melody walked to the house and stepped up on the front porch, positioning herself to the side of the door. "Hey, Mark, this is Melody Preston. Can you hear me in there?"

"I can hear you, Sheriff," a distressed voice sounded from within, "but you're wasting your effort. I'm really going to do it this time."

"Are you off your meds again, Mike?"

It took long seconds before the reply came, "They don't do no good."

"We talked about that last time. Let's talk about it again. Can I come in, Mike?"

"I'm too embarrassed to face you,"

"No need to be, Mike. You know I understand life. I know what it can do to you. Now, I'm coming in."

Melody reached to turn the knob and pushed the door open without exposing herself. Now she could hear the man inside softly sobbing. "Can I come in, Mike?"

"You know I would never hurt you, Sheriff. Come on in."

Melody stepped into the doorway to find Mike Perry sitting on his couch with a revolver pressed to his right temple. He was shirtless, wearing a pair of jean shorts and sandals.

"Hello, Mike."

"Howdy, Sheriff."

"Mike, you've known me since high school. I wish you'd just call me Melody."

Tears streamed down his thin face. "Okay, Melody."

Melody walked into the neatly kept little living room and took a seat on a cheap recliner across from the distraught man. "Damn, Mike, have you been working out? You are looking buff, my man."

Mike allowed a slight and tortured smile. "I've been on a diet."

"It's working for you," Melody smiled back.

"I'm a piece of shit, Melody. I don't deserve to live."

"Now, why would you say something like that, Mike? Jessica is crazy about you. You work hard, and you've provided her this nice place to live."

Mike shook his head and dropped his eyes to the floor. "I don't deserve to live and I certainly don't deserve her. I've been doing her wrong lately."

"We talked about things like this before, Mike. You know when you get off your meds, you see things differently."

"Not this time, Melody. I feel like I'm cheating on Jessica."

"I know you'd never do that," Melody whispered softly.

He squirmed in his seat, but did not lower the gun from his head. "I think about other women . . . when we're . . . you know . . . making love."

"Oh, Mike, that's all this is about?"

"That's part of it. Makes me feel awful."

Melody leaned forward and lowered her voice, "Do you know what I've come to learn about love making?"

He sheepishly raised his eyes to meet hers. "No. What's that?"

"There's no wrong way to do it."

"Do you really believe that?"

"Do you hurt her, Mike?"

"Oh, no, I'd never," he blurted.

"If she doesn't feel hurt, Mike, it's all good. No one can say what is right and what is wrong when it comes between a woman and a man. It's very complicated. Love and love making always is. Believe me, some people do things in bed that are . . . well, much more . . . uh, *different* than thinking about someone else while making love."

"They do?"

"Believe me, good friend, *they* certainly do. Now, will you please get the gun away from your head?"

"You won't tell Jessica what I told you?"

"Oh, no, I'd never," Melody mimicked with a smile and a wink.

Mike Perry lowered the gun, and handed it to Sheriff Preston.

* * *

"I ain't hitched a ride since back in the forties," Clint said to Bob.

"Well, how you get it done ain't changed, Clint. You just hold out your thumb and wish for the best."

Bob stood with Clint alongside Highway 62 on the outskirts of Anadarko. The small bag at Bob's feet contained all they'd need once they got where he wanted to be.

"It can be dangerous nowadays," Clint said. "So many nuts out running around."

Considering what the bag held, Bob knew there couldn't be any nuttier folk out and about, but he didn't want to dwell on that. Clint had tried hard enough to dissuade him, and he couldn't lean toward dissuading himself.

"What are they going to do, Clint? Rob us? We ain't got a dime. They going to do bad stuff to us? Hell, we already had beads stuck up our asses."

"I thought we weren't going to talk about that no more," Clint whined.

"We ain't. I'm just pointing out that what we're doing can't do us no worse than what's already been done."

Clint seemed to ponder that for long moments. Bob enjoyed the silence, but knew it would not last.

"When someone picks us up, if they ever do, why don't we just steal that car?"

"I swear, Clint, you listen about like a wife. I done told you. We are standing right outside town, people are passing who know us. Out there, nobody will see us."

"You say the deer will walk right up to us?"

"Old lady Bowden feeds them daily, Clint. Like I told you, they're like pets."

"It's a damned crazy idea, Bob."

"Shut up, Clint, and get your thumb up. Here comes another car."

* * *

They'd only been up an hour, and Bo opened and took a swig of his fifth beer. His refrigerator contained little less, but Bo had graciously made all available to Marvin, who fought the urge to drink right along with Bo until he passed out drunk. However, he now sipped only on his second beer. He couldn't afford a loose tongue that might release all that banged away at his mind and conscience. He'd already fought those demons all night while tossing and turning on the bare and stained mattress on the floor of the spare bedroom. While Bo talked about one thing and then another, Marvin sought peace in knowing he'd not yet betrayed the man. Maybe, he so hoped, he'd find the balls not to.

"And another thing I've been thinking about . . ."

Bo sure proved to be a talkative morning person, although noon lurked right around the corner. So far, he'd not made mention of Marvin having little to say in return.

". . . is, hell, Marvin, we can't rob the four dumbasses' damned card game."

Marvin fought hard not to exhale a sigh of much needed relief and scream "Thank God!" to the heavens. In a blink of an eye, he now had nothing more than dope smoking to relay to the asshole Eastridge. Why bother a busy cop with something so insignificant?

"Hey! Marvin!" Bo said forcibly.

The two words shook Marvin out of deep contemplation over his sudden delight.

"Uh, yeah, Bo?"

"Damn man, you sleeping or what? I asked do you know why we can't rob them?"

"Oh, I was just thinking on it."

"Well, first of all, their next game is tomorrow night. That's too soon. Hell, man, that doesn't give us enough time to get guns."

Guns? Holy shit!

"Why you looked so surprised? What were you planning on using? Knives? Clubs? Our dicks? Like, 'Get your hands up and give us the money or we'll fuck you!'" Bo chuckled, and then seemed to wonder why Marvin didn't laugh too.

"I guess I thought you had guns," Marvin lied.

"Well, I don't, but I know where we can get some."

Marvin didn't want to, but knew Bo would expect him to ask, "Where's that, Bo?"

"From Troy Rubottom."

Marvin almost choked on a sip of beer, but didn't, and wished he had to the point of choking clear to death.

* * *

"Lord Jesus help us. This is a terrible idea."

"I am damn tired of hearing that, Clint. Besides, it's worked so far."

"It was like shooting a puppy dog," Clint moaned from his hiding place behind a tree.

Bob, hiding behind another tree couldn't see Clint. "You got your bandana on?"

"Yeah," Clint barked, "I got the silly fucker on."

Bob adjusted his bandana and cowboy hat and knew he best tell Clint to do the same. "Make sure it covers your nose and pull your hat down tight. All you want showing is your eyes."

"You think I'm an idiot?" Clint growled back. Then seconds later finished with, "Guess I am. I'm here doing this with you. Lord Jesus help us."

It had been so long since the two old partners did anything other than sitting on a park bench that Bob forgot how hard Clint could be to work with. He'd first said they wouldn't catch a ride, but they did. He then said he doubted they'd even see a deer on old lady Bowden's spread of land, but they did. He also said he'd bet neither of the two old Colt revolvers would even shoot, but Bob's sure did. Now a fine and freshly dead buck lay positioned beside the county road, just waiting for some hick to stop and try to load it in the back of a pick-up truck.

"I ain't shooting nobody," Clint called out.

"Hell, we won't have to. You just follow my lead and keep your damned mouth shut." Bob now wondered why he'd even included Clint. Why hadn't he thought to just do this by himself? That way, it would be only him enjoying the pleasures of Nancy on a road trip. But then again, he'd been helping Clint enjoy life for over a half a century. It seemed too late to stop doing so now.

* * *

Melody Preston walked into the Dixie Diner and spotted Robert Morton waiting at a booth in the back. She made her way through the lunch crowd saying hello to someone at nearly every table and booth. She returned a wave to the town mayor across the dining room, and told the ailing Theresa Pierce that she was glad to see her up and about.

"Aren't you the social butterfly?" Robert said with a smile when she finally reached his location.

"Just politicking," she smiled back as she sat down across from him.

"This town needs a better selection of eating places," he said.

"This town needs a lot of things," she returned.

For the next few minutes they made small talk, ordered their drinks, and perused the menu. She knew the fine-looking doctor didn't relish trivial exchanges and just as she made her selection, he got to the point of their lunch date.

"I had a most interesting, uh, patient, yesterday."

"Is this going to be kinky?" she winked.

"If it was, I wouldn't share it," he winked back. "You know I never violate the principles of patients' rights."

"You are so noble," she giggled.

"It was your mother."

The waitress had just dropped off their drinks, and Melody took a hearty swig of sweet iced tea before mumbling, "Oh, shit."

"Yeah," Robert nodded and smiled.

"I'm guessing she complained of more than vaginal discharge?" Melody deadpanned.

"Oh, she only insisted that I make an honest woman out of you," he deadpanned back.

They put the topic on hold to place their order. Melody appreciated the break to get her thoughts and emotions in check. She didn't approve of anyone meddling in her personal life, especially Margaret Stinney.

"Make an honest woman out of me?" She forced a smile. "Is this where you slide out of the booth, drop to one knee, and pop that dastardly question?"

It surprised her when Robert somewhat grimaced at her words. When he didn't immediately respond with a witty quip, but instead started looking around the room, Melody felt a tickle in her guts. Not all tickles being good tickles, she noted that he didn't simply look at those around them, but seemed to study their interactions intently.

"I envy you having roots here," he finally commented. "You know people, and they know you. It must be nice really belonging to a community. I've never had that."

"It can be a real pain in the ass. Take my loving mother for example," Melody said to relieve what suddenly felt like tension.

He looked her sharply in the eye. "I'd like to put down some roots, Melody. Would you marry me?"

"Are you talking hypothetically?"

He reached across the table and took her hand. "No. I'm popping the 'dastardly question.'"

He squeezed her hand. She did not squeeze back. Robert looked down at their hands.

"That's not an encouraging response," he mumbled.

"Do I have to give you an answer right here and right now?" she asked softly.

He slowly released the grip on her hand. "I don't believe that would work in my favor."

"It's sudden, Robert. You took me completely by surprise. For now, would you accept a maybe?"

He offered a slight if not pained smile. "Maybe is better than an immediate no, Melody."

She no longer felt hungry for the meal she ordered, but did so want to wring her mother's neck.

* * *

Henry Beals spotted the deer beside the road too late to stop immediately, and had to back up to get a better look. A fresh kill could feed his wife and three kids for weeks. Henry left his ten-year-old Toyota truck running as he got out and crossed the street to examine the carcass. He bent to feel the condition of the deer when he heard abrupt rustling in the brush alongside the roadway. Henry looked up, and then jumped back. Two men wearing battered cowboy hats and colorful bandanas as masks had sprung upon him. Well, springing wasn't exactly the word for it, but they did have large and old revolvers pointed in his direction.

"What the hell are you doing?" he responded.

"Reach for the heavens!" the man out front demanded. His voice sounded old. He didn't seem to move real well, and neither did the other, but they held the guns steady enough. Henry threw his hands in the air.

"What the hell are you doing?" he repeated. No other words seemed to come to mind.

"This is a robbery," the lead man, wearing the yellow bandana, announced.

"You're robbing me?" Henry gasped.

"That's what you do in a robbery," Yellow Bandana huffed.

"Yeah, dumbass," the man in a red bandana chimed in.

"Shut up, uh . . . Jesse," Yellow Bandana shouted at Red Bandana.

"Fuck you . . . uhhhhhh . . . Frank," Red Bandana shouted back.

"Hey, guys, I ain't got nothing but fifty bucks on me," Henry relayed.

"Get it out then," Yellow Bandana ordered. "And we'll be taking your truck as well."

"My truck? Hell, mister, I can't do without my truck. I have to get back and forth to work to feed my wife and three kids."

Yellow Bandana pulled back the hammer on his revolver. "You damn sure can't feed them if you're dead. Now pull out your money."

Henry pulled at his wallet in a back pocket when Red Bandana stepped up to his partner. "Man says he has three kids. We ain't taking his damned money."

For just a second, Henry thought Yellow Bandana might turn his gun on Red Bandana, but instead just said a bunch of really nasty words. In a flash, well, not exactly a flash, both men moved toward Henry's truck, but kept their guns aimed at him.

"We could have used that damned fifty bucks," Henry heard Yellow Bandana hiss.

"I don't cotton to children going hungry," Red Bandana replied.

Henry watched his truck pull away, feeling some anger, but mostly glad to still be alive, have his money, and a freshly dead deer.

* * *

"Mind if I join you, Gabe?"

Gabe did mind, but didn't need more conflict in his life by turning Troy Rubottom away. He already had enough drama with his mother, Bob and Clint, and knocking Junior on his ass two days earlier for bringing up that ugly incident from his past.

"Pull up a chair, Troy."

Hell, Gabe thought, any man truly wanting to be alone with his miseries should do his drinking other than in the Spurs and Saddles Bar. If one of the other three had to show up, he'd just as soon it be Troy. They all shared financial interests, but Troy was also his brother-in-law.

Troy took a seat and asked what Gabe was drinking. Gabe told him Jim Beam, so Troy hailed a waitress and ordered a double for them both.

"Poker game's tomorrow night," Troy said.

Gabe nodded and grunted his acknowledgment of the date. It'd be his first time seeing Junior since laying his drunk- ass out cold.

Strangely enough, Troy pointed to Gabe's left hand as the thought of Junior still toyed with his insides. "Damn, that's one swollen set of knuckles," Troy said with arched eyebrows. "What did you do? Slug a rock?"

"Something like that," Gabe mumbled.

"Kind of coincidental, I guess, but I ran into Junior this morning. Looks like his chin collided with a rock."

"You don't say," Gabe grumbled.

"Uh huh" Troy grinned. "Been sometime since one of us slugged the other. Reckon it's been a long time in coming."

"I ain't going to tell you about it, Troy."

"Oh, didn't figure you would. Didn't figure Junior would either. So, I didn't even ask, but it sure gets a thinking man to wondering."

"You're always wondering about one thing or another," Gabe sighed.

"I am indeed cursed with deep thinking," Troy nodded.

"I hear tell you done some target practice with your rifle about a week ago," Gabe said, imitating Troy's arching of eyebrows.

"At least I wasn't shooting at somebody in our tight little group of four."

"Is that what we are, Troy? A tight little group?"

The waitress approached with the drinks, and Troy handed her a fist full of bills, telling her to keep what he didn't owe. He then took a hearty swig of his whiskey. "You ever wonder, Gabe, when it's all going to come unraveled? When we pounce on each other like the wolves we are, and just tear each other to shreds?"

"Don't know that it will ever come to that, Troy," Gabe said as he took his turn at a swig.

"Oh, hell, it's in our nature. Bound to happen one day."

"We'd all stand to lose a hell of lot, Troy."

"Yup, but we're a self-destructive lot. We started with nothing, and I'll bet that's how we'll go out."

Gabe preferred not to think along those lines, and it was apparent that one way or another, he'd have to get Junior lined out on letting the past belong to the past. He preferred not to go out with nothing. Thankfully, he didn't have to dwell on such for long. Troy abruptly pointed across the room.

"Would you look at that? Why, hell, that ain't right."

Gabe looked in the direction of the pointed finger, and observed two good-sized men sandwiching a noticeably smaller one. It appeared they intended to play catch with the smaller man, and he wanted to no part in it. From what Gabe could deduce, he was nearly begging to be left alone.

"All this talk, Gabe, has not put me in the mood to watch bullies at work."

"Guess you're thinking about intervening," Gabe grinned.

Troy stood up and pulled his cowboy hat down firmly on his head. "Nope. Done made up my mind."

Gabe stood as well. "I might not be much help with just one good hand."

"You know me, Gabriel. I don't tend to need much help."

Gabe followed as Troy led the way through the other onlookers. "I don't know the two doing the shoving," Gabe said, "but the one being shoved works at Wal-Mart."

"Strangers. Probably oilfield trash," Troy said over his shoulder.

A few more steps placed Troy right alongside the main attraction. All those in the vicinity obviously knew Troy because they hurriedly backed away. The sudden clearing of the masses caught the attention of the two strangers, and they both turned away from their prey to face Troy. Gabe stepped up to stand next to him.

"Can I help you cowboys?" the bully on Troy's left asked with a snarl.

Troy pointed to the Wal-Mart employee in the middle. "He's quite a bit smaller than you two ol' boys," he said calmly.

"Yeah," the bully on the right chuckled. "About your size."

"Then I'm assuming you won't mind me taking his place," Troy said.

The first bully, the one on the left, grabbed the smaller man in question, and simply tossed him aside. "Don't matter to me," he grinned, "But what role is that big Indian next to you going to play?"

"He's only here to pick up the pieces," Troy answered.

Gabe eyed the second bully, the one on the right. By the look in his eyes, his bravado seemed to be dwindling.

"Hey, uh, John," this one said to his partner, "Maybe we ought to just be on our way."

"Bullshit, Ed," the bully named John thundered. "I don't appreciate assholes in cowboy hats sticking their damn noses in . . ."

Speaking of noses, Gabe flinched when Troy all of sudden turned John's nose into a spray of blood and snot with an explosive left jab. Gabe didn't know if Ed even intended to help his friend, because before he could, Troy drove his right elbow into the man's Adam's apple.

John fell back into the bar, and tried to grab it to remain upright. Ed just crumbled to his knees, grasped his throat and started sucking for air. Gabe figured Troy simply didn't want John remaining upright because he quickly planted his right knee between John's legs. For reasons any man with balls could understand, John joined his buddy Ed on the floor.

"Hell, Troy," Gabe chuckled, "That didn't take long."

"Never does with these types," Troy responded before turning and starting back to his whiskey.

Times like this, Gabe thought, reminded him that if he had to be eternally tied to three other men, he could do worse than Troy Rubottom, Johnny Conwoop, and even Junior Pernell. Because, in the same situation, any of the three would have performed with the exact results.

Chapter Seven

Marvin had one more day. Eastridge would expect a call tomorrow. The thought of how that conversation might go caused Marvin to tighten his sphincter to keep from shitting his pants.

Yeah, well, Officer Eastridge, all I have to report is that we stole guns from Troy Rubottom so we can use them to rob the four horsemen of their gambling money next month. I'll let you know how that goes if I'm not dead.

Of course, they had not yet stolen the guns, but they were damn sure on their way to do so.

"And you're positive he won't be there?" Marvin asked from the front passenger's seat.

"Jesus Christ, Marvin," Bo said through gritted teeth. "I done told you. There's a big horse auction in Oklahoma City. That's where he'll be. If he ain't, we'll see his pick-up at the barn. If so, we'll just keep on going. Fuck man, you need to learn to relax."

Relax? Oh, if Bo only knew. But if he did know, he'd likely just kill Marvin. After spending what time he had with Bo, Marvin now felt sure this man was just crazy enough to do that. Marvin bit his tongue to keep from asking, yet again, about the possibility of Troy's wife being home. For now, he'd just have to believe Bo knew *for sure* that every Wednesday morning, Mrs. Rubottom did her grocery shopping for the week.

* * *

Paralegal Kathy Arthur sat at her desk with a phone to ear when Melody walked into the law office. Kathy silently asked Melody for a moment by raising an index finger and smiling sweetly. Within seconds she completed the call.

"You could have gone on back," Kathy smiled again, "but I didn't want you to catch him with his trousers around his ankles. He was watching porn when I went in a few minutes ago."

"Lord, Kathy," Melody giggled, "I don't know how you put up with the man."

"I don't date him," Kathy giggled back.

Melody knew Kathy didn't intend it to, but the comment kind of stung for a couple of reasons.

"I'm not even going to knock before entering," Melody said, brushing aside her newfound sensitivity.

"Serves him right," Kathy giggled again.

Brad Smith didn't have his trousers around his ankles, but was staring intently at his computer screen.

"Cops should never enter a room without knocking," he grinned at her.

"Defense attorneys shouldn't be watching internet porn before noon," she grinned back. "But, guess in your line of work you'd consider it continuing education."

"No. Just prepping for our next date."

There it went again. Another sting. Like the one in the outer office, it revolved around her "dating" Brad, or maybe not dating Brad. Which brought Melody immediately to the point of her visit.

"Robert Morton asked me to marry him."

Smith's jaw dropped. "Damn. Nothing like kicking a man in the balls while he's watching porn."

"I couldn't think of a subtler way to tell you."

"Tell me you immediately told him no, like you have me a dozen times before."

Melody took a deep breath. "I told him maybe."

Smith shot up from his chair. "Are you shitting me, Melody?"

"No," she barely whispered.

Smith ran first one hand and then the other through his thick hair. "Jesus Christ," he mumbled.

"I just felt I should tell you as soon . . ."

"Are you going to marry him?" he interrupted in a near moan.

Melody took another deep breath and shrugged her shoulders. "*Maybe.*"

Smith plopped back into his chair. "Wow," he sighed.

Melody nodded her head. "Yeah. Wow."

Smith looked down at his desk, took in a deep breath, and exhaled it slowly through his lips. "I always thought you'd one day tell me yes." He repeated the deep breath and lip-blowing thing. "I'll never find another woman that does . . . the things . . . you do for me, Melody."

Melody's shoulders involuntarily slumped. "I expect to hear the same from Jerry Eastridge."

Of course, had she given a "maybe" to Brad or Jerry, she'd expect the same from Robert.

* * *

"Mom? Hey, Mom? Open the damned door!" Gabe felt annoyed, but not yet concerned. He'd spent this amount of time before trying to get Nancy to open her door. Maybe she was in the shower. Or, maybe Bob and Clint were in the shower with her.

Now he knocked more consistently and shouted louder. When it came to the point of him pounding on the door, Gabe grew concerned. Not about Bob and Clint. If they were in there, he'd hear them screaming at each other by now.

Oh, Dear God, what are we going to do now, Bob?

Shut the hell up, Clint!

No. They weren't in there, but something seemed very wrong. Gabe took two steps back before delivering a powerful kick to the door. It took a second one to send it flying open.

"Mom?" he shouted as he bolted into the house. "Mom? Are you okay? Where are you?"

It took only seconds to make it throughout the house, and the same length of time to determine she wasn't in there. In her bedroom he found drawers pulled out from the dresser and clothes strewn across the bed along with a couple of pieces of luggage.

"Where in the hell would she have gone?" Gabe thundered.

* * *

Kadie normally looked forward to her shopping Wednesdays. Today she went as far as getting in her car, and pulling it into the garage. She could not remember the last time she'd put the car in the garage, and did so today only to make Lori Sarver think she'd already left for town. When Lori came by, on her way to town, and saw Kadie's Cadillac in the drive, she would most likely stop and suggest they drive in together. Kadie liked Lori, but didn't care to see her today. She didn't care to see anyone today.

Troy left early for Oklahoma City and a horse sale. Hopefully, he wouldn't return until after dark. Kadie would have the day to herself, and intended to spend every single hour of it in bed. If damned lucky, she'd sleep. If she couldn't, she planned on propping up on a pillow to watch old movies. Although, that wasn't a good definition of what she expected. Watching implied a mental escape from reality. More aptly, Kadie would simply stare at the screen. For Kadie, escaping any form of reality did not seem an option.

How many days had she now felt this way? And how many days had Troy failed to notice? Kadie had lost count. Of course, she'd done just enough chores and cooking to keep her husband from noticing. As long as he was fed, had clean clothes and a tidy house, Kadie could just continue to fade away inside. And the terrible thoughts of a single solution to her unhappiness would continue to plague her.

Why can't I just die?

Better yet . . .

Why can't he just die?

* * *

"Why this asshole?" Gabe mumbled to himself as the Anadarko police car pulled up in front of Nancy's house. Of all the cops on duty, why did they have to send Jerry Eastridge?

"What's going on, Saupitty?" the cop asked as he stepped up on the porch.

"The dispatcher didn't tell you?" Gabe replied as distastefully as Eastridge asked.

"Yeah, she told me. And now I'm asking you, what's going on, Saupitty?"

Gabe took a deep breath to steady his temper. He'd learned a long time ago down in south Texas, that you can fight a cop, and you can whip his ass, but you are not going to come out the winner.

"She's gone, and I don't know where she is, Eastridge."

"And you looked around real good inside?"

"Of course, I did. You think I call cops for the fucking fun of it?"

Eastridge chuckled. "Come to think of it, I've never known you *Four Horsemen* to call a cop for a damned thing."

Gabe humbled himself with a deep breath. "But this is serious. She's not right in the head. If she took off, she's not safe. I need help finding her."

To Gabe's surprise, his tone evidently rubbed a layer of rough edges off the huge cop. "Don't guess she has a car, Gabe?"

"No. I took it away from her several months back."

"Okay. Let's get a good description of her. If there's pictures of her in the house, that'll help. I'll get a Silver Alert broadcasted, and I'll start combing the area with other units."

Gabe nodded his head, gulped down even more humble pie and said, "Thanks Officer Eastridge."

* * *

"Damn, Bo, that's making a lot of noise."

Bo stopped pounding with the tire-tool he'd taken from his trunk, and wheeled around to face Marvin. "You know any better way to beat open a stout door, asshole?"

Marvin didn't want to push Bo to using the tool on him. By the sound of his voice and the look on his face, that could be a possibility. "No. Sorry, Bo. Just nervous."

"You see any houses from here?"

"Just the one over there that you said is Troy's."

"Exactly. We're in the middle of nowhere. Ain't nobody going to hear shit. Now, do you want to do this, or do you want to keep your mouth shut while I do it?"

"I'll keep my mouth shut, Bo."

Thankfully, Bo turned his rage from Marvin back to the door. Every blow sounded like a cannon going off. It seemed to take forever, but Bo finally managed to beat the door open. Bo clearly acted out of breath, but it was Marvin who sweated like the proverbial pig. Just like Bo said it would, the door led to a good-sized office within the cavernous barn. Bo flipped a light switch, and Marvin's mouth fell open. Rifles and shotguns lined the far wall.

"That's a lot of guns," Marvin exclaimed. "Seems he'd have this place alarmed."

Bo fell against the closest wall to catch his breath, but chuckled all the same. "Don't need one. Who's crazy enough to steal Troy Rubottom's guns?"

Marvin didn't find it funny, and just wanted to get on with it and get the hell out of there. "Which ones are we going to take?"

"Find the two shortest shotguns. We want automatics, but pumps will do. They'll be good for close work. I'll look around for handguns. Might be in the desk."

Marvin wasn't sure he'd know an automatic from a pump, but didn't care to prolong the stay by asking for clarification. He hurried toward the wall as Bo started for the desk. The long guns were in wooden gun racks. Marvin started picking through them while Bo made a terrible racket at opening and tossing drawers aside. Only seconds passed before a female voice sounded from behind them.

"Bo? Bo Conwoop, what in the hell are you doing?"

Marvin spun around and so did Bo. An Indian woman in a bathrobe and slippers stood in the open door. More importantly, she held what looked like an assault rifle pointed in their direction.

"Kadie," Bo whined. "I thought you were gone."

"What in the hell are you doing, Bo?" Kadie asked again.

Marvin thought she sounded eerily tranquil, and instead of helping to calm him, it frightened Marvin even more. Somehow, he would have preferred a hysterical woman with a gun.

"We came to steal some of Troy's guns, Kadie," Bo exhaled with slumped shoulders.

"Why would you do that?" she asked.

"To be honest with you, we need money. We intended to use them to pull some robberies."

Marvin couldn't believe Bo would be so honest, but if he had to do the talking, he didn't know what he'd say any differently. If you got caught with your pants down around your ankles, Marvin had once heard said, you might as well go ahead and shit.

"Who is he?" Kadie asked with a nod of her head toward Marvin.

"He's Marvin Purdy. Marvin, this is Kadie. Troy's wife."

"Uh, hello, Mrs. Rubottom," Marvin squawked.

Kadie did not respond, but suddenly looked deep in thought. "How much money you need, Bo?"

"Well, Kadie, we were hoping to raise about fifty-thousand a piece."

It surprised Marvin that the sum did not seem to surprise the woman.

"How would you like to make a hundred thousand each?"

"Why, shit, Sadie," Bo clearly joked, "How many people would we have to kill?"

"Just my husband."

Bo looked at Marvin, and seemed confused. He then looked back at Kadie. "Are you serious?"

"Dead serious."

Bo exhaled hard and rubbed both hands through his long hair. "Okay. Yeah. We'll kill him, but it will cost you a hundred and fifty thousand a piece."

"Hey, uh Bo, I think we should . . ." Marvin tried to object with his hands waiving in the air.

Bo explosively barreled up within inches of Marvin's face. "If you are going to fuck this up, I'll kill you right along with Troy. That would mean three-hundred thousand just for me."

Marvin had no reason not to believe Bo, and it felt as if the contents of his stomach suddenly turned to soup. He cradled his belly in his hands as he nodded his understanding.

"I'll pay the three hundred thousand to one of you, or one hundred and fifty thousand to the both of you. I don't care who ends up dead, as long as Troy does too," Kadie said. "But you can't use his guns. I'll give you a thousand in advance to buy the guns you'll need." She lowered the rifle. "Get in your car and meet me up at the house."

* * *

Melody had used her cell to call Jerry Eastridge, and now pulled into the parking lot where they agreed to meet. She spotted his city patrol unit and pulled her cruiser alongside and up close to it, aligning her driver's window with his. She lowered her window, and winked at the ruggedly handsome face that grinned back from a mere two feet away.

"Is this a booty call, Gorgeous?" Eastridge asked.

"Official business," she giggled before killing her engine. "What can you tell me about Nancy Saupitty gone missing?"

"Not much. No more than I put out in the alert," he said with an air of disappointment. "I know your uncle is sure upset. Made me almost feel sorry for him."

Melody knew Eastridge disliked her Uncle Gabe and the rest of his bunch, but knew he also took his job very seriously, and would do his best to help find Nancy. "I know something you might not," she said.

"Surprise me."

"Bob Nettle and Clint Avants have, I guess for some time now, been fucking Nancy."

"Are you shitting me? Damn, that's gross."

"I didn't figure Uncle Gabe would offer that up," Melody chuckled.

Eastridge chewed on the info for a long moment before responding, "I don't blame him. That's not something I would want out about my mom. Two old men screwing one old woman? Damn, that's despicable."

"And you are going to cast stones?" Melody teased.

"You're the one that wanted to keep this official. So, keep it that way," Eastridge grimaced. "Besides, we're not old and disgusting."

"Well, we're not old," Melody had to add before dropping it. "Anyway, Nancy might be found with those two."

"The two old perverts live together over on Oak Street. I'll check that out."

"I already have. They're not there. And I might have more."

"What?" Eastridge barked.

"Yesterday, one of my deputies took an armed robbery and auto theft report out near Mrs. Bowden's farm. Really a strange deal. Two men wearing bandanas as masks robbed the victim of his pickup when he pulled over to look at a freshly dead deer alongside the road. He couldn't see anything but their eyes because of the bandanas and cowboy hats they were wearing. The kicker is, he said they talked and moved like old men. Now, I'm putting two and two together."

"Wow," Eastridge grinned. "The two old bastards stole a truck and then kidnapped Nancy Saupitty?"

"I'm guessing she went voluntarily," Melody said.

Eastridge slapped his steering wheel with both hands and threw his head back to laugh. "I can't wait to inform your uncle of that possibility."

"Would you let me do that, Jerry?" Melody asked in a tone she knew he couldn't refuse. "Please?"

What started as a frown morphed into a cocky smile, "Okay. But you'll owe me big."

Melody quickly decided this was not the time or place to tell Jerry about Robert Morton's proposal. When upset, Jerry could be a very *bad boy.*

* * *

"What is it, Kadie?" Troy answered his cell gruffly.

No "hello, honey." No fondness in his voice. No kindness. No tenderness. And, Kadie could not help but smile.

"Do you have something to tell me about your office in the barn?" She asked.

"My office? What the hell you talking about?"

Since he couldn't see it, Kadie allowed herself another smile. "So, you don't know?"

"I'm in the middle of this goddamned auction, Kadie. Tell me what you're talking about because I'm not in the mood for games."

You best get in the mood for some, Kadie thought. But then said, "I went out to do some bookkeeping for you. The door's kicked in, and your desk drawers are tossed all about."

Troy threw a fit on the other end of the call. The black, ugly, nasty, kind of fit that normally panicked Kadie, but not this time.

"Is anything missing?" he bellowed.

Kadie struggled not to sound too calm. "I can't tell. Do you want me to call the police?"

"Fuck no. I'll handle this shit myself."

Just what she expected. Just to taunt, she wanted to warn her husband against being so predictable. Tell him that it could be dangerous for his health. Of course, she didn't.

"What you can do is call Red Winfield. Tell him I won't be at the card game tonight."

Kadie said she would, and he hung up. No "Goodbye, honey." No, "Thanks, I love you, baby." No fondness in his voice. No kindness. No tenderness. And Kadie smiled again.

* * *

"Where are we going, Bob?"

Thankfully, this time, Clint provided the answer, "Why, Nancy, Bob's done told you three times just today that we're going to wherever the road takes us."

Nancy responded the same way she had each time she asked before. She smiled and said, "I like that. It sounds so romantic. But I don't have but one thousand dollars."

Bob grinned from his place behind the steering wheel. A thousand bucks, if spent right, could buy a lot of gasoline, meals, and motel rooms. A thousand bucks could carry them a long way from Anadarko, and Gabe Saupitty.

They'd picked Nancy up the night before just after dark. She at first seemed confused on whether or not to go with them. Bob told her it would be an adventure of a lifetime, and Clint promised they would stop for fried chicken down the road. Bob still didn't know if it was an adventurous spirit or a hunger for chicken that convinced her, but she decided to go. They'd spent the previous night in one room at a Motel Six with a king-sized bed. Neither Bob nor Clint bothered Nancy for loving. It seemed robbing, grand theft, and whisking maidens away in the night proved enough excitement for them both in the course of one day. Bob did dream in the middle of the night that he and Nancy were going at it, when all of a sudden, she whipped out a string of beads. He'd not slept well the rest of the night. His restlessness was compounded by the fact that fried chicken had given either Clint or Nancy a terrible case of fart letting.

Now the Texas border laid about thirty miles up the road. Once they hit the Lone Star state, Bob would start looking for a place to call it a day. A lot of sunlight still remained, but Bob felt ready to get out of the truck. Nancy more than likely felt the same because she'd fallen asleep and was lightly snoring.

"Say, Bob," Clint said to interrupt his thinking.

"Yeah?"

"Will crossing the state line put us in any more trouble than we're already in?"

Bob did not want Nancy waking to hear any of this. He and Clint decided it best not to tell her how they got the truck. He answered in a hushed tone.

"Don't know. I figure the law, if they get a chance, will arrest us no matter where we are. And I figure it don't matter how many state lines we cross if Gabe gets hold of us. He can only kill us once."

"Yup, but there's fast dying and there's slow dying," Clint mumbled.

"Yeah, well the way I see it, Clint, we been slow dying since the day we was born. Maybe it's time for a change."

Bob chuckled. Clint didn't.

* * *

"First time I've ever been summoned to this particular sheriff's office," Gabe said as he lumbered through the door.

"The message I left on your phone asked you sweetly to meet me here, Uncle Gabe. Hardly a summons," Melody giggled as she stood up and moved around her desk to greet him. She'd always held a tender spot in her heart for the big man, and knew he felt the same. She threw her arms around him and he pulled her into his thick upper body.

"I'm so sorry to hear about Nancy," she said once the hugging subsided.

"I'm hoping you have news?" He asked.

The look of worry in his eyes tugged at Melody's heart, but she knew that look was about to turn stormy.

"I got a hunch, and you're not going to like it."

Gabe took a deep breath and held it before asking, "Tell me."

"I think she's with Bob Nettle and Clint Avants."

Gabe bellowed like a bull while he wheeled about in place as if looking for something to kick or toss.

"Please don't tear up my office, Uncle Gabe."

For long, tense moments he just made the animalistic grunts and growls. "Where are they?" he finally seethed.

"Don't have a clue." Melody then told him about the hold-up and the stolen truck.

"Jesus Christ, they could be anywhere by now," he thundered.

"They may be far, but then again they might be near. I've put out all the necessary information to every local and state agency, including the FBI. I asked them to handle it as a possible abduction."

"Abduction my ass! They kidnapped her!"

"Basically, the same thing, Uncle Gabe."

Eventually, the broad shoulders slumped. "Ain't a damned thing I can do . . . but wait."

"That's about it."

Then he straightened. "But I'll tell you what, my dear niece, should I come across them, you will be putting me in a cell."

Melody certainly hoped it would never come to that.

* * *

Woop walked through his rambling house looking for Rheta, and found her in her upstairs sewing room reading a book.

"Howdy White Woman," he said as he leaned in the doorway.

"Well, hello there, you Comanche savage," she beamed up at him before dog-earing a page and closing her book.

"Why do you call this your sewing room when all you do is read up here?"

"What are you doing home? This is your gambling night at the cabin."

Woop walked into the room and took the only other available chair. "I decided I'd rather spend the evening with my loving old lady."

"That's bullshit."

"Yeah," he chuckled. "It is."

Rheta playfully tossed the paperback at him. He caught it in mid-air, and studied the title. "Why you read this kind of shit?"

"Why aren't you gambling?"

"Why do you read this shit?" Woop repeated.

"I have to get my romance someplace," she smiled. "Now, why are you home?"

Woop tossed the novel back into her lap. "Red called. The game is cancelled."

"Cancelled? Did one of the other three die?"

"I couldn't be that lucky," he grunted. "No. Someone broke into Rubottom's office, where he keeps all his guns, and Bob Nettle and Clint Avants kidnapped Nancy Saupitty."

Rheta's mouth fell open, but she still managed to ask, "Are you kidding me?"

"On which account?"

"Jeez, Woop, on both. Who's stupid enough to try and rob Troy? And, damn, Woop, Gabe will surely kill those two old men."

He took a second to think over her response. "Yeah. Must have been somebody who didn't know whose place they were breaking into, and, yup, I don't hold much promise for Bob and Clint if Gabe catches up with them."

Woop watched as Rheta processed. He thought she looked pretty doing so, but didn't like what it produced.

"Woop, are you boys losing control?"

"What are you talking about? Losing control of what?"

Rheta scrunched her face. "Well, think about it. There was a time, and I don't know when it went away, but there was a time no one in these parts would dare cross any one of you four."

Woop gave it some thought, and it stung. "Maybe it's just coincidence."

"And maybe you four are losing control."

He scratched at his chin before coming to his senses and making light of it. "Control? Shit, woman, I'm still in control. And I'll prove it. Go fix me some supper."

"Go fix your own supper."

Woop cocked his head and gave her a stern look.

"See?" Rheta chuckled. "Control is a slippery animal. Once it gets out of your grip . . . it's gone."

Chapter Eight

Morning's first glow teased at the window above the mattress where Marvin sat crossed-legged, swaying to and fro. He expected Bo to be sleeping off last night's heavy drinking, and hoped he'd be doing so until at least noon. That would give Marvin plenty of time to slip out, find a payphone, and call Eastridge. The act was planned. What he would say was not.

Only two things seemed certain. One, Marvin surely wanted the one hundred and fifty thousand dollars. Two, he didn't want to kill for it. He could bring himself to rob and burglarize, but murder proved a whole different matter. It seemed to Marvin like comparing a pimple on the ass to a cancerous tumor on a vital organ. The amount of money in question would make him a rich man. He could do things with that money he'd never dreamed of doing. In a nutshell, the problem seemed to be that Marvin simply was not the murdering type. Bo, on the other hand, expressed no qualms over carrying out the awful crime. Marvin felt so convinced of the fact that he knew Bo would surely kill him dead if he even thought Marvin had any kind of dealings with Eastridge.

So, the long hours of sitting cross-legged and swaying had yet to provide Marvin with the solution of how he could keep from murdering without being murdered. Yes, he could run, but could he escape both Eastridge and Bo? Yes, he could completely spill his guts to Eastridge. But, could he truly trust Eastridge to somehow keep Bo from killing him? Why would he even think Eastridge would give a damn if Bo did kill him? So many questions, and no good answers.

With his mind spinning and his heart racing, Marvin forced himself from the mattress and quietly out the door. Right now, he knew the only thing he must do was find a phone.

* * *

Red Winfield strolled up to the booth in his fine business suit and stuck out his right hand.

"Thanks for coming, Red," Woop said as he leaned forward in his seat and shook the out-stretched hand.

"I don't pass up a free breakfast," Red grinned as he scooted in across from Woop. "And, you sounded concerned on the phone. Now, that I'm here, you look concerned. You know, you got that concerned Indian look on your face."

"Any Indian looks concerned when meeting with the white man that controls all of his assets," Woop smiled. Honestly, he didn't know he sounded concerned earlier or looked that way now. It didn't say much for that stereotypical "stoic" bullshit. He'd have to work on that.

"I hope to hell it's not money you're worried about, because you have tons of it."

"It's along those lines," Woop nodded in a more "stoic" manner. "Guess I'll get right to the point. Red, do you think me and the others are losing control?"

Red laughed before responding, "Losing control of what, Woop?"

"I don't really know," Woop frowned.

Red laughed again. "What the hell are you talking about?"

Woop squirmed in his seat. "Oh, shit, it's just something my wife said. I told her why the card game was cancelled, and she asked if I thought we were losing control. Maybe she meant respect. I mean, who would break into one of our places, or kidnap one of our loved ones, Red?"

"Oh, I get it," Red said while nodding his head. "But maybe what she was saying, was that people no longer fear you four."

"I've never wanted to be feared," Woop grunted.

"Well, too late for that. I'm scared to death of you four idiots."

Woop laughed this time, but countered it with, "I'm serious, Red. Who around these parts don't know Troy, and don't know better than to fuck with him? And you'd think Bob and Clint would damn sure know better than to cross Gabe."

The two men put their conversation on hold to order their breakfast.

"Bring me the Dixie Diner breakfast special, and cut off a slab of raw buffalo meat for Tonto, here," Red grinned and winked at the young waitress.

"I'll take the special, too," Woop mumbled.

"Did you see the look on her face, Woop?" Red asked as the waitress moved off. "It terrorized her that I'd refer to the great Johnny Conwoop as Tonto. See, you still got it."

"Fuck you, you funny fucker," Woop sighed.

"Okay. To answer your question, I don't know anyone stupid enough to break into Troy's office. As to Bob and Clint, if you took away all their stores of stupid, there would be nothing left but two empty sets of old cowboy clothes."

"Maybe the four of us just need to band closer together," Woop said more to himself than to Red.

"That would be an unusual change of pace," Red chuckled. "But, honestly, I think you're making too much of this. Whoever hit Troy's place either don't know Troy, or didn't know it was his place they were hitting. I'd call it coincidence."

"That's what I told Rheta."

"See, great minds do think alike." Red then took a sip of coffee before asking, "By the way, what's going on with Bo? What's he up to nowadays?"

"Yet another coincidence," Woop grumbled.

"How's that?"

"Well, when it comes to that boy, Red, I've lost all control."

* * *

Junior pointed to a chair in the office of his barn. "Have a seat," he said to Craig Johns.

Johns sat down and then said, "I guess I could have told you what I have on the phone."

"I'd rather hear it face to face," Junior replied before plopping down in the chair behind his desk.

"I have good news, and I have bad news," Johns said. "Which do you want first?"

"Surprise me," Junior sneered.

"Okay then, Junior, I'll start on a positive note. I think you'll be pleased to learn that I may not be gay after all."

Having his elbows propped on the desk in front of him, Junior automatically dropped his head into his hands. From this position he fought off the urge to say nasty and hurtful things, managing to mutter instead, "Do tell, Craig." And didn't know why he muttered it, because he really didn't want Johns to tell another damn thing about it.

"Yup, I think I was just what you call bi-curious."

Junior raised his head to look wearily at Johns. "I have no idea what you're . . ."

"It means I might have bi-sexual tendencies and was simply curious what it would be like to have sex with a man."

"Awww, jeez. Fuck me . . . I mean . . . jeez, I don't mean that!" Junior blurted.

Johns broke into laughter. "I just wanted you to know. Thought it might make you feel better about me."

"It doesn't," Junior moaned as he threw up palms to stop any further discussion. He relished the moments of silence to collect his thoughts, and purge them.

"So, Craig, the bad news is about the investigation?"

Johns turned serious in a wink of an eye. "I was able to find out all I have by simply using the Internet. And, actually, it's not all bad."

Junior sucked in air. "Let's hear it."

"First of all, none of the reports I could find list suspects."

Junior's outlook brightened. "That's damn good news," he almost smiled.

"Yes, it is. And, far as I can tell it's now filed as a cold case. In other words, there's no ongoing investigation."

"Why, shit, I might just dance a jig, but probably won't," Junior nodded.

"Yeah, don't dance just yet, because on the other hand, it's almost as bad as you expected. There were three people in the car. A mother and father and their infant son. Only one survived."

"Which one?"

"The baby. Who, of course, is a man now."

Dear God, alongside that road . . . I did hear what I thought I heard.

Junior could only shake his head as Johns disseminated the awful truth. "What do you know about him?"

"Not much. I'd have to go to Colorado to learn more."

Junior looked Johns hard in the eyes. "Then go."

"I will have to be damn careful how I go about it. We don't want the case reopened."

"By all means, Craig, do be damned careful."

* * *

"Yes ma'am, Miss Sheriff Lady," Jerry Eastridge said while standing at an exaggerated position of attention while offering a salute with the wrong hand. "Officer Eastridge of the Anadarko mounting police reporting as directed."

"Mounting police," Melody grinned from her desk chair, "That's clever."

"Hoped you'd think so. Now, why the hell did you want to meet in your office?"

The grin melted from her face. She didn't at all want to do this.

"Well, this is where I delivered the bad news to Uncle Gabe yesterday, and he took it fairly well. Didn't wreck anything. I'm thinking, with any luck at all, you won't either."

"That damned sure sounds ominous," Eastridge grimaced before settling in a chair across from Melody's desk. "You have some kind of bad news for me?"

"Probably so," Melody said softly. "Robert Morton asked me to marry him . . . and I'm going to tell him yes."

The big cop suddenly looked like a blow-up doll stuck with a pin. "Probably so? Goddamn, Melody, why didn't you just pull your gun and shoot me in the heart?"

"No good way of saying it, Jerry. Besides, you've never asked me to marry you."

Eastridge dropped his head to stare at huge hands. "Tried being married three times. I'm not good at it." Then he looked back up and into Melody's eyes. "I never took you for the marrying type anyway, Melody."

"Every woman is the marrying type sooner or later," She exhaled heavily.

The look in his eyes grew quickly nasty like an approaching storm. "Fuck, you're only marrying him because he's a doctor. I ought to break the little motherfucker in three pieces."

"Awww, now there's the response I was waiting for."

Eastridge jumped up from the chair and flung it aside. "Fuck it! If that's what you want, that's what you deserve. It won't last. A woman like you will go through that wimp like a dose of salt."

As Eastridge stomped toward the door, Melody searched for words, but none seemed appropriate. Jerry was the just type of man who could only express pain as anger.

He stopped at the door and wheeled around. "And when you're finished with him," he seethed, "Don't come running back to me. I won't have you."

At a loss for appropriate, Melody chose inappropriate, and slung them at his back. "Fuck you, Eastridge!"

He turned around a final time. "You'll never enjoy that privilege again, bitch!"

* * *

Troy looked up at the sound of something outside the destroyed door to his office. The sight of the figure in the doorway didn't startle him, but did surprise him. He could not remember the last time the big man paid him a visit.

"Come in, Woop. I'd ask what brings you out, but that would be a stupid question to ask. I'm not in the mood for stupidity."

Woop walked in and stood to look around the office. "You have any idea who to lynch for this?"

"Not really. Kadie went to town yesterday to do her shopping. We're guessing the sound of her approaching car scared them away. I spent the night in here hoping they'd try again."

"Police might be able to get some prints, Troy."

"Fuck the police. I'll find out who did it."

Woop nodded his understanding. "You had any trouble with anyone lately?"

"I taught two oil-field trash types a lesson on picking on little fellers a couple of days ago in the Spurs and Saddles. I wouldn't think they'd want more of me, but guess they'd have to be my prime suspects. I'll be looking them up."

"Looks like all your rifles and shotguns are still in place," Woop observed.

"They didn't get anything. Guess they didn't have time. Sure glad Kadie didn't walk in on them."

"That could have been really bad," Woop grunted with a nod of his head. "Hey," Woop said after a slight pause, "what about those two you shot at for dumping trash about a week back?"

"I didn't shoot at them. I shot at their truck. And I damned sure hit it, too. But, I met one of the two face to face. Hell, his eyes gave away the fact he has no balls. Don't think it was them."

"Well, we need to start getting the word out. Someone will know something."

"We?" Troy asked.

"Hell yes, we, Troy. It was once well known, but I think there now needs to be a reminder. You fuck with one of us, you get fucked by all of us."

Troy took a few moments to think on Woop's words before saying, "Well, Woop, that sounds like a declaration of solidarity. And I like it. It's kind of like the 'Four Horsemen Ride Again.' Sure has a ring to it, but do you think Junior and Gabe feel the same? I heard about Gabe knocking Junior on his ass."

"Yeah, I'm guessing that was over some personal business from a long time back. Hell, all four of us have one time or another laid hands on the other. I'm sure they'd both find it in their best interest to, uh, what words am I looking for, professor?"

"In their best interest to reestablish our reputation?"

"Yeah, that's what I'm talking about," Woop grinned.

"It's good to have friends," Troy summated.

"Yup," Woop grinned again, "even if they ain't all that friendly."

* * *

With every single ring on the other end, Marvin fought to keep from hanging up the pay phone. Still, even now, he did not know what to say when Eastridge picked up. With any luck at all he wouldn't answer, but Marvin didn't get to finish the thought.

"Who is this?" A very mean sounding voice answered.

Who answers a phone like that? Now Marvin really wanted to hang up. It sounded like Eastridge was terribly pissed before Marvin even uttered a word.

"It's Marvin Purdy," his voice trembled and quaked. Eastridge said nothing in return. Maybe he didn't hear him? "Officer Eastridge? This is Marvin . . ."

"You best have something really fucking good, Purdy."

We broke into Troy Rubottom's barn.

His wife caught us.

She wants us to kill Troy.

Bo might kill me.

I could end up running from you and Bo and maybe even the Four Horse . . .

It struck Marvin like a fart turned to shit. But, this wasn't shit. If it was, it was good shit. Or maybe something real close to good shit. At the very least, it presented another opportunity other than going to jail, killing, or being killed.

"He smokes dope. I haven't seen much of it around. I don't think he sells it, because if he did I'd see a lot of it . . ."

"That's all the fuck you got?" Eastridge stormed.

That's not all I got, but all you're going to get, Fuck in the nose.

"Shit, Officer Eastridge, it's only been three days. I can tell he don't trust me yet. If I had more time . . ."

"You got three more days, you scum bag piece of decaying dick! By then, you better have more."

Eastridge hung up on him, and Marvin moved the receiver from his ear to stare at it. "Scum bag piece of decaying dick?" He repeated out loud. Then, for the first time in three days, Marvin laughed. He laughed until tears trickled down his cheeks.

* * *

Saupitty sat upon his tall buckskin gelding and glanced over at Woop. "Good idea coming out and riding this land. No better way to get acquainted with it than on horseback."

"Yup, that's what I was thinking when I suggested it, Gabe," Woop nodded from atop his sleek Paint mare. "Three thousand acres of it to get acquainted with. Glad Red finally closed the deal."

"Would have closed it much sooner if not for that ugly motherfucker, Junior," Gabe growled.

Woop nodded and chuckled.

"Me being an Apache, and you being a Comanche, looks like one of us would have scalped that son of a bitch long ago, Woop."

"Way I see it, in light of our monthly poker games, we've both scalped him a number of times."

Gabe grunted as he tried to turn his mind to poker. "Hated having to be a part of cancelling our last get together."

Woop looked over at him. "You couldn't help that. Damn sorry to hear about your mom. Any word on her whereabouts?"

"None. But I'll tell you what, if I get the chance, I'll damned sure scalp those two old bastards that stole her away."

"That's another reason I suggested coming out here, Gabe. Nothing takes bad shit off a man's mind like bouncing a butt on a horse's back."

Gabe pulled in a deep breath of the fresh country air and scanned the big chunk of land with tall grasses and rolling hills. It didn't have a lot of big trees, but enough to shade cattle from the harsh summer sun. "Entire place will need new fencing," he observed.

"Yup," Woop said with a nod.

They kept their horses at a walk, and neither spoke for another hundred or so yards of riding.

"There's another reason I wanted to get you out here, Gabe," Woop broke the silence. "It has to do with your mom, and Troy's break-in."

Gabe did not look at Woop, but said, "Surely you don't think the two situations are related."

"In a way, I think they are."

Gabe now turned his head to stare at Woop. "You're thinking Bob and Clint tried to steal Troy's guns?"

"Oh, hell, no. They're both at least smart enough not to screw with two of us at the same time. But, Bob and Clint and someone else did give us a screwing."

"Us?" Gabe grumbled.

Woop turned to meet his stare. "Hell yes, us. I've been talking with Troy. Me and him are going to do what we can to help you find your mother. And I'm going to help him to find out who broke into his office. I'm hoping you'll help me do that. And . . . I'm hoping you will reach out to Junior to help us all."

Gabe felt his guts clinch. "I'll do what I can to help Troy, but fuck that shit on reaching out to Junior, and fuck him, too."

Woop let out a loud sigh. "Now, see, we're getting to the heart of the problem, and why it was all of us who took a screwing. I believe folks are sensing that we no longer stick together. That we no longer have each other's backs."

Gabe's immediate inclination was to deny that the four of them had ever stuck together and watched each other's backs. But he knew that would be a lie. All four had always battled each other in a tight little circle, but no one else dared put a foot in that circle. Until recently. As he pondered the decline, his eyes fell upon a bank of dark clouds assaulting the horizon. He pointed at the clouds.

"Looks like a storm is brewing."

Woop never looked up from the ground in front of him, but nodded his head. "I do fear you are right."

* * *

Melody didn't bother calling first. She wanted to surprise him, and when he opened his front door, she could tell she had.

"I have a warrant for your arrest."

"What law did I break?"

"Touching too many titties, and looking at more pussies than any man should have a right to."

Dr. Robert Morton chuckled and shook his head. "You have such a lovely way with words." He stepped to the side and motioned Melody in. "If you have to strip search me, I would prefer you do it out of view of my neighbors."

Melody stepped in and smiled at him. "Looks like you'd want the widow Folgers across the street knowing there's much more to you than just a handsome face."

Morton closed the door and took Melody into his arms. "There's only one woman I care to get naked in front of."

Melody tiptoed to give him a warm kiss. "And who would that be?"

"Hopefully my fiancé."

Melody kissed him again. This one longer and more intense. Then she pulled away from his arms and strolled through the entryway to the lavish living room. The doctor had a wonderful sense of design, and expensive tastes. She sat down upon a plush sofa of rich leather.

"It's this fiancé thing that I'm here about."

Morton was moving toward a matching recliner, but stopped, apparently thinking he'd rather be upright to hear what she had to say.

"I've given it a lot of thought, Robert, and I'm about to destroy your life."

His head dropped and he exhaled heavily. "I feared as much."

"No, you didn't, because I'm going to marry you."

His head shot up, and a broad smile lit his face. "You are such an ass."

"Yes, and we've not even set a date yet. Just wait until I get a ring on my finger."

He pulled her from the couch and escorted her toward the staircase.

"You need to know, Robert, that Jerry Eastridge is most likely going to whip *your* ass."

He leaned to whisper in her ear, "It's been whipped before, sweetheart."

Chapter Nine

Bob sat naked on the side of the other queen-sized bed in the motel room and stared at the wall two feet away. He sniffed at the air in the room. It smelled of nasty old-people sex. Sooner or later, one of the three would have to give into bathing. He reached for his chewing tobacco on the nightstand and stuffed what remained of it into his sagging facial pouch. The bed behind him squeaked rhythmically as if objecting to the part it played in Clint and Nancy's early morning getting-it-on.

"Nancy," Clint moaned. "I done told you three times, my name ain't Seymour."

The squeaking stopped.

"Who are you then? And why am I fuckin' you?"

Bob shook his head and sighed. Nancy seemed to be getting worse by the minute. He looked down at the purple bruise around his left nipple. The night before, during his turn with her, she suddenly went all crazy-eyed, screamed "RAPE," and clamped down on his nipple with bared teeth. Getting her to let loose proved as difficult as removing a tick from the cheeks of your ass without benefit of a mirror.

"Where you going, Nancy?" Clint asked.

"To find Seymour. He's going to whip your ass for sure."

"Awww, hell, Nancy, once this thing goes down, don't know when it will come to life again!"

Bob cradled his head in his hands. He kept it there until he felt a tap on the top of it. Bob turned to look up at Nancy.

"Do you know where Seymour went?"

He pulled in a deep breath before responding. "Sure do, Nancy. He stepped out for a cup of coffee. Said you should shower while he's gone."

Nancy turned without a word and started for the restroom while scratching at a saggy and badly wrinkled ass. Bob waited until he heard the water running.

"Clint," he said as he turned in place, "We got to get her . . ."

Clint had pulled the covers up, but there was no doubting what he performed beneath them.

"Fuck, Clint, aren't you a little old for that shit?" Bob groaned.

The pumping activity beneath the sheets ceased.

"I'm a little old for all kinds of shit, Bob. I want to go home. I miss our bench in front of the drugstore."

Bob grabbed his jeans and pulled them on. "Glad to hear you say that. Get up and let's get dressed."

"Where we going, Bob?"

"Soon as Nancy gets cleaned up, we're taking her back to Gabe."

"Why, shit, man, he'll kill our asses. And the rest of our damned bodies as well."

Bob couldn't find his socks and struggled to pull his boots onto bare feet. "Maybe, and maybe not. Just maybe he'll be so relieved to get her back that he'll forgive us for our stupid-assed mistake."

"Wasn't my idea in the first place, Bob," Clint said as he started grabbing for his clothes.

"Yeah, well, you went along with it. One thing is for sure, if he catches us before we return her, he'll damn sure kill us both."

"You seen my underwear, Bob?"

"No, and I ain't lookin' for the damned nasty things. Go without them. Now, I'm going to walk across the street and get us all some coffee. You get yourself and Nancy ready to go."

* * *

"I don't know what the hell you want, but I really don't care to have you here," Junior growled.

"Well, get the *hell* over it. Besides, I called and asked if I could come by, and you said yes. Now, here I am, so deal with it."

Junior set behind his desk in the barn office and watched as Gabe Saupitty casually pulled up a chair. Junior now wished he'd not given into his curiosity. Just laying eyes on the long-haired Apache angered him even more than he anticipated. Should have told him, "Shit no, you can't come over, asshole!"

Junior thought Gabe might just want to discuss their sins committed long ago in Colorado, and already decided he would not yet share the information Craig Johns supplied. Knowledge certainly equated to power in this situation.

"You got any whiskey in that desk?" Gabe asked.

Junior grunted disapproval, but opened a drawer and pulled out a new bottle of Johnny Walker Black. "I don't have any glasses," he snarled.

Gabe grabbed up the bottle and twisted off the cap. "For nearly two-hundred years, we Apache have been drinking white man's whiskey straight from the bottle. Don't need no damn glasses."

Junior sat silently as Gabe took one long swig from the bottle, and then another. He then held the bottle out for Junior.

"Here, take a bump. Might improve your disposition."

Junior grabbed *his* bottle and took two swigs more mightily than had Gabe just to prove he could. He then placed the bottle on the desk between them.

"Why are you here?"

"Because you invited me . . . in a sense," Gabe grinned before grabbing up the bottle and taking another chug.

"I ain't drunk this time. I might just whip your ass. Leave you lying on the ground like you did me."

Gabe pushed the bottle toward Junior. "Here's you some courage."

Junior scooped up the bottle and took another hearty swig. "Don't push me, motherfucker. What do you want?"

"I want your support."

"You running for office? I wouldn't vote for you as dog catcher."

Gabe threw back his head and laughed, and Junior wished he hadn't. It took off the edge. "What kind of support?" he sighed.

"Did you hear about somebody breaking into Troy's barn?"

"Yeah, I heard about it. That's some crazy shit."

"Exactly, Junior. It's some unbelievable shit that shouldn't have happened. Not to one of us! That's where I need your support. I'm going to be asking questions about it, and I hope you will as well."

"What kind of questions and to who?" Junior asked before sliding the bottle back to Gabe.

"To the types that know those kind of types. To the low lives. We got plenty of those here in Caddo County. By, doing so, we show . . . uh . . . *solidarity*. It will remind those types that the four of us stand together." Gabe took the bottle and another gulp before passing it back to Junior.

Junior knew his next question, and took a hit off the bottle for emphasis. "You talking about types like that worthless son of Woop's?"

"You bet. Him and the types of women he associates with."

"Don't you bring my daughter into this, you motherfucker," Junior growled.

Gabe's eyes narrowed into a mean squint, but then he took a noticeably large breath and exhaled it slowly. "Woop will talk to Bo, but you will need to talk to Cassie."

"I'll talk to who I see fit to talk to."

"So, you're in, Junior?"

"Well, what about your situation, *Gabriel,* are you wanting my help to find your mother?"

Gabe repeated the deep-breathing process. "I'd appreciate any help you could lend. I want her back."

"All right. I'll do my part for Troy. As for you, I'll help there too, but I want your word no harm will come to Bob and Clint."

"Why do you give a fuck about those two bastards?"

"Same reason you should. None of us four would be worth a stinking pile of shit had they not taken us under wing."

Gabe took one more long hit off the bottle before pushing to his feet. "I won't give you my word on that."

Junior stood as well. "Then I'll give you my word on this. You hurt either one of them too awfully bad, you'll be dealing with me. And I won't be drunk the next time, but I will have my gun."

Gabe snarled out a snicker, and turned to walk toward the door.

"One more thing, Gabe," Junior called out. "Back on this business of the low-life thing. You surely believe every one of us fall into that same category."

Gabe didn't bother turning back, but said over his shoulder. "Why of course we do, but the four of us? Hell, we are the aristocracy of the low-lifes."

* * *

Bob walked past their Toyota truck in the motel parking lot. With his hands full of three Styrofoam cups of coffee, he kicked on the door of room 38 with the toe of his boot.

"Open the damn door, Clint."

Clint didn't open the damn door even though Bob called out a couple more times. Grumbling profanities, he stooped to put the coffee on the concrete, and reached into the right front pocket of his jeans for the room key. Not finding it there, he dug into his left one.

"Well, hellfire," he grumbled before reaching with both hands into his back pockets.

"I got my key, Bob."

Clint's voice suddenly at his back startled Bob, and he kicked over two of the cups of coffee. He spun on Clint. "Now look what the hell you made me do. Where is Nancy?"

"I left her in the room to walk to that grocery store down the street for some Prince Albert. I'm sure she's still in there."

"Well, she ain't answering the damn door."

"You probably don't sound like Seymour, Bob."

"Open the damn door, Clint."

Clint opened the door and Bob wobbled inside. She wasn't on one of two beds, so he headed toward the bathroom.

"Oh, Jesus, Clint, she ain't here," Bob moaned.

"Are you sure?" Clint asked from behind him.

Bob spun on him a second time. "Well, do you see her? You think she's hiding under a goddamned bed?"

Clint lowered himself to his knees and scurried to check under both. "You can't get under these beds, Bob."

"No shit, you blamed idiot. Oh, dear Jesus, she's gone."

"What are we going to do, Bob?"

"Why hell, Clint, we're going to call the police."

"Really?"

"No, not really, you idiot. Get your ass out there. We got to find her."

Clint started for the door. "I'm about tired of this 'idiot' bullshit."

"Well, I ain't the idiot that left her here alone."

"Well, I ain't the idiot that kicked over two of the three cups of coffee. Was one of those mine?"

"Yeah, Bob, I had three cups of black coffee, and I just happened to kick over the two that belongs to you and Nancy."

"Can I have a sip of yours?"

* * *

Marvin stood beside Bo as he pounded on the door. "You sure she's home, Bo?"

Bo didn't bother giving an answer, but hollered, "Open the door, Cassie! I know you're in there!"

To Marvin's surprise, the door opened. A woman looking to be about his age stuck a sleepy looking head out the door. Her bleached blonde hair looked a mess, all tangled, and sleep tousled.

"What do you want, Bo Conwoop?" she grumbled.

"I want to come in, Cassie."

The woman turned unfriendly green eyes on Marvin. "Who the fuck are you?"

"Uhhhh," Marvin started, "I'm Marvin . . ."

"I'll make the introductions once we're inside, Cassie," Bo rudely interrupted.

"My daddy is paying me to stay away from you."

"Fuck Junior Pernell. I got business to discuss with you. I plan on paying you some money, too."

"Look at this new house, Bo. It's damned nice. Daddy bought it for me. You going to pay me that kind of money?"

Marvin had already noticed that this house looked a hell of lot better than what Bo lived in. "It is a nice house, Cassie," he smiled.

"Shut the fuck up, Marvin," Bo hissed. "Cassie, he don't have to know I was here. Come on, let me in. Let's talk."

Cassie stuck her head further out the door to scan up and down the street. "Okay, but you can't stay long."

She walked back into the house, and Bo followed her. Hesitantly, Marvin followed Bo.

"Cassie this is Marvin Purdy. Marvin, this is Cassie Pernell," Bo said.

"Nice to meet you, Cassie," Marvin grinned, and offered his right hand for shaking.

Cassie looked at it as if it held a turd. "Uh huh," she said before plopping down on a couch nearly buried in clothes and litter.

Where the outside of the house looked dandy, Marvin thought the inside looked as if occupied by a swarm of filthy pack rats. Even if invited to do so, he wouldn't care to sit on any exposed surface he could see.

"Cassie, me and Marvin here got a big job to do. It pays big money. You help us out, I'll toss you a thousand once the job pays off."

"You taking down a bank?" Cassie snickered.

"Something like that," Bo grinned. "Only bigger."

"What do you want from me, Bo?"

Bo shoved a heap of all kinds of shit from an armchair and took a seat across from Cassie. "You once told me you know some dudes up around Oklahoma City that sells guns that can't be traced. I want to meet those dudes."

Cassie leaned forward and moved a bunch of fast food wrappers and other trash around on a coffee table until locating a pack of Marlboros and a pink Bic lighter. She tapped a cigarette out and flipped it between her lips. She thumbed the lighter wheel until a spark produced flame.

"You've always been so full of shit, Bo," she said before torching the end of her cigarette.

"Not this time. This is for real shit, and we need guns."

Cassie blew a plume of smoke in Bo's direction. "I'll set up the meeting, but it will cost you two thousand dollars. Not one."

Bo offered a most fetching smile. "Maybe we can talk it over in your bedroom?"

Cassie chuckled. "Not in the mood, Bo, but could be for yet another thousand."

Marvin fought back a grin. Cassie was slim with big tits. Might even be considered somewhat pretty if fixed up, but not a thousand dollars' worth of somewhat. He expected Bo would scoff at the offer. But he didn't.

"Give it to me on credit?"

"You good for it?"

"With the deal we got arranged . . . you can bet your sweet ass I am."

Cassie stood and said, "Come on then."

Bo turned to Marvin and grinned. "Make yourself at home. I won't be long."

* * *

"Get off me."

"What? Hell, I ain't even finished, and I'm paying for it, too."

"That's what I've been thinking about," Cassie admitted as she pushed Bo off her.

"You're thinking about that while we're making love?" Bo replied as he rolled onto his side to look at her.

"Bo, you're not a bad fuck, but you don't know shit about making love."

"So, you ain't going to let me finish?"

"I want to know what you're going to use the guns for. I need to know you can actually pay me three thousand dollars."

"Two thousand, Cassie. I ain't paying shit for half a fuck."

"Tell me what you have planned, and you can crawl back on."

Bo pushed himself up to lean against the headboard of her bed. "What I got planned will make one hundred and fifty thousand dollars, and the same amount for Marvin. But not sure he's going to hold up his end. In that case, I get three hundred thousand."

Cassie scooted up to sit next to him, and turned doubtful eyes on him. "Bullshit, Bo. How could you possibly pull off something to make that kind of money?"

"You're going to be shocked, and not sure you want to hear it."

"Sounds like to me that you don't want no more pussy."

137

"Kadie Rubottom is paying me that much to kill Troy."

Several thoughts and emotions struck Cassie like a bolt of electricity. She summed them all by robust laughter. "That's some unbelievable shit, but somehow I believe it. I never cared for Troy. Too arrogant. He always had that little man syndrome thing going on."

"So, you're all right with it?"

Cassie laughed again before sliding down on her back. "Crawl on up here, Killer."

All right with it? Hell, Bo had about a good a chance of killing Troy Rubottom that he did in making her have an orgasm.

* * *

Bob drove the old Toyota truck north, and was now nearly two hours closer to Oklahoma. He was leaving Texas with everything he took there, except Nancy, and a pair of socks. They'd looked high and low for her for over an hour, and searched every place they could think to search. Even questioned people they came in contact with. None admitted seeing an old woman who did not seem right in the head. While Bob drove, he committed more attention to thinking than driving.

"I now know what we got to do, Clint."

Clint has sat quietly for the past hour while staring out the passenger's window. He seldom kept quiet for that length of time, and Bob hated to get him going now, but knew Clint had a right to know what all his thinking produced.

"We're going back to look for her some more?" Clint asked.

"I done told you at least five times that we ain't going back. We didn't find her looking for an hour or more, and we ain't going to find her looking another hour or more."

"Then what are you talking about? What is it we got to do?"

"We got to strike first before we get struck."

"And what the heck does that mean?"

Bob took his eyes off the road to look hard at Clint. "We got to kill Gabe before he kills us."

Clint did not start babbling objections like Bob expected, but instead turned his head to stare again out his window. A few minutes later, he looked back at Bob.

"I need you to stop this truck and let me out, Bob."

"Why the hell would you want me to do that?"

"Because. I done stole away the man's mama, and sexed her as many times as I could. Then I let her get away, and I left her there by her lonesome. I've already done Gabe too much wrong to kill him on top of all that. So, this is where you and me split ways."

"And what are you going to do once I let you out, Clint?"

"I'm going to hitchhike my way back and keep looking for Nancy."

Bob slammed both palms against the steering wheel several times before pulling to the side of the interstate and stopping the truck. He put it in neutral, and turned in his seat to face Clint, who was already opening the passenger door.

"Just wait a minute, Clint," Bob said with as much calm as he could muster.

"Ain't no more to be said."

"Yeah there is. I don't doubt that you'll make your way back to that wide-spot in the road, but I'm going to tell you what you're likely to find. I'd bet by now that Nancy has wound up in the custody of the local police. I'm sure there's warrants out for you and me both. It won't be hard for them cops to find an old man wondering their streets. You'll end up in prison for the rest of your life, and Nancy will be sent safely home to Gabe. You see, she'll be okay in the long-run, but you'll just be fucked."

Clint turned and put both feet out the door. Then he just sat there. Long seconds later he mumbled, "There just ain't no good way out of this mess for us, is there, Bob?"

Bob pulled in a deep breath, and just could not find the energy to lie. "Nope. No good way out. Hell, our chances of killing Gabe before he kills us ain't worth a shit. So, we can die fighting, die running, or die in prison."

Clint swung his legs back in the truck, pulled the door shut, and pointed north. "Well, let's get to our dying."

"Are you going to try to help me get him?"

Clint stared at the road outside the windshield. "I ain't going to try real hard."

* * *

Craig Johns fell backwards into the bed of the Motel Six in Durango, Colorado. Not being in just real good graces with his wife, he'd left Anadarko within hours of last meeting with Junior Pernell, and drove nearly thirteen hours straight to reach Durango.

His wife had told him, "*I don't give a fuck where you go or even if you never come back, you queer bastard.*"

Even after all those hours on the road, her words had stung enough to help him ward off rest so he could immediately start his search for a man named Gary Langston. Computerized records revealed that Langston was raised by grandparents after the terrible automobile accident that killed his parents and put him in a children's hospital for nearly a year. As far as Johns could determine, Langston remained in the Durango area.

Johns had spent at least ten hours running leads and carefully asking questions pertaining to the whereabouts of Langston. Now, flat on his back, he felt the torment of his exhaustion, along with a sour feeling of apprehension about the man he sought. Information from those he approached had come haltingly, with obvious reluctance to tell what they knew. Jones had never tried to extract teeth from a conscious lion, but now felt he might know how difficult it would be. In his past experiences, he'd found that regular folk didn't mind sharing information about other regular folk, but balked when those sought tended to be *dangerous*.

One contact in particular responded, "So you need to talk to Gary Langston do you? You say he's a cousin of yours, huh? Well, let me tell you, mister, if the man I know as *Scar* cares to talk to you . . . he'll find you before you find him."

Scar?

The nickname did not leave Johns with a feeling that this case would be the easy open and close type he'd handled in the past.

Chapter Ten

Cassie Pernell acted damn quickly, and now Marvin's guts ached with dread. Bo just got off the phone with her, and she had set the meeting with the gunrunners for later in the day. Bo grabbed a joint to celebrate. Marvin grabbed his guts and hoped not to vomit. Meet gunrunners tonight, and contact Officer Ass-hole Eastridge tomorrow. Marvin might not only vomit, but thought he might shit his pants and pass-out at the same time.

Bo got only several hits into his marijuana when a sudden pounding sounded at the door.

"Oh, fuck," he moaned, "no mistaking that knock. It's my old man."

Marvin had not yet met Johnny Conwoop and didn't care to do so now. "What's he doing here, Bo?"

"How the fuck would I know, dumb-ass?" Bo hissed.

"Bo?" A loud voice called from the front porch. "Open this goddamned door, or I'll kick it down!"

Bo moved quickly to the door, but held on to his joint. "Hold the fuck on. I'm coming," he hollered.

Bo opened the door and stuck his head out. Suddenly, the door flew open and Bo stumbled backwards. One big and mean looking Indian in a cowboy hat stepped through the opening.

"Fuck, Dad . . ."

"Shut up, Bo." Then the man turned hostile eyes on Marvin. "Who are you?"

The last time Marvin tried to answer that question, asked by Cassie, Bo shut him up. Marvin did not offer a response this time.

"Best get to telling him, dumb-ass," Bo sighed.

Marvin stammered his answer, "I'm Marvin Purdy, Mr. Conwoop."

The man most called Woop looked down at the joint in his son's hand. Then he glared at Marvin. "You the one who sells him his dope?"

"Oh, no sir, I'm just a . . . "

"Shut the fuck up, Marvin," Bo interrupted. "No, Dad, he's just a friend. I'm letting him stay here with me . . . but I'm charging him rent."

"Yeah, I just bet you are, Bo. Well, I'm glad he's here. Gives me a chance to talk to two of your types."

"About what?"

"I'm looking for whoever broke into Troy's office."

Marvin suddenly thought his rectum and his throat were going to collide. He fought to keep his knees from buckling. Bo, on the other hand, didn't miss a beat.

"How the fuck would I know anything about that?"

Woop gave his nastiest look yet at Marvin. "Might be the company you keep."

"Oh, bullshit, Dad. You know I'm not a thief, and I know Marvin isn't either."

"I don't put nothing past you, Bo. You've given me no reason to. I know you associate with the low-life types, and know the low-life types can't help but brag about their low-life shit they pull. What have you heard?"

"I ain't heard shit. Fuck, if I did, Troy is like an uncle to me. I'd be letting him know."

"I'm actually your father, asshole, and you don't ever tell me shit."

"Well, I would this time. Hell, whoever did that was fucking with family. I wouldn't stand for that."

"Yeah, I know, Bo. You're nothing if not the upstanding family type." Woop moved up close to Marvin. "You need to tell me anything, boy?"

At that very moment, Marvin had to fight off the first urge to smile since he didn't know when.

Oh, you bet I do, sir . . . just not right here and now.

"Mr. Conwoop, I don't even know who the Troy is that you're talking about, sir."

Woop clearly studied Marvin for long seconds before responding, "Son, you do seem to harbor some respect. So, what the hell are you doing with Bo?"

* * *

"You been acting different the last day or so."

Kadie Rubottom looked at her husband and offered an actually sincere smile. "How's that, Troy?"

Troy pointed at her smiling lips. "Like that. You smile more. You act . . . well, happy."

Sadie considered his statement, and the smile broadened.

Imagine that. Me happy?

"Can't imagine what you're happy about all of a sudden. But, guess you have figured out what happiness is. Can't be me. I ain't doing nothing different."

No shit.

Honestly, Troy had been harder to live with than ever before since Bo Conwoop and his friend broke into Troy's office. He'd been moody and self-absorbed. Sharp tongued, and clearly bent on revenge. The small but mighty Troy Rubottom showed all the signs of a man violated. Kadie fought off a giggle.

Troy moved away from where she stood at the kitchen counter preparing a sandwich for his lunch. He strolled to the nearby table and plopped down. He pushed his cowboy hat back on his head and let out a long sigh.

"You got a boyfriend or something?"

No. I have a husband. But not for long.

"Don't be silly, Troy. Guess lately I've just been . . ."

Excited about my future.

". . . concentrating on the positive instead of the negative."

Troy emitted a joyless chuckle. "Yeah, me too. I now have help in finding who broke into my office."

Kadie stiffened. "How's that?"

"The other three. They're pitching in. Asking questions and probing about. Woop is even supposed to talk to his piece of shit son today."

Kadie gulped a deep breath. Her heart suddenly pounded, and she felt as if an invisible hand had slapped her back to reality. For reasons she could not fathom, she'd never even considered Troy finding out about her arrangement with Bo. She'd only considered Troy being dead. Now she contemplated how he would react. What he'd do to or with her. Her mind filled with fog as black as smoke, and only one thought pierced it.

I have to get in touch with Bo.

* * *

Sheriff Preston pulled her cruiser to a stop just feet away from the round-pen where her Uncle Gabe worked at training a young colt to lead. She had not wanted to give him the news over the phone. Gabe quickly released the lead rope from the colt's halter and started toward her. Concern occupied his chiseled face.

She stepped out of the car to holler at him. "It's not bad news!"

Gabe nodded in apparent relief before crossing through the two horizontal bars of the pen. Melody walked up to meet him.

"It's good news, Uncle Gabe. Nancy is safe. She was found by locals in a small town south of Borger, Texas."

Gabe grabbed her and applied a bear-like hug. Then she felt his large body release a load of tension.

"She's okay?" he asked as he released his grip.

"Disoriented, but physically sound," Melody smiled.

Gabe looked to the heavens and took a deep breath. "Thank you," he said with his eyes looking upward. Then he looked down, and his eyes narrowed.

"What about those two old perverts?"

"No news on them. I gave the officer the description of the truck we assume they stole. They haven't been able to locate it. Sounds like it's a damned small place. If it was there, they'd found it pretty quickly."

"What are you saying, Melody? They dumped her off and left her there?"

"Looks like they did."

"Sons of bitches!" Gabe thundered.

"Well, at least we know where she is. I can send a deputy to transport her back."

Gabe thought for a moment, and then shook his head. "Appreciate the offer, but I best go get her."

"I can go with you, Uncle Gabe."

"Sweet of you, but not necessary. Who knows, I might just bump into Bob and Clint on the way there or back. Wouldn't want no law woman with me should that happen."

Melody giggled as she reached behind his head and jerked on his long braid, "You behave yourself. Don't let that Apache temper get you into trouble."

Gabe gave her a fetching grin. "I ain't going to make promises I can't keep to my favorite niece. Thanks for coming out here, sweetheart."

They hugged again, and Melody started back to her car, but then remembered something else. "Uncle Gabe, do you know a Seymour?"

Gabe scrunched his handsome face. "Don't ring no bells. Why you ask?"

"Nancy told the officers there that she had been with a man by that name. And that he's black."

Gabe looked skywards again. "Oh, dear God . . ."

* * *

Marvin peered over the front seat and shook his head at the two men standing beside a big pick-up truck parked on a county road in a heavily wooded area. "Don't look very friendly to me," he sighed.

Bo turned from his place behind the wheel to glare at Marvin. "We ain't here to make love to them."

Cassie Pernell didn't look at Marvin from the front passenger seat, but did say, "They see the money, they'll be friendly enough."

Bo and Cassie got out of the Camaro at the same time. It took Marvin long seconds to decide to push the seat back forward and unfold himself from the cramped rear compartment. If he knew Bo wouldn't object, he'd rather have remained in the car.

"You got some money to show us?" a tall and rotund redneck type asked Cassie.

Cassie pointed to Bo. "He's got your money."

"Let's see it," a smaller redneck type barked at Bo.

Bo looked hard at the smaller of the two. "You telling or you asking?"

The big dude took an aggressive step forward, and Cassie stepped in front of him. "Pull your dicks in boys," she chuckled. "No sense in this being anything but easy."

She glanced over her shoulder at Bo. "Bo, this big feller is Don and this is his partner Oscar. Don and Oscar, this is Bo and Marvin. Get the money out, Bo."

Bo pulled a wad of bills from his pocket and handed it to Oscar, who went through it with thumbs and index fingers from both hands.

"It's all here, Don."

Don reached beneath an untucked denim shirt with both hands and pulled out two handguns. "Glock 40 millimeters, just like we agreed on." He handed both guns to Bo.

Bo looked them up and down like he knew what he was doing. Marvin hoped he did, because he didn't know shit about guns.

"The serial numbers are filed down," Bo said.

"Of course they are," Oscar hissed. "We don't deal in new firearms."

"Means they can't be traced. Right?" Bo asked.

Don provided the answer. "No. Just means they can't be traced to me and Oscar. Cops have a method for pulling up the numbers. That means you best be damned careful about keeping them out of the hands of cops."

Bo handed one of the guns to Marvin. "We aren't fucking idiots," he said to Don as he stuffed his gun into the waistband of his jeans.

Don turned to Cassie and smiled in a friendly manner. "Get them the fuck out of here, Cassie."

Cassie smiled back at the big man. "Good advice, Don. Thanks for dealing with us."

Marvin could tell Bo didn't appreciate being sent on his way in such a manner, and Cassie must have expected a reaction. She quickly wheeled on Bo. "Don't say a damned word. Don's brother, Dan, is somewhere real close, and you can bet your ass he's got a gun trained on you at this very moment."

"Fuck, Cassie," Don chuckled, "There you go spoiling all the fun."

Bo took a second to glance around the woods that surrounded them on both sides of the road. Without a saying another thing, he went back to his car and got in. Marvin hurriedly did the same.

He didn't take another easy breath until Bo pulled away from the rednecks. Marvin glanced at the gun in his hand, and then turned to look out the rear window in time to see a third man stepping onto the roadway. This experience told him one damn thing for sure. Bo knew no more about this kind of shit than Marvin did. It served to confirm that Marvin had only one chance in hell of living through this entire mess.

* * *

Additional long hours of asking questions in and around Durango, Colorado, netted no better results than the day before for Craig Johns. Having gone through the drive-thru to grab a dinner consisting of a Big Mac and fries, Johns pulled into a parking space in front of his motel room. He got out of the car with his bagged meal in hand, being careful not to bump the door into the Harley he parked next to, even though the rugged looking machine already touted numerous dings and marks. The bike sported skulls on many of the engine parts, and stickers that gave explicit warnings. One read, "Fuck with me and Die." Various mementos were adhered to the Harley, including a horrid looking doll's head, and a crucifix with a skeleton attached. In Oklahoma, these types of cycles were referred to as "Rat Bikes," and were ridden by the hard-core brand of bikers. Had there been a string of them in the parking lot, Johns would have been finding another room for the night.

He opened his door with the card, and used the heal of his sneaker to shut it once he'd stepped inside. Johns took the few short steps to the little round table in almost total darkness, set his food down, and turned to fumble for the light switch. When he turned toward the interior, he gasped and his body nearly convulsed at what the light revealed. Johns' mouth flew open, but he didn't get a chance to utter his surprise.

"You better not scream, motherfucker," a deep voice threatened.

Johns quickly shook his head and displayed the palms of his hands to the hulking figure sitting on the side of John's bed not more than four feet away. Heavily muscled arms covered in tattoos hung from a black leather vest decorated with soiled white patches. The big hands resting on the man's jean clad knees bore silver rings on every finger. A few displayed turquoise, but most exhibited different variations of skulls. Thick and oily dark hair hung down to the man's shoulders, covering some of his face, but not the wicked and jagged scar on the left cheek that snaked up to a terribly maimed eye socket. A milky white eyeball filled the socket, even though it moved, it looked long dead.

"Why the fuck you asking around about me?" the man asked, flashing stained and jagged teeth.

Johns gulped in air and released it in a question that came out as a fact. "Gary Langston."

"That did not answer my question, motherfucker. I know who I am. Who are you, and who sent you?"

"My name is Craig Johns. I'm a private investigator," Johns managed without stammering.

Langston looked Johns up and down. "Thought you might be a bounty hunter. But you look too big a pussy for that kind of work. I won't ask the second part of my question again before ripping you to bloody pieces."

Johns preferred remaining in just one piece, but knew he best not reveal that Junior Pernell sent him, and the reason for him doing so.

"My client means you no harm. As a matter of fact . . ."

Maybe it was a look in Langston's one good eye, or maybe he twitched, or maybe it was just Johns' imagination, but he thought Langston intended to stand. Johns bolted for the door.

He made it to the door, and no further. A powerful grip fell upon the back of his neck, and in a flash, Johns' back collided with the far wall of the room. He'd been flung like the proverbial rag doll. The impact knocked the breath from him, and he slid down the wall to land hard on his ass. Langston jerked him to his feet and threw him against another wall. Johns' head took the brunt of this toss, and he nearly passed out.

When his vision cleared, he could see the huge man standing over him, and he saw the hunting knife in his right hand.

"Don't know what all you've learned about me, but hope you know enough to believe I'm about to cut your balls off and cram them down your throat."

Even if Johns knew nothing about the man, which was close to what he'd been able to pull from others, just his appearance and displayed brutality would suggest him capable and willing to castrate. Johns' balls had brought him recent troubles, but he dearly cared to hang on to them. He started talking and didn't finish until Langston knew exactly who and what brought him to Durango.

Langston took seconds to process the information before opening his mouth. "That's all you know about the accident that killed my mom and pop and . . ."

Langston brought the terrifying knife to his face and traced the scar on his face.

". . . marked me for life?"

"He didn't go into specifics, Mr. Langston. He just sent me to find you."

Langston took a few steps back before inserting the knife into a sheath on his belt. Then he reached inside his vest, and pulled out a cell phone. Johns fought off the need to curl into a ball as Langston placed a call.

"Hey, Stoney, he's here, and I got him. Bring a car. Also, want you, Thumbs, and Sarge to take a road trip to Oklahoma with me.

Yeah, Oklahoma. No, not club business. It's personal. Very fucking personal."

Langston looked down at Johns once the phone was tucked back into his vest. "You're going to take me to this Junior Pernell."

"Don't guess he'll be the one getting the first chance to kill me?" Johns' moaned.

"You saying he's capable of killing with other than a car?"

Johns looked to the ceiling and tried to calm his breathing. "There's four of you going. He also belongs to a tight knit group of four. Like you, and I'm sure your friends, they're not four dudes I want to fuck with. I'm betting I die whichever way it goes."

Langston laughed for the first time. "I wouldn't bet against you, *Mr. Private Investigator.*"

* * *

Woop felt Rheta tugging and shaking on him, but he tried his best to ignore her.

"Woop! Damn it, someone is at the front door," she insisted. "Wake up!"

"What time is it?" Woop groaned.

"Nearly two. I fear it's the police. Maybe, Bo . . ."

"Yeah, yeah, I'm awake." Woop threw back the covers and swung his legs off the side of the bed.

Bo.

He knew his wife lived with a dread of being awakened deep in the night to get the news that her only child had finally once and for all screwed up big time. He reached for the gun on the nightstand and struggled to his feet. It might be the police, but it might not be. It could be someone just needing shot. If it turned out to be Bo, he intended to club him with the heavy revolver.

Woop stumbled and nearly fell twice just getting down the stairs. It served to intensify his anger at being so rudely awakened. He jerked the door open with his gun at the ready.

"Jesus Christ, Mr. Conwoop! Please don't shoot!"

Woop shook his head to clear his mind and vision. "What the hell are you doing here?" He didn't remember the kid's name, but knew the face and where he knew it from.

"Who is it, Woop?" Rheta called from the top of the stairs.

"Go back to bed, woman," Woop hollered up to her. "I'll explain when I get back up there." Woop kept his gun trained on the trembling face as he stepped out the door and shut it behind him.

"You best get to talking, boy. And I don't remember your damned name."

"Marvin, sir. Marvin Purdy. I'm in a terrible mess, Mr. Conwoop, and Bo is about to fuck up in a really big way. I don't know where else to turn."

Woop lowered the gun. "What's going on?"

"Do you know the cop Eastridge?"

"Yeah, I do."

"He wants me to be his snitch. He wants shit on Bo . . . and I got big shit, but damned sure don't want to give it to Eastridge."

Woop used his free hand to rub at a sudden pain in his guts. "What kind of shit?"

The kid in front of him looked as if he felt the same pain right between his eyes. "It was me and Bo that broke into Mr. Rubottom's barn."

Woop looked down at the gun in his hand. He wanted to put it to use. He just didn't know if he wanted to put it to Purdy's head, or his own.

"That ain't the worst of it, Mr. Conwoop," Purdy blurted.

Woop thrust his face within inches of Purdy's. "Boy, I don't know how it can get worse than that."

"Mr. Rubottom's wife, don't remember her name, she caught us in that barn. She had a rifle on us, but only let us go because Bo promised to kill her husband for her."

Woop reached with his empty hand to steady himself against the bricks of the house just to remain upright.

"And there's a lot more to it than that, sir," Purdy concluded in a whimper.

Woop pointed his pistol at the porch steps. "Have a seat, Marvin."

Marvin did as told, and Woop carefully lowered himself to sit beside him. "Tell me everything."

Woop listened as Purdy told about the initial plans of robbing the monthly poker game, the amount of money Kadie Rubottom offered for the killing of Troy, the cash she'd provided to purchase guns, and finally, how the guns were now in hand.

Woop struggled to find the strength to ask, "Anything else I need to know, Marvin?"

"One more thing, sir. I have to call Eastridge tomorrow to tell him what I know."

Woop nearly smiled at the only good news he'd heard. He at least was left with one card up his sleeve.

"Don't call him, Marvin. I can take care of Eastridge."

Chapter Eleven

For the first time since he'd been staying in the house, Bo got up first and now stood over the mattress toeing Marvin in the ribs.

"Wake up, damn it. Kadie Rubottom has called a meeting."

Marvin jerked upright. "What about?"

"Don't know. She said it can't wait. Get your clothes on so we can get out of here."

Marvin returned late from his conversation with Woop. Bo had been asleep when he left, and was thankfully still asleep by the time he got back. A little over two hours of rest left Marvin feeling numb. His mind for once seemed just incapable of racing.

"Where we meeting her?" he asked from the passenger seat.

"The cabin."

Fuck me.

When they were in the car and moving, fear overtook the numbness. Marvin wanted to scream objections, but knew they would only bring wrath. He sat quietly and looked out the passenger window hoping the car would break down. Hell, he'd even settle for a head on collision. But nothing kept them from reaching the cabin. Kadie's car was parked in front of the small structure.

When Bo pulled in behind the car, Kadie sprung from the driver's door and sprinted to the Camaro. She stopped so close to Bo's door that he rolled down his window.

"We've got to call this off," she blurted.

"The meeting?"

"No! The killing!"

"What the fuck for, Kadie?"

"Has Woop talked to you?"

"Yeah, he talked to both of us . . ."

"You didn't tell him anything did you, Bo?"

"About us going to kill Troy? Why, fuck no, I didn't. He just wanted information on the burglary. You think I'm stupid enough to tell him me and Marvin did it?"

Kadie bent low to look in at Marvin. He shrugged his shoulders and shook his head, hoping she could not sense that he truly liked where this was going.

"All four are out asking questions. It's just too risky to go on with it now, Bo." Kadie said as she backed away from his door.

Bo threw his door open and jumped out. "Bullshit, Kadie. What about the money?"

"What about it?"

"You promised us three hundred thousand dollars!" Bo shouted.

"That was to kill Troy. Now, you can't kill him."

Marvin could only see parts of Bo and Kadie from his seat, but he could see enough to realize Bo was taking aggressive steps toward Kadie. Marvin quickly got out of the car. They were practically off the hook. He didn't know exactly what to do, but he didn't intend to let Bo mess that up.

"Bo, she makes a good point," Marvin hollered over the roof of the Camaro.

Bo spun to glare at Marvin. "Best get your fucking ass back in that car."

"You act like you're going to hurt Kadie," Marvin groaned.

Bo cocked his head as if in thought, but did not take his eyes off Marvin. Bo took in a deep breath, and then let it out slowly. "Hell, I ain't going to hurt her." But he did turn back toward Kadie.

"You still got to pay us."

"What's say we just postpone it for a while, Bo? I still want him dead. But we got to wait until some of this blows over."

That seemed to appease Bo, but dampened Marvin's hope of escaping the horrible deed, but all was not totally bleak. Marvin had dreaded that Kadie called them out only to insist that they kill Troy immediately. Now, it simply meant Woop would have more time to intervene.

* * *

Woop took his hat off upon entering the beauty salon. Every head in the place turned to acknowledge his presence making him feel like a fish out of water. He did his best to ignore the feeling as he scanned the different stations for the woman he hoped to find. Luckily, he spotted her, but unfortunately, she stood at the far end of the salon. Woop weaved through the stations, nodding at the women he didn't recognize and greeting those he did. He eventually made it up to Cindy Wade with his hat literally and figuratively in hand.

"Howdy, Cindy, hate to bother you while you're working, but I need to talk to you about something."

"Why hello there, Mr. Conwoop. Couldn't imagine what you are doing here. What you got on your mind?"

Woop looked down on the elderly lady reclined in Cindy's chair with her head in a sink. "Well, Cindy, it's a private matter, so if you . . ."

The elderly woman craned her neck to look up with apparent hostility, but then cut her eyes to Cindy. "Young lady, whatever this man wants with you, it can't be good. Johnny Conwoop was a trouble-maker in school, and talk has it he still is."

Only then did Woop recognize the old crone. "Howdy, Mrs. Cockrill," he groaned.

"I also hear you went and got yourself rich, Johnny. Lord knows how. You were the most naturally stupid kid I ever taught . . . or tried to teach."

Woop glanced at Cindy as she chuckled at the exchange. "Mrs. Cockrill was my math teacher throughout high school. Whatever she's having done here today is on me."

"Well, Johnny, that would certainly make up for some of the hell you gave me in all those classes. Cindy, he'd probably pay extra if you held my head under this water until I stopped kicking."

Woop grinned for the first time since entering the salon. "A lot extra, Cindy."

"Can't do that, Mr. Conwoop, but can take a break once I get Mrs. Cockrill washed out."

Woop nodded his thanks and started away.

"Johnny, don't you forget I know Rheta. Your motives best be honorable. Now, why that sweet Rheta ever married a type like you, I'll . . ."

Woop walked away as she talked. He'd once had to listen to her, but he'd come a long way since those days, no matter how despicable the topic he needed to discuss with Cindy Wade.

* * *

"Now, Mom, we got a long ride ahead of us. Why don't you just lay back your seat and try to get some rest."

"I ain't your mom, you motherfucker! Done told you that three times," Nancy Saupitty babbled.

Gabe drew in a deep breath and held it as long as he could. A local doctor had given Nancy a sedative, and now he only wished the hell it'd kick in.

"Where you takin' me?"

"Back to Anadarko. Home."

"Anadarko? You think that's were Seymour went?"

"Don't know no Seymour. Done told you that *three* times."

"You gonna know him. He won't appreciate you kidnapping his woman. That big black buck has a terrible temper. You'll see."

Gabe only wanted to see his way out of Texas. Nancy fell silent, but started clawing at her unmentionable regions with both hands.

"What are you doing, Mom? What's wrong?"

"My play-pretty itches and burns."

Gabe moaned at the mentioning of the unmentionable.

"Those other two bastards more than likely deposited bad seed."

Oh, dear Jesus.

Gabe wanted to get both their minds off what itched. "You have any idea where those two bastards might have gone?"

"I hope to hell. Shit, I don't even know their names."

"Bob and Clint, Mom."

Nancy bolted upright in her seat and turned wide eyes on Gabe. He could see the gears barely cranking in her feeble mind. It took her long seconds, but she uttered a response.

"By God, it was Bob and Clint. Oh, Lord, Gabe, what have I done?"

"Ain't worth worrying about now, Mom. But I can tell you, you ain't done but barely worse than what I intend to do."

* * *

Woop declined the cigarette that Cindy Wade offered, but did take the lighter from her hand to ignite the one she stuck to her lips. He'd given up smoking ten years earlier, but still had an eye for pretty women. Cindy fit the category. She was tall and slender, big in only the right places. Woop forced all that from his mind. No good could come from thinking such about a woman young enough to call him gramps. He glanced around the alley just outside the back door of the salon while thanking God he was not ten or so years younger.

"Thanks, Mr. Conwoop," Cindy said as she took the lighter from Woop's hands. "Now, what in the world did you come to see me about?"

"First, please call me Woop. Everyone else does."

"Okay, Woop," Cindy said with a sweet smile.

"I don't know if you'll remember, but two, maybe three years ago, I saw you in the Boots and Saddles. You were drinking heavy because of a bad break-up with Jerry Eastridge."

"Oh, that sick bastard," Cindy said as she exhaled a puff of smoke tinged with disgust.

"That's what you called him that night."

"Do you know, Woop, he still brings me misery? Hell, every time I meet a new man, it won't be but a matter of days until Jerry stops him leaving my house. No telling how many tickets he's written to my lovers, and does so until they are no longer my lovers."

"That's a sorry thing to do, Cindy."

"He's a sorry son of a bitch."

"Well, uh, you told me that night that if I ever needed something on him . . . you had plenty. I find myself needing something on him."

"How about a video tape?"

"Of what?"

Cindy stomped out her cigarette before giving Woop a wink. "Oh, you'll see." Then she paused to give Woop a grin he could only interpret as seductive, "But you'll have to see me naked as well."

Woop wanted to bite his tongue, but just couldn't do so. "I don't think I'll have a problem with that, Cindy."

She took a pen and pad from her smock pocket and scribbled on it. She tore off the small sheet of paper and handed it to Woop. "Here's my address. I get off at four."

* * *

Craig Johns would have preferred leaving earlier in the day, but it seemed that Scar and his wicked looking friends considered afternoon as their early hours. He drove alone in his car, but wasn't all by his lonesome. He constantly glanced in his rearview mirror to observe the four bikes following close behind. Scar, along with Stoney, Thumbs, and Sarge held a tight formation not two car lengths behind Johns. Leaving them in his dust was not an option. On its best day, his old truck was no match for the powerful bikes that tailed him.

Scar advised him that they'd drive straight through to Oklahoma. When the bikes with their smaller tanks needed fuel, one would pass him and escort him off the interstate. Johns didn't have to be warned about doing anything stupid. He'd watched the four prepare for the trip, and knew all were heavily armed. At this point, his mind frantically searched for ways he could give Junior Pernell a warning, but his efforts produced not a damned thing.

As it now stood, they'd reach Junior's home at about nine in the morning, and Junior would be a sitting duck. Whatever the four bikers did to him would be Johns' fault, and he didn't care to have that on his conscience. Johns really didn't know just yet how to categorize Junior Pernell, but did not consider him to be all in all a bad man. He'd come to believe that Junior roughing him up on the side of the road had been fate. Had that not happened, Johns might have never come to the realization that he wasn't truly gay. Just a man, who like Junior, made some mistakes in life. Somewhere between this long stretch of interstate and Junior's ranch, Johns would have to take drastic actions.

* * *

I am too old to be having such ridiculous fantasies.
And I have a damn good woman at home.

Woop silently thanked God that Cindy Wade did not open the door completely naked or even scantily dressed.

You silly old fucker.

She did have a thumb drive in her hand, and she didn't invite Woop in to view it with her.

"I hope you can put this to good use, Woop."

Woop took the thumb drive and studied it for a long moment. "Uh, probably best that I don't even look at it, Cindy. You, know, me being of heart-attack age. You mind telling me what's on it, so I can at least act like I've seen it?"

Cindy giggled like a schoolgirl and then set about turning Woop's face a flushed color of red.

* * *

"What the fuck are you doing coming to my house?"

The huge man was clad in a wife-beater and boxer shorts. He held a glass in his hand that looked to contain iced-tea, but Woop knew better. Only three feet stood between Woop and the off-duty cop. Woop could smell the alcohol on Eastridge's breath.

"Well, this ain't no social call, Eastridge. I'm here about Marvin Purdy."

Eastridge squinted his eyes into a mean glare. "That bastard was supposed to contact me today. He didn't do it."

"I know that. I told him not to do it."

Eastridge had stood holding the outer glass door open. Now he stepped out on the porch, letting it slam shut behind him. Woop held his ground to stand almost face to face with Eastridge. The man had six inches on him, and about fifty pounds of muscle.

"What gave you that fucking right?" Eastridge hissed.

"Purdy works for me. He's only with Bo because I pay him to keep an eye on him. He don't have shit to report to you. I'm here to ask that you just let him be."

"Well, you've asked. And my response is, fuck you, Conwoop. I'm going to put that worthless piece of shit son of yours away for one thing or another. Purdy is going to make sure I do. Now, get the fuck out of here."

Woop faked a grin. "I tried asking. Now, I'm going to tell you something. Right here in my pocket," Woop said as he patted the right thigh of his jeans, "I have some evidence I'm sure you don't want getting out."

Eastridge did not have an immediate response, but seemed to try clearing his head of near drunkenness before asking, "What the fuck you think you got on me?"

"I have a thumb drive that contains a video. One you didn't know was being taken."

Eastridge bared and gritted his teeth as his face contorted in rage. "Where did you get it?"

Woop sincerely grinned this time. "Cindy Wade gave it to me."

Eastridge emitted a long growl before abruptly bringing the glass to his lips. He drained the contents and then flung the glass at the far wall that ran adjacent to the porch. The sudden motion and shattering of glass caused Woop to tense and flinch, but he readied himself for an attack.

Instead of attacking, Eastridge grinned back at him. "So glad you are stupid enough to share that with me. Because now, I'm going to twist your head off before I take that thumb drive from you."

Woop had not fought too many men larger than himself, but learned long ago that doing such provided certain advantages. For one, it elevated critical parts, making them more accessible. He reached with his left hand to grab Eastridge's ball sack while his right hand shot out for his throat. He gripped with all his might with both hands. With the asset of surprise, he used the handfuls of flesh to thrust Eastridge back against the glass door, and pinned him there. Eastridge bellowed in pain and used both his hands to try dislodging the grip on his balls. Within seconds of being deprived of air, both hands shot up to claw at the grip on his throat. Woop lowered his head and drove it into Eastridge's face. The huge man slumped against the door, and Woop continued to squeeze while bending at the knees as Eastridge slid down the door into a sitting position.

Woop lightened the grip on both throat and balls from crippling to maintaining. He leaned to put his lips closer to Eastridge's ear. "Hey, *Jerry*, want me to take you inside now? Maybe strap you naked to the bed? I've whipped a lot of men's asses before, but never spanked one. If I need to do that to get my message across, I'm wearing a good stout belt."

Eastridge sucked in air in great gulps, but managed to shake his head no. Woop pushed up to his feet and started down the steps and off the porch.

"Conwoop," Eastridge gasped.

Woop turned back to face him.

It took some effort for the slumped man to get his words out. "You will pay for this, motherfucker."

Woop damn sure knew he'd have to watch his step and his back from here on out, but he couldn't let a threat go unanswered. "When and if that time comes, Eastridge, suggest you don't underestimate me a second time."

* * *

"I've given this a lot of thinking, Marvin."

"I don't think you've given it enough, Bo."

Bo pointed to the gun butt protruding from Marvin's waistband. "You know, you've gotten awful cocky since wearing that thing around. Seems to me you're getting downright disrespectful."

Marvin looked down at his gun. "Fuck, man, I only wear it because you insist I do."

Bo reached to the small of his back and pulled his automatic. "I'm starting to believe you might just want to take charge, Marvin."

Bo didn't have the gun pointed, but Marvin threw his arms in the air all the same. "Bullshit! I ain't challenging you, dude. I was just pointing out that Kadie said not to do it."

Bo studied the gun in his hand while reaching with his other to grab the can of beer next to his chair. He took a mighty swig before placing the gun in his lap. "And I'm saying she said she still wants it done. That's why I'm saying tomorrow, or the next day, we just get it done. Then she'll have the money to pay us."

Marvin forced a response. "But what about your dad and the other two? If Troy ends up dead, they're going to search high and low for who killed him."

Bo responded first with laughter. "That's the beauty of it, man. They won't know to look immediately right at us, but we know to look at them."

"What does that mean? What are you saying, Bo?"

"Goddamn, Marvin, isn't it obvious? See, if we can take out one, we can take out all one by one. Once we start killing, ain't no need to stop until all they have is ours."

It suddenly dawned on Marvin that if that was how obvious worked, he obviously needed to pull his gun and shoot Bo right here and right now. Woop would immediately want to strike out at Marvin, but once he heard what his son planned, he'd let Marvin live. Only two things kept Marvin from going for his gun. One, he did not yet know how to work the damned thing. And, two, he simply didn't believe himself to be the killing kind.

* * *

When Gabe pulled into the drive it was near midnight. He got out of the truck and stretched and moaned miserably before bending down and looking back inside.

"I know it's not your house, Mom. It's my house. I can't allow you to stay at your place alone. Now, come on and get out of the car."

Nancy called him yet another awful name before aiming the middle finger of her right hand at his face.

"Awww, Jesus," he bellowed before slamming his door and starting around the front of the truck to drag Nancy out if need be. He took only a few steps when a searing pain erupted in his left shoulder and shot down his left arm. He spun and slumped back over the chrome grill of the big Dodge.

My fucking heart.

He thought the obvious.

But instantaneously with the pain, he'd saw a flash of sparks, but not from within his head. It'd spewed from the darkness of the side yard.

Only now, in the passing of less than a second, did he hear the tremendous eruption.

BOOM!

He tried to push away from the truck when an invisible force tore into his guts. And for a second time . . .

BOOM!

Gabe crumbled to his knees, gagging at the taste of blood that surged from the back of his throat and spilled out his mouth. It was dark to begin with, but quickly started growing even darker. He toppled face forward, just conscious enough to make out frantic shouted words.

"Run, Clint! Let's get the fuck out of here!"

Chapter Twelve

He'd seriously considered calling in sick, but didn't care to spend the day pacing around his house, getting drunk, and wanting revenge against . . .

Melody Preston and . . .

Bo Conwoop and . . .

Marvin Purdy, and last but far from fucking least . . .

Johnny Conwoop.

Thankfully, Eastridge made it in for the morning shift line-up. Had he not, it might have been hours before he heard about Gabe Saupitty being gunned down in his driveway. Upon hearing the news delivered by the shift commander, Eastridge was the only cop in the room to bellow laughter and clap his hands. Fuck the rest of the pussies. He was the only one to express outright what the others felt as well. Saupitty, like the other three he associated with, was a thug. The captain conducting the line-up gave Eastridge a sharp look, but didn't have the balls to reprimand him. Fuck him, too. The captain approached him after dismissing his shift from line-up.

"What happened to your face, Jerry?"

"I tripped over my dog, boss," Eastridge had smirked.

Now, an hour later, Eastridge sat in his parked car along Main Street with his window down watching the sparse flow of traffic. He hoped for any opportunity to relieve his pent up energy. God have mercy on anyone who crossed him today.

Eastridge heard the roar of loud motorcycle pipes before observing the source. Moments later four outlaw types of bikers came into view, following right on the ass of a beat up truck that looked familiar.

Only when Eastridge could clearly see the driver did he recognize Craig Johns, the silly-assed wannabe Magnum P.I. At the exact moment, Johns turned his head and spotted Eastridge. What Johns did next, left Eastridge with his mouth hanging open, and set his blood to boiling.

* * *

Johns could have avoided leading the trailing Harleys through Anadarko, but time was running out, and now he sought just any opportunity to escape the four bikers. He'd initially hoped he could lose them in heavy traffic. Then, surely as gift from God, he spotted Patrolman Jerry Eastridge. With only a moment to think, only one solution came to mind. He quickly cranked down his window, extended his arm and a middle finger right at Eastridge.

"Fuck you, pussy!" he shouted before stomping down on the accelerator.

Eastridge had his overhead emergency lights on in a flash. Johns looked into his rearview mirror and observed Scar and the others breaking formation and splitting to the right and left to take side streets. Once they were out of sight, Johns slammed on his brakes and pulled immediately to the curb. He bailed from the cab and put his hands high in the air just as Eastridge pulled in behind his truck.

The giant cop jumped from his patrol car with gun in hand.

"I surrender, Officer Eastridge! I'm ready to go to jail!" Johns shouted.

Eastridge pointed his service weapon and ordered. "Turn around asshole, put your hands on the back of your head, and get on your knees!"

Johns immediately and quickly did as told. In a blink of an eye, cuffs were clamped brutally to his wrists. Eastridge then grabbed him by the throat, jerked him to his feet, and nearly ran him back to the patrol car. The patrolman threw him across the hood and started frisking him with the tenderness of a Grizzly searching for food.

"You must have fucking lost your mind, Johns," Eastridge hissed.

"Yes sir, I must have."

Eastridge jerked him off the hood and shook him like a misbehaving child before tossing him in the back seat of the cruiser.

Once behind the wheel, and breathing heavily, Eastridge turned back to stare at Johns. "Did this have anything to do with those maggots on Harleys?"

"Sir, it had everything to do with those maggots on Harleys."

"You best tell me what's going on, fuck dummy."

"Sir, for right now, that's all I'm saying. I'm going to exercise my right to remain silent."

"And I might exercise my right to beat what I want out of you, fuck scum."

Johns pulled in a weary breath before saying, "We both know you're not going to do that. Please, just get me on to the jail so I can get my one phone call."

Eastridge continued to call him all kind of fuck names, but at least he did it on the way to the city jail.

* * *

It took Scar nearly an hour to round up his crew. With all now in tow, he pulled into the parking lot of a closed-down mom and pop grocery store. They each put kickstands down and killed their engines before gathering in a tight circle.

"I can't wait to get my hands on the little shit bag," Sarge grumbled, "but that was one smart move."

"Yeah," Scar mumbled, "but kind of leaves us fucked right now."

"I want to know what he's telling that cop," Stoney said.

"He ain't telling him shit," Scar replied. "But you can bet your ass, he'll be calling Junior Pernell to give him a warning."

"We need to find a phone book, Scar," Thumbs suggested. "Maybe Pernell is listed and we can get an address."

"Good idea, Thumbs. If that don't work, we'll just start asking around," Scar nodded. "Ain't much of a town. Bet everyone knows everyone else."

Scar started for his bike, signaling the others to do the same. This not being club business, the others were only obligated by friendship. Scar had learned long ago that friendship only stretched so far. If things didn't start working in his favor soon, he'd be at this task all by himself.

* * *

Sadie stood next to her husband's bed holding his hand when her twin sister walked into the small ICU room. Kadie stopped just inside the door and scanned her eyes over all the tubes running from

Gabe's body. It took her a few seconds, but she did walk up to the bedside. Sadie, expecting a hug, turned to face her.

"I wish that was Troy dying there in that bed."

Sadie stiffened and her mouth fell open. She'd struggled throughout the night to fight back bitter rage, and now had to fight even harder to keep from unleashing it upon her sister. Instead, she bent to put her head close to Gabe's head. "You don't listen to her, Gabriel. You're not dying, baby. You're too damn tough and mean to die."

"He's unconscious. He didn't hear me, Sadie."

Sadie wheeled to put her face even closer to Kadie than she had Gabe. "You don't know that. How dare you," she hissed while struggling to keep her voice down. "You don't offer me a hug or words of encouragement. You just babble that horrible bullshit. What the hell is going on with you, Kadie?"

"I'm sorry," Kadie mumbled, but still did not offer comfort.

"I've called you and texted you dozens of times this past week. And you don't have the decency to respond? I want to know what is going on in that brain of yours."

Kadie looked her dead in the eyes. "Believe me, no you don't."

Sadie intended to push further for an explanation, but Red Winfield burst into the room. He grabbed Sadie and pulled her snugly into his chest.

"I was attending a conference in Tulsa. Started for home the minute I got the word, Sadie."

Out of the corner of her eye, Sadie watched as Kadie solemnly walked out of the room. For the first time since finding Gabe lying in the driveway, Sadie completely melted down, sobbing uncontrollably.

"Let's step outside, honey," Red said as he gently moved her toward the door. He held her tightly in the hall until Sadie cried herself out.

"What happened, Sadie?" Red whispered in her ear.

She fought to catch her breath, but did not attempt to move her head from Red's chest. "Don't know. The shots woke me up. I found him in front of his truck. I couldn't accompany him in the ambulance because I had to find someone to watch over Nancy. All I know is that he was shot twice. Once in the shoulder and the other in the abdomen. They don't know if he's going to make it through this, Red."

Winfield squeezed her even tighter. "The strong bastard will be just fine, baby. It'll take more than just two bullets to finish Gabe Saupitty."

Sadie nodded her head over and over. She so wanted to believe that.

"Do you have any idea who might have done this, Sadie?"

"None. He was out when I found him, and has never regained consciousness."

"Oh, he will. I know him too well to believe otherwise. We'll worry about who did it later. For now, let's just go back in and be with him."

Sadie again nodded her head and let Red escort her back into her husband's room.

* * *

Junior Pernell did not recognize the number calling his cell, but answered it any way. It could be someone calling about Gabe Saupitty.

"Junior, this is Craig Johns."

"It didn't show your number. Where you calling from?"

"The city jail."

"Anadarko city jail? What the hell did you do, Johns?"

"Junior, I need to know where you are right now."

"I'm at home. Getting ready to head to the hospital. Don't know if you know it, but someone tried to kill Gabe Saupitty."

"Junior, listen to me. You stay at home. You arm yourself, and you stay at home."

Junior's thoughts went to mush. "What the hell are talking about? What the fuck is going on here?"

"There are four bad dudes in town right now. I do believe they are going to try to find you and kill you. The leader of the four is the man you sent me to find."

"Johns, are they ones who shot Saupitty?"

The pause on the other end lasted nearly long enough to launch Junior into a tirade.

"When was he shot, Junior?"

"From what I've heard, somewhere around midnight."

Another infuriating pause before Johns responded, "Couldn't have been them. They followed me into town at about eight this morning . . . Why would you think they shot Saupitty?"

This time Junior provided the lapse in precious time. "Gabe was driving the truck the night we hit that family."

"It wasn't them, Junior. Now listen, I need someone to bail me out of here, and it shouldn't be you. As soon as I'm out, I need to go home and grab something that I hope to hell I won't need, then I'll head to your place and explain all."

Junior fought through the haze that filled his thinking and asked the only thing that came to mind. "Johns, after I've heard all you have to say, am I going to want to kill you?"

"More than likely so, Junior. But only if the other four don't get to me before you do. That's the reason I need to get to my house first."

* * *

Red walked into the ICU waiting room to find Troy and Woop sitting side by side.

"Where's Junior?" He asked.

"Don't know," Troy responded. "I called him with the news. Said he'd be here."

"Did he act surprised?" Woop asked.

"About Gabe being shot?" Troy asked.

"Yup."

"Why, hell yes, he acted surprised. What kind of question is that?"

"Well you know, he went after Gabe with a gun just recently, and Gabe knocked him on his ass."

"Why, if you think Junior . . ." Troy started with a growl.

"Move over Woop," Red interrupted. "I best sit between you two so we don't have another shooting."

"I don't have a gun on me," Woop said.

"You damn sure know I do," Troy hissed.

Woop got up and moved two chairs down, and Red plopped into the one he vacated. "Now, boys, we all know Junior might do just about anything, *except* shoot a man down under the cover of darkness. If he was stupid enough to shoot Gabe, and we all know

Junior, he'd been stupid enough to do it in a less cowardly fashion. Hell, Woop, it wasn't."

"Then who the hell did it?" Woop asked.

"Don't know," Red replied. "But I tell you what, when you leave here, Woop, you should head home and get your gun. If someone wanted to kill Gabe, I'd be betting they'd want you two dead as well."

Red watched as Woop and Troy mulled that over. Woop broke the moment of silence.

"What do we do if he dies?"

"He ain't going to die," Troy blurted.

"I don't think he will either," Red responded. "But if he does, Woop, we'll throw him one hell of a funeral."

"I'm talking assets here, Red," Woop said.

"That's a hell of a thing to be worried about," Troy bristled.

Red held up a palm toward Troy. "It's a fair question, but we've got it all down in writing. We take care of Sadie so she doesn't want for a thing the rest of her life, and the rest you three split up."

Woop leaned past Red to look at Troy. "Hell, it ain't that I want him to die."

Red watched Troy take a few cleansing breaths.

"Shit, I know that, Woop," Troy nodded. "We're just all on edge right now, with damn good reason to be so."

"That's a good way to put it, Troy," Red said. "I'm going to head out and contact Melody Preston. Sadie said she spent most of the night here with her Uncle Gabe. I'll see if there's anything she knows, and if we can do anything to lend a hand."

"I'm going to head out and get a gun," Woop said.

"Think I'll just hang out here a while with my sister-in-law," Troy mumbled.

Red looked around for Kadie, and didn't see her. Seemed rather strange to him that she wasn't hovering nearby.

* * *

Bob Nettle sat with Clint Avants in the Toyota truck they'd stolen just one week earlier on the far side of the county from a man simply wanting deer meat. Bob felt as safe as he possibly could be on the secluded road that was barely more than a one-lane trail. Even so, he moaned out a long sigh.

"No shit," Clint grumbled. "Sitting out here like a couple of sorry-assed criminals, which we now just happen to be."

"Don't feel like hearing it, Clint."

Clint started to nod his head as if he had a bee in his ear. "Oh, I'd feel like shit too if it'd been me that killed poor Gabe."

Bob turned his head away from Clint to stare out his window. "You just better hope I killed him. A wounded Grizzly is a dangerous thing to face."

"Hell, I ain't got no worries. I didn't do the shooting."

Bob wearily turned his gaze back on Clint. "But you did help steal his mama away, and did more than your fair share of fucking her."

Clint moaned a sigh this time. "Poor thing, just sitting there in that truck while you gunned down her only boy."

Bob slumped over the steering wheel. "Honestly, Clint, it's all your fault. You should have shot me before I shot him."

Clint didn't offer a response, and for torturous seconds, Bob only had to deal with his own thoughts.

"What are we going to do now?" Clint eventually asked.

"Have no damned idea."

* * *

"Hey, dude, you by any chance know a man by the name of Junior Pernell?"

Ryan Cornish was under the hood of his old truck. He'd just two days ago replaced all the windows Troy Rubottom shot out. Now it was broke down on the side of the road. He'd heard the bikes approaching, and heard them pull over. Cornish figured the riders were going to the little bar he'd broken down in front of. He pulled his head out from beneath the hood, and fought to keep from gasping at the man standing next to him.

"Uh, I know who he is, but I don't know him," Ryan replied to the big man with a terribly disfigured face.

"You know anybody who does know him?"

Three other intimidating types walked up to stand beside the scarred man. Cornish felt bullied just looking at the four. He feared simply telling them no, would not send them on their way. Somehow, a thought popped into his mind, and he couldn't help but smile.

"Yes, sir, I just might be able to help you. My brother-in-law's name is Marvin Purdy. He lives with a man named Bo Conwoop. Bo's father is best friends with Junior."

The biker did not return the smile. "No shit? How do we find this Bo dude?"

"Well, my wife tells me he lives on Seventh Street just east of Broadway. Don't know the address or the exact house, but do know he drives a damned sharp red Camaro. I don't know of another one in town. You find that car, and you'll find Bo. He can tell you all you want to know about Junior."

The heavily tatted big man with the awful eye nodded his head. "Okay. Can you point us in the general direction of Seventh and Broadway?"

Cornish provided the directions, and grinned as the four walked away.

"Fuck you, Marvin Purdy," he whispered under his breath. Folks in these parts did not appreciate extending a helping hand to only have it shit in.

* * *

Right in the middle of her own county, someone gunned down her uncle. Sheriff Melody Preston took that as a personal affront. She'd spent the night with her Uncle Gabe in the hospital and now her body wanted sleep, but her mind wanted answers. Mainly, who wanted Gabe Saupitty dead? Considering what they'd already done, Melody had to look toward Bob Nettle and Clint Avants. But, really? The two had practically raised Gabe. Still, she assigned a deputy to watch the shack the old men claimed as home. If one or both showed up, they'd be brought in on the existing charges and questioned about the shooting.

In a small town, the word of anything the least bit exciting or unusual spread like the plague. She'd heard of the recent confrontation between Junior Pernell and her uncle. She didn't know what it stemmed from, but decided she'd personally pay a visit to Junior. Melody didn't expect a lot to come from that. The *Four Horsemen* were notorious for infighting. She didn't consider Junior any more of a suspect than she did Bob and Clint. But at this juncture, the Sheriff did not intend to leave any stone unturned. As far as that went, it was no secret that Gabe and Sadie's domestic disputes could get rather ugly.

Jesus Christ, Aunt Sadie?

Melody so often wished she'd been born to some other family in some other place.

Chapter Thirteen

Woop pounded on Bo's door a second time. It wasn't yet noon, so he knew Bo was still in bed. That irked him. No man should be in bed at this hour of the day, unless he worked all night. He raised his big fist to pound a third time just as Marvin Purdy opened the door.

"Where's that worthless friend of yours?" Woop asked.

"In bed."

Woop leaned in close and lowered his voice. "I'll be talking to you in just a few minutes." He then pushed past Purdy and stomped into Bo's bedroom.

"Get your lazy ass out of that bed," Woop boomed.

Bo jerked upright and flinched at the sight of his dad. "What the fuck?"

"Gabe Saupitty's been shot. That's what the fuck. You get up and get down to the hospital to pay your respects to Sadie. She kept you as a toddler back when your mama still worked. It's the right thing to do."

Bo rubbed at his eyes, but made no other motion to follow the demand.

"You need me to help you get out of that bed?"

"No. But wish you'd step out while I get dressed."

"Do it quickly," Woop said as he walked out of the room.

It didn't really make a damn if Bo went to the hospital or not. Woop just wanted him out of the house. There would be no reason for Marvin Purdy to accompany him to the hospital. Soon enough, Bo stepped out of his bedroom.

"Come on, Marvin, we're headed out to do the right thing."

"He ain't got nothing on but his jeans," Woop said, "And I don't have the time for him to even put on a shirt and shoes. You get on to the hospital, boy."

Bo clearly wanted to object, but knew he stood within grasping distance of his old man. He shot Purdy a distinct look of warning before turning and walking out of the house. Woop waited until his car pulled out of the drive. He then reached into his back pocket, pulled out a cell phone, and handed it to Purdy.

"I'm pretty damn sure I have Officer Eastridge off your ass. I put my number in that phone. You keep in contact with me. Understand?"

"Yes, sir," Purdy nodded. "But there's something I need to tell you already."

"Get to telling."

"We met with Kadie yesterday. She postponed the killing of her husband, but Bo plans on doing it anyway. Maybe as soon as tonight or tomorrow."

"Oh, shit," Woop moaned.

"And that's not all, sir. Bo's talking about taking you all out one by one."

"Even me?" Woop helplessly blurted.

"Yes, sir. Even you. He wants everything you four have to become his. What do I do, Mr. Conwoop?"

Woop didn't know why the revelation surprised him. Bo clearly hated him, even as a small boy. He removed his cowboy hat and rubbed his head wearily until a possible solution came to mind. "You point out to Bo that, with the shooting of Gabe Saupitty, we are all on high alert. That truly ain't no lie. I can promise you, Troy is expecting just about anything. You make him believe that. If you can't, you call me on that phone."

Purdy didn't seem all too confident with the role he had to play, but nodded his head all the same. "Okay, Mr. Conwoop. I'll do that."

* * *

"Come on in and get to talking."

Junior stepped aside to let Craig Johns into the office of his horse barn. He pointed at a chair, and Johns took it. The shaggy headed investigator looked worn to near exhaustion. Junior took a seat behind his desk.

"I feel like I let you down, Junior."

"Maybe. Maybe not. I won't know until you tell me what happened." Junior pointed at an angry looking bruise on Johns' forehead. "Guessing that lump on your noggin tells some of the story."

Johns leaned forward while dropping his head and moving his long hair aside. "He did this first. Threw me around like a Nerf ball."

Junior could clearly make out the huge handprint on the back of Johns' neck. "So he thinks he's a badass, huh?"

"Sir, he is a badass. I didn't tell him a damned thing until he pulled a knife to cut off my balls. I damn sure believed he would have done it if I hadn't talked."

"What did you tell him?"

Johns cleared his throat. "Everything I know. I'm damn sorry for bringing them here."

"How did that happen to be?"

"Him and three of his thug friends followed me on their bikes. I thought all the way back on how to lose them, and get a warning to you. I didn't get any good chances to do so until coming through town this morning. I saw that cop, Eastridge, flipped him off, and called him a pussy. When he came after me, the bikers split. I knew I'd get a phone call from jail to give you the warning."

Junior sat silently while processing the information. Then he started to nod his head. "Well, I wish they weren't here, but I don't fault you. You did okay under the circumstances."

"I'm pretty sure they are going to try to find and kill you, Junior."

Junior pushed to his feet. "Four bikers in town should not be that hard to find. They don't know what I look like. I intend to find them before they find their way here."

"I'm going with you."

"No. They damn sure know what you look like. But I do need a favor."

"You name it."

"Before I leave, I got to go in the house and tell my wife what's going on. She has no idea what happened way back when. Once I leave, I'd like you to stay here and keep guard over her. You got a gun?"

"No, sir."

Junior grinned at Johns. "Not a problem. I got plenty."

"Junior, the man's name is Gary Langston. You can't miss him. His face is badly maimed." Johns then drew in a deep breath, and let it out slowly. "He's been that way since the wreck. He goes by the name of Scar."

"That's truly a pity," Junior said, and meant it. "But, he's a big boy now. I don't intend to die over an accident that I had no control over. If given a chance, I'll let him know of my remorse for what happened. If that's not good enough . . . he can carry his scars to hell with him."

* * *

Jolene Pernell sat watching television with a freshly lit cigarette when she heard Junior come in the back door.

"Jolene?"

She turned up the volume on the television with the remote. He knew she hated interruptions while watching her afternoon soap operas. Of course, that did not stop him from stepping right in front of the television once he located her in the big house.

"At least move your ugly ass aside so I can pause it," she said with a plume of exhaled smoke.

Junior stepped aside and she hit the pause button. "It's too early for you to be hungry, so what are you looking for that you can't find? If it's one of your tools, I ain't had it."

"I ain't looking for nothing but you."

There seemed sadness in the declaration, but Jolene followed her nature and made light of it. "Damn, Junior, that sounds almost romantic."

Her husband just stared at her. The unusually thoughtful look in his eyes prompted her to snuff out the cigarette and move forward to the edge of the couch.

"What's up, Junior?"

He plopped down in his recliner across from where she sat. "I've got something I need to tell you."

"Oh, shit. You've found a younger woman. And she's blind." Jolene hoped for one of those moments when Junior fought off a smile. She didn't get one.

"There's a man out back in the barn. His name is Craig Johns, and he's going to stick around here to protect you."

Jolene's stomach instantly turned sour. "Protect me? Against what?"

Junior seemed to suddenly have trouble swallowing. "Many years ago, when I was still on the rodeo circuit, I was riding with Gabe in his truck up in Colorado . . ."

Jolene held her stomach with both hands as Junior forced her into his past.

* * *

"You need to slow this son of a bitch down, Saupitty. You're drunker than shit, and it's snowing like a motherfucker."

"Maybe you just need to drink more," Gabe chuckled.

Junior grabbed the bottle of Jack Daniels sitting on the bench seat between them. He choked down one mighty swig and chased it with another.

"I'll drink to that," Gabe chuckled. "Hand it over to me, Junior."

"Fuck that."

"Don't make me pull this truck over and spank you like a baby."

"We're in the damned mountains, in the snow, and you're already driving like a madman. Only way I'm giving up this bottle is if you slow down."

Gabe stomped on the accelerator.

"You crazy dog-eating Apache motherfucker!" Junior bellowed. "Go ahead and pull this truck over. I will whip your ass just so I can drive!"

Gabe belted out his arrogant way of laughing. "Ain't never seen no horse or road I can't handle!"

Junior reached with both hands to grasp the dashboard. At that very moment he noticed the oncoming lights approaching at a very disturbing angle.

"Sharp curve, Gabe!"

Gabe applied too heavy of a drunken foot abruptly on the brake pedal. The truck slid to the right. Had it not, they'd have hit the car in the other lane head-on. The right side of Gabe's truck collided with the left side of the other car, sending the passenger car off the steep edge of the mountain road. Junior screamed curse words until the truck finally came to a stop.

"What the hell have you done?" he bellowed

"I can't see no taillights," Gabe moaned as his head jerked from one rear-view mirror to the other.

"That's 'cause they went off the side of the fucking mountain!"

Junior threw open his door and bailed from the cab. The whiskey and the treacherous footing prevented him from running, and it seemed to take hours to make it across the road and back to the spot where the car parted ways with it. With each step he dreaded how many hundreds of feet the car must have plunged down the side of the mountain. Once he reached the edge, he spotted the car's taillights and felt little relief seeing that it came to rest only about forty-feet below him, because all he could see of the car was the underneath side.

Fearing the car might burst into flames, he listened intently for the sound of a running engine, and thought he heard an even more dreadful sound.

Gabe stepped up beside him. "Fuck! It's upside down!"

"SHHHHHHH! Listen!" Junior hissed.

Gabe only remained silent for a second or two. "What did you hear?"

"Please shut the hell up . . . I thought I heard a baby crying."

"Oh, dear Jesus," Gabe moaned.

Junior didn't hear it again. "I'm going down there."

Nearly too drunk to stand, Gabe peered over the edge, teetered, then quickly adjusted his weight to fall back on his ass. "Shit, man, it's a good fifty feet straight down. You'll break your neck."

"I can't just leave them down there."

"You might make it down, but you won't make it back up, Junior. What good can that do?"

"Then what the hell *are we going to do?*"

"We got to get to a pay phone. Call help for them."

Nothing better came to Junior's mind. "You go. I'll stay here."

Gabe struggled to his feet. "Junior, I'll make the call, but I'm not coming back here. I'm drunker than shit. Police find me here, I'm going to jail. If someone down there is dead, I'll be going to prison. Probably for the rest of my life. I'm sorry as hell about this, but I ain't going to prison."

Junior did not like what he heard, but he understood. "Let's get the hell to a phone. I'm driving."

"Hell, I ain't so drunk I can't . . ."

Junior wheeled and grabbed the lapels of Gabe's jacket, spinning him around to thrust him backwards toward the steep drop off. "Say one more word, Gabe, and I'll put you down there with them."

Gabe nodded his inebriated head. Junior then used the grasp to shove him toward the truck.

Thirty miles later down the road Junior finally spotted a pay phone.

* * *

"You just left them there?"

Junior pushed out of his recliner and looked down at his wife. "Yeah, Jolene, we did. Now you know why I've been crying at night."

"Why are just now telling me this?"

"Hell, I just realized a week or so back what was bothering me."

"No, Junior, I mean why didn't you tell me about it when it happened?"

The truth made Junior want to lie, but he'd been dishonest about it all for too long already. "I didn't get back home for a good month after it happened. I don't like admitting it now, but truth is, after that much time passing, it just wasn't that big a deal to me. Guess I convinced myself they'd all lived. That, or I just buried the memory so deep it's just now coming back to haunt me."

"Do you even know how many were in the car?"

"I do now. The man waiting in my office is a private investigator. I had him check it all out. There was a mom, dad, and a baby. The baby lived. The parents didn't."

Jolene took her eyes off Junior to glance around the living room as if searching for something. She swiped at tears starting to trickle down her cheeks before turning back to Junior.

"Damn. Just when I thought I'd figured out how much of an asshole you are, Junior, you surprise me by being more so than I calculated."

190

"Well, if you're pissed now, Jolene, prepare to be more pissed. That baby grew up to be a man wanting vengeance. He's in town now with three others. I'm going out to find them before they find me."

Jolene shot to her feet. "And what the hell are you going to do when you find them, Junior?" she practically screamed.

"I'll start with an apology. The rest is up to him."

Jolene leapt at Junior and wrapped her arms tightly around him. "No! No, you're not going. You are for sure an asshole, but you're the only asshole I have. I can't let you do this."

Junior craned his neck to kiss her gently on the forehead before prying her loose and holding her at arm's length. "Jolene, sadly enough, you don't have a say in the matter. This is man business. I got myself into it, and now it falls on me to get myself out of it."

Junior walked out the front door to the sound of Jolene sobbing.

* * *

Marvin jumped to his feet at the sound of Bo's Camaro pulling into the drive. He tugged his t-shirt down low to conceal the phone in his back pocket. Bo came in the door with anger painted all over his face.

"How long did that bastard stick around after I left?"

"Shit, Bo, he left right after you did."

"So you and him didn't discuss anything?"

"What the hell would we discuss?"

"Oh, fuck, I don't know. Maybe the plans to kill his good buddy Troy?"

Marvin threw his arms in the air. "Jeez, dude, you don't trust me anymore than that? You think I'm that fucking . . ."

A loud knock on the door interrupted Marvin's fake plea of innocence. Bo spun to face the door.

"I ain't in no mood for another visit from that fuck," he thundered before jerking the door open.

Bo's body blocked most of Marvin's view of a hulking figure standing on the porch, but didn't interfere with him hearing the question asked.

"Are you Bo or Marvin?"

"Who the fuck are . . ."

Bo didn't get to finish his question. Marvin just saw motion, but heard the sound of fist colliding with flesh. He jumped aside to keep from being hit by Bo's body in flight. In the next instance the small living room was filled with four big bikers. The first one that came through the door, a man with a mangled face, turned his one good eye on Marvin.

"Now I will ask you. Are you . . ."

"I'm Marvin," he blurted. "The dude on the floor is Bo."

Bo lay on his back with both hands cradling his bloody face. One of the other bikers bent over and jerked him to his feet.

The one with the scarred face moved to place it next to Bo's. "I hear you know a man named Junior Pernell?"

Bo looked barely conscious, but managed to nod his battered head.

"Then we need to talk. Sarge, make him comfortable on that couch."

The man holding Bo upright slung him like a sack of potatoes. Bo landed almost in a sitting position on the couch.

The leader turned to Marvin. "Have a seat there beside him."

"Yes, sir."

"Bo and Marvin, you can call me Scar. These dudes with me are Sarge, Thumbs, and Stoney. Not a one of us has the least bit of tolerance for bullshit. Now, tell me where I can find Junior Pernell."

"You going to kill him?" Bo moaned.

Marvin scooted a foot further away from Bo.

The one pointed out as Stoney stepped up beside Scar. "Shit, Scar, maybe you hit him so hard you fucked up his hearing."

"No, no that's not it. I'm not bullshitting," Bo said as he held up his hands in the surrender mode. "It's just that Junior is one of four dudes that stick together. Me and Marvin here are out to kill one of them, too. Being paid big money to do it. Might just go ahead and kill the other three while we're at it. Just thinking maybe we could work together. Hell, we'd split the money."

Marvin could not understand how it came down to this so damned quickly.

"How big a money you talking about, Bo?" Scar asked.

"Three hundred thousand."

Scar grabbed the only other chair in the living room and pulled it up close to Bo. He took a seat and lit a cigarette. "Bo, I want you to educate me on these four men. I want to know everything you know."

Bo started talking, and Marvin longed to do the same. Only he wanted to talk into the telephone hidden in his rear pocket.

* * *

Junior was just driving around looking for four men on Harleys when his cell phone started ringing. A quick glance identified Red Winfield as the caller.

"What do you need, Red?"

"Just wanted to hear your sweet voice, asshole. Where are you?"

"Out and about. What do you want?"

"Wanted to know why you didn't show up at the hospital today."

"Long story and none of your business."

"See why I called you asshole? Anyway, doubt if you care, but Gabe came to. Looks like he's beat the worst of it."

Junior did in fact care. "I'm headed over there right now."

"No. Visiting hours are over. But it would be decent of you to make a showing in the morning."

"I don't need you telling me the decent thing to do, Red," Junior growled.

"Junior, as always, you need all the help you can get."

You don't know how right you are this time, Red.

Chapter Fourteen

Junior had relieved Craig Johns of his security duty just a few minutes past midnight. Junior told him he'd been looking high and low for Scar and his crew. Johns silently thanked God that Junior didn't find them. He didn't doubt Junior could hold his own against any one of the four, but damn sure doubted he'd stand a chance in hell against all four. Before leaving, Johns handed over the handgun and shotgun Junior supplied for Johns' duty of keeping watch.

"I also left you a present in your office, Junior. A little something that was always too big for me anyway. It might help get you through this awful shit."

"Please tell me it ain't one of those helmets shaped like cowboy hats that trail riders use nowadays."

The comment had made Craig laugh. "Something like that, Junior."

"I think you ought to take that .45 auto with you, Craig," Junior had offered.

"Best not, I'm not licensed to carry. After the stunt I pulled in town with Eastridge, I could be on the whole department's shit list. But I would like to make a suggestion."

"Go ahead."

"I think you ought to bring the other three in on what's going on with those four asshole bikers. I'd feel better if Mr. Rubottom and Mr. Conwoop helped us out with this. Of course, Mr. Saupitty can't be of help, but if he survives, he should know about it."

"Yeah, I could go to them, Craig, and they'd help any way they could. But this is my mess, and I just don't care to get them tangled up in it. Hell, I feel bad enough about pulling you into it."

"Oh, don't worry about me, Junior. I shook them once and figure I can do it again if need be. You just be safe."

"You do the same, Craig."

Now, forty minutes after leaving Junior's ranch, Johns pulled into his drive. The spot where his wife parked her car was vacant. He slumped over the wheel and moaned out loud. She'd said she wouldn't be here when he returned. Sure looked like she meant it. After long minutes of sitting and hurting, Johns wiped the tears from his eyes and crawled out of the car. He didn't care to enter the empty house, but no other options came to mind. He opened the front door with his key and walked directly into an ambush.

Johns bellowed an objection, but could not break the strong bear hug of his attacker. He felt himself being moved with ease toward the living room. The lights in the interior room came to life, and Johns observed Scar, Stoney, and Thumbs sitting casually in his living room. Sarge released his grip and shoved him to the middle of the room.

"Where's my wife?" Johns asked angrily.

"Wife?" Scar grinned. "Don't know shit about a wife. No one here when we kicked in the back door."

"You ain't seen her? She's not here?"

"You ought to know by now, old friend, that if we found a woman here, we'd use her to add to your torment."

Johns' mind quickly left a loved-one for what he liked to consider a friend. "Now, that I know you don't have her, I don't give a shit what you do to me, asshole. I'm not telling you where to find Junior Pernell."

Scar threw back his head and laughed heartily. "No longer need you for that, Johns. Same person who told us where to find your house has already provided all we need to know about Pernell."

Johns' shoulders drooped, and he dropped his head to stare at the carpet. "Guess there's only one other reason for you being here."

"You guessed right," Scar grinned as he stood and pulled his dreaded knife.

Stoney and Thumbs jumped in and took hold of Johns to hold him in place.

"I'm going to start by making your face and one of your eyeballs look like mine."

Craig Johns tried with all his might not to scream as Scar started to carve.

* * *

Junior rolled over in bed and grabbed the ringing cell phone. Without benefit of his reading glasses, he couldn't check to see who was calling.

"This is Junior," he grumbled.

"Junior . . . they are forcing me to call you."

The voice sounded just awful, but Junior recognized it all the same.

"Craig? What the fuck's going on?"

"They got me . . . say they will get you next . . . I didn't want to call . . ."

197

Junior swung out of his bed. "Craig, what have they done to you?"

"Cut me . . . a lot . . . face . . . everywhere."

"Craig! Where are you?"

The only response Junior got was the reverberating sound of an explosion.

"Craig! Craig?" Junior screamed until someone on the other end disconnected the call.

* * *

The Dixie Diner opened its door at six sharp, and Junior walked in a few minutes later. He'd just returned from a round trip to Oklahoma City where he'd dropped his wife off with her brother and his family. Junior had time for only one sip of coffee before Red Winfield walked through the diner's door.

"Was really pissed at you for calling so early, Junior. But now that I see you, I can tell you had a need to call early. You look like shit. I mean, even more so than usual."

"I feel like shit, Red. Been up all night. I couldn't think of anything else to do but call you."

"What's going on?"

"It's bad. God awful bad. Do you know a kid here in town named Craig Johns?"

"Small time private investigator?"

"That's him."

"Yeah, I know him. I've financed a few junk cars for him and his wife."

"Well, I'm pretty sure he's dead, and it's all my fault."

A waitress set a cup of coffee in front of Red, and asked if they were ready to order.

Red cleared his throat. "Don't think we'll be eating this morning, Darla"

The moment she walked away, Red leaned over the table as close as he could get to Junior. "What the fuck are you talking about?"

Junior took a big gulp of the strong black coffee. "It's a long story. But thought I best tell you before I end up dead as well."

* * *

Marvin snuck out of the house as the sun peeked over the horizon. Bo would remain dead asleep for at least another three hours. He'd drank and smoked dope long after the bikers left the house. Marvin helped him to his bed only three hours earlier. Sleep had not been an option for Marvin. He walked a block away from the house before pulling out the phone and dialing Woop's number.

"Up early, aren't you, boy?" Woop answered.

"Didn't go to sleep, sir. Knowing what I know, I couldn't."

"What *do you* know, Marvin?"

"Jesus Christ, Mr. Conwoop, there are four bad dudes here in town from Colorado. They've come to kill Junior Pernell. They probably killed a dude last night named Johns. And now, Bo has set them up to kill the rest."

"The rest of who?"

"Mr. Rubottom, Mr. Saupitty . . . and you, Mr. Conwoop."

The pause on the other end lasted so long that Marvin asked, "Mr. Conwoop, you still there?"

Still seconds ticked by before Woop responded. "I'm here. Where are you, Marvin?"

"A block away from Bo's house."

"You get your ass to that Conoco station up on Broadway. Wait there until I pick you up. It'll take me about ten minutes to get there."

Woop hung up before Marvin could offer a response.

* * *

Junior finished telling all he had to tell and fell into a slump in the booth he shared with Red.

"Lord have mercy, Junior," Red exhaled, just as his cell started to ring.

Junior watched Red pull his phone and look to see who was calling.

"It's Woop."

Junior figured it much too early for a social call from yet another of Red's famed associates. He sat upright to glean what he could from the upcoming exchange.

"Good morning, Woop."

Junior watched closely as Red listened. Whatever Woop imparted didn't seem to heighten the mood Junior dampened.

"Can't you give me more than that, Woop?"

Long pause.

"Okay, okay, Woop, relax. I'll make it happen."

Junior waited until Red tucked the cell back inside the breast pocket of his high-dollar suit. "What's that all about, Red?"

Red flexed his neck and shoulders in an apparent attempt to relieve stress. "Woop wants all of us still standing to gather at the cabin for an emergency meeting."

"What for?"

"Don't really know, Junior. All I know is that if the four of you hadn't made me filthy rich, I'd told you long ago to go fuck yourselves."

* * *

Melody Preston leaned over Gabe's bed. "Uncle Gabe, you feel like talking?"

"My throat's really sore from that breathing tube."

He sounded weak, but looked a hell of lot better than the last time Melody saw him.

"Other than that," he moaned, "just feel like I was run over by a truck and then raped by a rhino."

Melody laughed. It did her heart good to see he still clung to his sense of humor.

"Uncle Gabe, I've been beating the bushes, and haven't come up with a damn thing. Haven't heard anything back yet from the Oklahoma Bureau of Investigation on the slugs removed from your body. Basically, I don't have shit on who did this."

Gabe closed his eyes and made an attempt to adjust his head on the pillow. Melody gently fluffed the pillow beneath his head. It gave her seconds to consider his body language. She believed had he been well and sitting upright, he might have averted his eyes for just a second instead of closing them. A sure sign of avoidance.

She decided to come right to the point. "Did you see who shot you, Uncle Gabe?"

He pulled in a deep breath and let it out slowly. "No. Too dark. Just saw the flashes."

"Did you notice anything or hear anything that might help me in my investigation?"

Gabe took long seconds to respond, and then did so with only a slight shake of his head.

Melody had conducted too many interrogations to believe Gabe, but knew this was not the time or place to push further. "Okay, Uncle Gabe. You just rest and continue to get better. I'll check in on you later."

"You look like you could use some rest."

"I'll catch up on my sleep after I find out who did this."

Gabe Saupitty closed his eyes again and didn't open them the few seconds Melody remained in the room.

* * *

"See, I told you so, Clint," Bob whispered from their hiding place in the woods. "Now maybe you'll have a little faith in me. I knew they'd be gathering here sooner or later."

Clint was stretched out on his belly right next to Bob, but he leaned in even closer. "I don't mind telling you you're right when you're right," he whispered back, "but if they find us here, we'll both be dead. I'll damn sure be talking to you about that in hell."

"They ain't gonna be checking these damned woods. When Woop gets here, he'll do just like the others. He'll step inside the cabin without even a glance around."

Bob and Clint had to only wait on their bellies a few more minutes before Woop pulled up in his truck.

"Who's that with him, Bob?"

"Hell, some kid. Never seen him before."

Bob waited until Woop and the stranger entered the cabin before turning to look at Clint. "Red opened the windows for a little air in there. I'm going to creep up and hear what they have to say.

"That's about a stupid assed thing to do," Clint objected. "If you creep up there, I'm creeping back to the truck."

"You can't go nowhere. I got the keys."

"Well, if I hear you screaming out in pain, I'll have just that much of a jump on getting away on foot."

"You are one hell of a partner, Clint," Bob snarled as he began to crawl forward.

* * *

"He looks familiar, but can't place him," Troy said to Woop while staring at Marvin. "Who the hell is he?"

Woop pulled up his chair and took the liberty to point to Gabe's empty one. "Take a seat," he said to Marvin.

Once seated, Woop turned his attention to Troy, "I'll get to who he is as I explain why we are here." Woop started to say more, but Red jumped in.

"Boys, we're here because Woop wanted this meeting, but it turns out that Junior has a bellyful that he needs to discuss as well."

"I guess the fuck he does," Woop grumbled as he turned a hostile look on Junior.

"You keep looking at me like that, Woop, and I'll cut them ugly eyes out of your Comanche head."

In damned sure no mood for additional threats, Woop started out of his chair, but Red made it to his feet first.

"Goddamnit, boys, I don't know what Woop has, but Junior damn sure has a mess on his hands. We can't start off like this. One more ugly word, and I'm out of here. You can handle Woop's shit and Junior's shit without my involvement."

Woop forced himself to remain calm. "Okay, Red. You're right. Knowing what I know, which I'm sure is part of Junior's problem, we are going to need your help."

"All right then," Red nodded as he sat back down, "Why don't you start with what you have, Woop?"

Woop's mind had spun on what to say and how to say it. He turned his eyes on Troy. "This here is Marvin Purdy, Troy. He's the one you shot at for dumping trash, and the one who later approached you in the Spurs and Saddles."

"Oh, yeah, now I remember. What's the piece of shit doing here?"

Woop took a few seconds to tame his tongue. "The kid has his downfalls, but all in all, he's proving to be a decent enough type. Decent enough to care whether or not you live or die, Troy."

"What the does that mean?" Troy glared.

"This is going to be damn hard for you to stomach, Troy. And there ain't no good way of putting it. So, I'm just going to put out there, and I'd ask that you remain as calm as possible."

"Then why don't you get the hell on with it?" Troy growled.

"Marvin didn't want to be part of it, but it was him . . . and that worthless piece of shit son of mine that broke into your office."

"Goddamn you!" Troy bellowed at Marvin as he jumped to his feet.

"Red!" Woop thundered, but unnecessarily, because Red shot to his as well and stepped in between Troy and Marvin.

"I'm sure there's more to hear, Troy, and I beg you hear Woop out," Red said.

It took long seconds and more talking for Red to get Troy back in his seat.

Woop leaned in close to Troy. "Red's right, Troy, there's a hell of a lot more to this, and I haven't even got to the truly ugly part yet."

Troy looked hard at Woop, but Woop could see the worry that mingled with the anger.

"Kadie interrupted them in their attempts to steal from you, Troy."

Troy took on a look that suggested he'd not heard Woop correctly. He then turned the same look on Marvin. Finally, he moved his eyes back to Woop.

"Go on," Troy mumbled.

"Bo told Kadie that they'd intended to steal guns, so that they could rob us here at one of our poker games."

Red let out a long and mournful sigh at the same time Junior released a foul word. Troy remained silent. Woop could tell his mighty thinking skills were churning away.

"Then what happened?" Troy asked in a near whisper.

Woop cleared his throat before drawing in a deep breath. "Kadie offered them three hundred thousand dollars to kill you, Troy."

"Jesus Christ!" Junior blurted.

"That surely can't be the truth, Woop," Red objected, turning a leery eye on Marvin.

"It is the truth, Mr. Winfield," Marvin nearly whimpered.

Troy held up a hand to silence the others. It took him several seconds before he said, "Kadie's been acting awfully strange since the break in. I don't doubt what you're saying, Woop."

Woop breathed a sigh of relief. "Troy, she also gave them money to buy the guns to kill you with. They've already got them. Junior, your daughter set up the deal for the guns."

"Oh, hell," Junior hissed.

Troy looked down at the table and shook his head miserably. "Why did you come forward with this, Purdy?"

Marvin cleared his throat before saying, "I ain't no murderer, Mr. Rubottom. I didn't want to break into your office either. Truth is, I was just too scared of Bo to stand up to him."

Troy shook his head again in the same pitiful manner.

Woop desperately needed a break. "Junior, this would be a good time to tell us what's going on with you. Once you're finished, I have a final piece to add."

Junior let out a moan and slumped forward to rest his elbows on the table. "Many years ago, when we were all very young and traveling from one rodeo to another, me and Gabe ran a family off the road up in the Rockies. We basically left them there to die. That started wearing on me not long ago. That's why I ended up pulling a gun on Gabe.

"I decided to hire a private investigator by the name of Craig Johns to look into who was in the car and what happened to them. Come to find out, it was a man and woman and their baby boy. The mother and father were killed in the accident, but the child lived. He grew up wanting vengeance. He found Johns during his investigation up in Durango, Colorado. Him and three of his buddies, all outlaw bikers, forced Johns to bring them back here. They're here now looking to find and kill me. I'm fairly certain they've already killed Craig Johns."

"Well, Junior," Troy grumbled, "Looks like you and me are in about the same boat."

"We're all in that boat," Woop said.

"How you mean that, Woop?" Red asked.

"Those four bikers showed up at Bo's house. They wanted information on how to find Junior. Bo, uh, well, he brought them in on his deal, and upped the ante. Bo offered them the entire three hundred thousand to see to it that me, Troy, Junior, and Gabe are all put to death."

"My God," Red moaned.

"I damn sure didn't want to bring you and Troy into all this," Junior said to Woop.

"You didn't, Junior. My own flesh and blood did."

"What in the hell do we do now?" Junior asked while looking at the faces around the table.

"I really don't know. I'm open for suggestions," Woop responded.

Red jumped in. "Junior thinks if they killed Johns, they probably did it at his house. An anonymous phone call to the police could possibly take care of the four outsiders."

"I don't want the police involved," Troy said abruptly. "It might eventually fall back on Kadie. I'll have to deal with that, but I don't want the police involved."

"Okay," Red nodded before turning to Marvin, "Are you willing to go back and keep further tabs on Bo and the bikers?"

Marvin emitted a tormented hiss of air. "If Bo, or any of those other dudes find out, they'll kill me for sure. I would . . ."

"What if I was to pay you the three hundred thousand that was to go to those fuckers?" Troy interrupted.

Marvin looked sheepishly at Troy, "I wasn't going to say no. I was going to say that I'd do it for Mr. Conwoop. He saved my ass from Officer Eastridge."

The three other faces turned to Woop. "Long story," he said with a shake of his head.

"I'd still pay you that amount, Purdy," Troy said.

"I think it's safe to say the others would pitch in to help with the money," Red inserted.

Woop nodded his head, and then Junior did the same.

"I have done my own share of bad shit. I don't need to be paid to make it right," Marvin said.

Woop placed a hand on Marvin's shoulders. "It would just be the right thing for us to do." Then, he turned to the others. "I suggest we monitor the situation with the information Marvin supplies. When the time is right, we set a trap for the five of them. Whatever we do will be self-defense."

"You're including Bo?" Red asked.

"I'm hoping he won't have to die in the outcome. But truth is, he's the one that put this all in motion. He made a man's decision. He has to accept a man's consequences."

Red solemnly nodded his head. "Let's get to planning this all out."

Chapter Fifteen

"What time is it?"

"It's a little after midnight, Gabe. It's a new day, old friend," Troy responded.

Gabe asked the time of day from a deep haze. He turned his head to look at Troy, trying to focus his eyes in the dimly lit room. "What are you doing here?"

"I sent Sadie home to get some rest. From this point forward, Woop, Junior, Red, or I will be watching over you until you get out of here."

"What the hell for?" Gabe knew who shot him, and knew they wouldn't be making another attempt. At least not here.

"Well, brother-in-law, we got a hit out on all of us for three hundred thousand dollars."

"What?" Woop thought maybe the drugs were messing with his hearing.

"Yeah. We have a bounty on our heads."

Gabe was thinking clear enough to know Bob and Clint couldn't put together three pennies to have them killed. "Who could pay that kind of money and why would they?"

"I don't yet know the why, but it's my dear Kadie who initially put the money up."

Gabe tried to raise his head to look around the room. "Is this a fucking dream?"

"It's no dream, Gabe, but it's damned sure a nightmare. You up for hearing the rest of it?"

"Kadie wants us dead?"

"No not exactly. She just wants me dead."

"I don't understand."

"I don't either," Troy chuckled, but it sounded hollow. "It's a long story, Gabe, but basically, Bo Conwoop wants us dead, and he's enlisted the help from someone out of your past."

Gabe shook his head to clear it. "If you are intentionally screwing with my mind, all the dope I'm taking don't need your help. Get to the point in plain English, or get out of here."

From that point on, Gabe did his best to listen, and make sense of some unbelievable goings-on. Once Troy finished, Gabe pushed the button for a nurse and more drugs. While he waited for an angel of mercy, only one comment came to mind."

"It was Bob and Clint who tried to kill me."

Troy moved in close. "Are you shitting me, Gabe?"

"No."

"Well, Good God Almighty, all the hell we needed was another twist."

* * *

"Why don't we just run away? We are already neck deep in shit, and now we're just looking for more to bury our faces in."

"Stop your bellyaching, Clint. This is the only way out for us. I done explained, we pull this off, we'll live high off the hog for what few years we have remaining."

"If Mike Jackson catches us out here, he'll kill us where we stand, Bob. I'd just as soon live longer than that, even if I have to live poor."

"He's still in bed. Won't get up until the sun does. That's a good two hours away." Bob then pointed to the Chevy truck sitting beside a barn about a hundred yards from where they stooped behind a chicken coup. "When we was mucking stalls for him last year, we learned he never takes the keys out of the ignition. It's ours for the taking. It's so far from the house up there that he won't hear it starting up. So stop fucking worrying."

"It's what you got planned for that truck that really worries me," Clint moaned.

"It's what I got planned for that truck that will make us rich. Now, come on. Let's go make a difference in a lot of people's lives."

* * *

Junior parked a block away, and now hurried on foot to take advantage of what little darkness remained. Johns' car was parked in the drive, and it didn't appear any lights were on in the small house. He rang the doorbell, waited long seconds, and then knocked a few times, but not loudly enough to draw attention from any neighbors that might be awake at this hour. He waited only a few seconds before deciding to go to the back door.

He walked around the house and went through an open gate attached to a chain-link fence. It really didn't surprise him to find the back door standing ajar, but did intensify his anxiety. He used the flashlight app on his cell phone to examine the back door. It clearly had been kicked nearly off the hinges. Junior used the toe of his boot to push the door open.

"Craig?" he called softly before entering. Getting no response, he took a few steps inside and removed his handkerchief from a back pocket. He used it to push the door closed behind him.

"Craig? This is Junior. Are you here?"

Fuck, I know you're here.

Junior paused to steady his nerves before going any further. He walked the few feet of a narrow hall that led to the kitchen. Even with little light, Junior could see that a bar separated the kitchen from a living room. He stepped over to the bar and from there could see the form lying on the living room floor.

"Oh, damn, Craig," he moaned.

He walked only close enough to the body so he could illuminate it with his cell phone flashlight. Craig lay face down with his phone lying next to him. Junior could see the blood matted hair on the back of his head. The mess nearly concealed the entrance wound. Junior thanked God he could not see the face. When a bullet entered, it normally made a small hole. When it exited, it tended to remove great chunks of bone and flesh. The pool of blood spanning from Craig's head suggested just that. Junior stood next to a wall that Craig no doubt faced before the shot was fired. Junior didn't dare turn his light on the wall. Instead, he backed away a few feet and turned off the light on his phone. Tears of fury blurred his vision.

"I'm so sorry, Craig. This is all my fault. I can only promise you this. Those bikers . . . I'll take them apart in little pieces."

Junior left the house and made his way to the most remote pay phone he could locate. He did his best to disguise his voice as he reported Craig Johns' dead body to the 911 operator. He hung up when the young man started to ask questions, and carefully wiped down the phone receiver with his handkerchief.

* * *

Marvin made his way to the front door in response to the early morning knocking. He pulled the door open and Scar with his henchmen walked in without an invite.

"Where's your buddy, Bo?" Scar asked.

"It's still early, Scar."

"Not inquiring about the time, asshole. Where is he?"

Marvin nodded toward Bo's room. "Still in bed."

"Fuck that. We got shit to do," Scar said before stomping off in the direction Marvin nodded.

Marvin heard Bo squeal. A few moments later, Scar shoved Bo into the center of the living room.

"You could have at least let me pull on some jeans," Bo grumbled as he pulled up his sagging underwear.

"I'm not one to lay in bed all day when there's killing to be done," Scar responded, "And I don't have any sympathy for those who do."

"I was about to get up," Bo groaned.

Scar smirked at Bo before saying, "Let's get this shit planned out. I intend to be on my way back to Colorado in less than two days' time."

Because he couldn't do anything else, Marvin nodded his head. Then the front door flew open, and two old men aiming big revolvers strolled right in. All four bikers reached to retrieve guns, but the old man in the lead took exception.

"I just recently shot a man I practically raised as a son. I'd damn sure plug any one or all of you nasty looking sons of bitches."

"Bob? Clint?" Bo hollered. "What the fuck?"

The lead man glanced at Bo. "We know what you boys got planned. Ain't going to let it happen. These old revolvers hold six rounds apiece. That's two for each of you bastards. Best get to saying your prayers."

After yesterday's meeting, Marvin let himself believe he might make it out of this mess alive. Now he could not help but blurt, "You're going to kill us?"

"Yup, and we'll make it quick if you let us," the lead man said. "Now, I want you fellers to get down on your knees, and put your hands up on your heads."

Marvin did not hesitate following the order. If he had to die, he preferred it to be quick. He knew none of the others he'd secretly betrayed would offer as much.

* * *

Patrolman Eastridge walked in the front door of the small house. He looked down at the body, and then turned his eyes on the officer assigned to the call.

"It's damn sure Craig Johns, Butler. He's wearing the same clothes he had on when I put him in jail two days ago."

"I figured as much, Jerry. This is his house, and the anonymous caller said we'd find him dead here." Tony Butler replied.

"Don't mean it couldn't have been somebody else," Eastridge snarled.

Butler shrugged his shoulders. "Guess that's true enough. Neighbor woman said him and his wife have been at odds lately. Think she did this?"

"Could have, I guess," Eastridge lied. He'd not put anything in his arrest report on Johns about the four outlaw types tailing him on rat bikes, and he didn't care to share the information with Butler. It'd been a tough five days for Eastridge. Melody broke up with him, and that asshole Johnny Conwoop had confronted him with his single deep and dark secret, breaking the grasp he held on Marvin Purdy that he'd hoped would land Conwoop's maggot son in jail. Pinning this murder on one or all of the four bikers would definitely boost his morale.

"Detectives are in route, Jerry. Best you clear out of the crime scene," Butler said.

"Fuck you, Butler, and fuck the detectives as well."

Butler once again shrugged his shoulders.

Eastridge had taken the liberty to find out who Johns placed his phone call to from jail. The number traced to Junior Pernell's cell phone. Somehow, Pernell, and therefore the other three, were tied to Craig Johns' murder. Without help from anyone else, Eastridge intended to find out the extent of their involvement. He'd have to tread lightly. He believed that what Johnny Conwoop knew about him Pernell, Rubottom, and Saupitty knew as well. Eastridge damn sure didn't want the entire county knowing that he occasionally liked having his ass spanked by a willing woman.

* * *

Marvin had only seconds to feel damned ridiculous. The others in the living room did not fall to their knees and place their hands on top of their heads. It was Sarge who reached in a flash to knock the gun out of the lead codger's hand. The other old man, instead of taking action, voluntarily tossed his gun to the floor.

"Jesus Christ, Clint!" the lead man bellowed, "Why didn't you shoot?"

"I'm sorry, Bob," Clint moaned, "but I've grown tired of following your stupid-assed ideas."

Stoney stepped around Bob and Clint to push the front door closed while Thumbs scooped up the two ancient revolvers. Scar stepped up close to Bob.

"Guess you know what this means, you stupid old fucker?" he hissed.

Bob stood tall. "Guess it means the cards have turned, you ugly motherfucker."

Scar backhanded Bob, and the elderly man crumbled to his knees. Clint shuffled to reach down and give his friend a helping hand.

"Please, Mister," Clint blurted, "Just let me get him out of here. This was a bad idea, but let us go, and you won't see us again."

"Afraid I can't do that, old-timer," Scar grinned. "But, I do want to know what ties you have to the so-called *Four Horsemen*."

* * *

"I don't want you here. Get your ass gone."

Junior pulled a chair up close to Gabe's bed and took a seat. "It's my turn to watch you. I ain't going no place, so deal with it."

Gabe pulled in a ragged breath, and released it slowly. They'd cut his pain meds, and the doctor reported he'd made a near miraculous recovery. But not yet miraculous enough to allow him to reach and grab Junior by the throat.

"A lot of the mess we now find ourselves in is your fault, asshole. You should have had the good sense to let the past remain in the past."

To Gabe's surprise, Junior nodded his head.

"You are right, Gabe. I now wish I'd done so. I had no idea it would come to this."

Gabe didn't know how to take a humble and repentant Junior Pernell. He'd never seen this side of the man he'd known most of his life.

"Tell me what all happened, Junior. Not sure at this point what I've been told and what I imagined because of all the drugs."

Gabe remained quiet through the entire story Junior struggled to deliver. The fact Junior started with plagued Gabe throughout the telling.

"Jesus, Junior, you were crying in your sleep?"

"I ain't proud of it, Gabe."

Gabe nodded his head several times before admitting, "I understand. And I ain't proud of the fact that I could so easily put the accident out of mind, Junior. I fear we both, and the others, are just reaping what I sowed. I'm wishing I'd not let you shoulder this all on your own."

Junior dropped his head and shrugged his meaty shoulders. "Ain't all our fault. We had nothing to do with what occurred between Kadie and Bo."

"Yeah. But you know, maybe we needed something like this to pull us all together, Junior."

Junior looked up and into Gabe's eyes. "I don't disagree, but I'd surely chose another path to making that so."

Gabe used the support device attached over his head to pull himself up in the bed. "Junior, I got to get the fuck out of here. My clothes are in that closet behind you. I'd appreciate you helping me into them."

"Not sure that's such a good idea, Gabe."

Gabe chuckled, and it felt good to do so. "It's too late now, old friend, to keep bad ideas from interfering with this fucked-up situation."

* * *

Kadie heard the front door open and close. She hurried from the back of the house to find Troy already seated in his recliner. "Where in the world have you been, Troy? I've been worried sick about you."

It wasn't entirely a lie. She'd called his cell numerous times, and he'd not answered. She could have more accurately stated her worry with another question.

Did you stay out all night because you know about my deception?

"I've been at the hospital keeping watch over Gabe," Troy responded without looking at her.

"Does this have something to do with who shot him?"

"In a round-about way," Troy mumbled without giving her even a glance.

"So, you know who shot him?"

"I do."

"And you think they're going to try again?"

Troy finally looked up and stared directly into her eyes. Kadie couldn't exactly put a name to what the eyes revealed. They seemed to display a combination of emotions.

"No. Don't believe that's the case, Kadie. Now there's others out to kill him. They're also aiming to kill me, Gabe, and Woop as well."

"My God, Troy, what's all this all about?"

Troy averted his eyes to stare at the far wall. "I'll get to that, but first, go get my checkbook."

Kadie appreciated the opportunity away from him to clear her thinking and deal with her dread. She grabbed his checkbook from the desk in the study and paused a minute out of his sight to take deep breaths. When she returned to hand it to him, Troy pulled a pen from his shirt pocket and started filling out the next available check. When finished, he handed it up to her without saying a word.

Kadie studied the check, and her breath nearly froze in her lungs. "You made it out to me?" She paused in order to calm her racing heart. "For the amount of . . . Three hundred thousand dollars?"

Troy pushed out of his recliner and moved to put his face close to hers. "Go pack a bag, Kadie. I want you out of here before I do something ugly. You can give all that money to Bo Conwoop as you promised, or you can use it to start a new life some where else."

"Oh, Troy," Kadie gasped as tears started to stream, "I don't know how or what . . ."

Troy put four fingers of his right hand to her lips to hush her mouth. "Get gone, woman. Do it quickly."

Kadie turned and hurried to their master bedroom. She threw what little remained of her life into a suitcase while sobbing out loud. In several rooms away, she heard Troy doing the same.

* * *

Marvin watched Scar as he processed the information he'd pulled from Bob and Clint. Marvin's mind spun with the information they'd provided. The two old men had once held close ties with Saupitty, Rubottom, Pernell, and Conwoop. But just recently, they'd abducted Saupitty's mother and then tried to kill Saupitty to cover their asses. Marvin suspected their crimes had spoiled their relations with the other three power brokers as well. He now waited anxiously to see what Scar would come up with. He didn't have to wait long.

"These two are damn fine bait," Scar announced. "We can use them to lure these so called Four Horsemen into one place at one time. They'll either show up to save them, or to do them harm. All we have to do is come up with the place to draw them in."

Marvin nodded his head along with Bo and the other three bikers. What else could he do?

"Bo," Scar said, "I want you to keep these two old fuckers here and out of sight. Fuck them up if they give you any trouble, but don't kill them."

"Me and Marvin can damn sure do that," Bo readily agreed.

"Well, there's still that stolen truck parked out front," Scar mumbled. "So, you are going to have to do without Marvin for a while."

Just hearing that caused Marvin's gut to clinch even before Scar turned his one good eye on him.

"Marvin, you need to get that truck out of here. Take it someplace, dump it, and get your ass back here with Bo."

It took long seconds for Marvin to realize the advantage of his assignment. All alone, he could use his cell to update Woop.

"Me and my boys are going back to the motel to talk this over," Scar said as he headed for the door. "Bo," he said over his shoulder, "you know these parts better than all of us. You come up with someplace we can lure those four assholes to."

"I'll do that, Scar."

Marvin followed the four bikers out the door. As Clint said it would be, he found the key in the ignition of the stolen truck. Marvin pulled the phone from his pocket as he drove and called the only number it contained under contacts.

"What's going on, Marvin?" Woop asked.

"Really bad shit, sir."

"Well, what's the hell is new about that?"

Marvin hurriedly told him what had transpired with Bob and Clint. It took long minutes before Woop offered a solution.

"Listen carefully, Marvin. Here's the lie I want you to relay to Bo."

Marvin listened and asked questions until he felt he clearly understood what Woop demanded.

"Okay, Mr. Conwoop, I got it down. And I think unless I get caught in this stolen truck, I can pull it off."

"You got that gun on you, Marvin?"

"Yes, sir."

"If you get pulled over by the police . . . use it to shoot yourself in the head. That'd most likely be your quickest and easiest way out of this mess."

Chapter Sixteen

Eastridge felt too keyed up to head home and to bed. At a quarter past midnight, he drove the city streets in his personal car and wearing civilian clothing. He'd been cruising past clubs, bars, and motels looking for the four bikes he'd seen following Johns on Main Street three days earlier. All along he'd fought back the urge to pay an unannounced visit to Melody Preston. Now he had only two more motels to check, and still did not feel certain he wouldn't then pop in on Melody.

And what if the good Doctor Morton is there?

Eastridge gritted his teeth and grumbled, "I will fuck him up."

The satisfaction of doing so played in his mind as he pulled into Anadarko's Motel Six. He imagined Morton screaming for mercy as he pulled to the back parking lot. The satisfying fantasy evaporated the moment he spotted the four parked Harley Davidsons.

Eastridge pulled up next to the bikes and parked his car. He unfolded from beneath the wheel to check the plates on the bikes.

Colorado?

He put a hand on the engines to feel for heat. They'd been parked long enough to cool. He scanned the rooms looking for interior lights. The types who rode these bikes certainly would be late night kinds of scum. He spotted only two rooms that emitted light from the inexpensive shades. He pulled his gun from a shoulder holster as he made his way toward the closest of the two. Eastridge could not see anything through the closed shades and stepped to the door to listen for noises from within. With his right ear pressed to the door, he suddenly felt the pressure of cold steel inserted into his left ear.

"Even flinch, motherfucker," a voice whispered from behind him, "And I'll paint that door with your brains."

Then his gun was jerked from his hand. Eastridge spun in place and barely got a glance of a man before the man's gun collided with his forehead. It took a second strike from the heavy firearm to buckle his knees and he fell back against the door. He tumbled backwards as the door opened behind him, and felt himself being dragged into the motel room. Just barely conscious, it took moments to realize his pockets were being searched.

"He's a fucking cop, Scar."

The declaration seemed to boom like thunder from a thick and dark cloud.

"I'm off duty," he managed to slur.

"Good job, Thumbs," a different voice said. "Glad we posted a guard. Get his ass up."

Hands grabbed him, pulled him upright, and slammed him down on a chair. He gasped and sputtered when cold water assaulted his face, but it did serve to rouse him to near senses. He looked up and into a face that made him think his vision might have been damaged from the blow to his head. The face seemed terribly maimed.

"What the fuck are you doing here?"

"Just, uh . . . nothing. Looking for a hooker," Eastridge managed to lie.

"I think you are looking for us, asshole."

Eastridge mumbled objections, but heard the man's voice drown out his.

"Strip him naked, boys."

He did his best to struggle, but body blows from numerous fists rendered him incapable. His own handcuffs were used to restrain his hands behind his back.

"You're one big cop," mangled face said. "Off duty and looking for us? Bet you're a rogue with a bad-assed reputation."

"I don't even know who you are," Eastridge groaned yet another lie.

"Don't believe that, but do believe you must be a man with one hell of an ego. Stoney, I want you to film this with your phone. Sarge, let's pull out our dicks and give this naked big cop a facial."

Eastridge tried to bolt from the chair, but a fourth man held him in place with a strangling grip on his throat. He closed his eyes and groaned pitifully as two penises were rubbed all over his face . . . to include his lips.

"You getting this, Stoney?

"Hell, yes I am," a voice laughed.

After what seemed hours, the two men stepped back and tucked away their stuff.

The maimed face leaned in close. "We can't right now stand the heat of a missing cop, and I don't think you're the type that can stand the humiliation of Stoney's video being shown around this small town. You think we can come to some kind of understanding?"

Eastridge felt rage along with utter disgust surging through his body, and feared he might just vomit. He choked it back and moaned, "What do you want from me?"

"We're leaving this town in two days' time. We don't want to see you again. We will put what Stoney filmed on all our phones. If we're taken into custody, we'll make sure the arresting cops see it. You know it will spread from there. You'll be ruined for damn sure."

Eastridge dropped his damaged head to his bare chest. "You won't see me again."

The apparent leader with the hideous face said, "Okay. Someone give him his keys, and nothing else."

The cuffs were removed and his keys were placed in his right hand. "What about my clothes? My badge? My gun?"

"I'm keeping all the rest as a memento," the scarred one chuckled. "Get him out of here."

Eastridge was tossed naked out the door. He stumbled and fell several times as he hurried to his car. Once inside, he slumped over the wheel and let go with great sobs of shame and indignation. Knowing that he was already ruined, he felt vital parts deep within him starting to die.

* * *

"It took you long enough to get the fuck back here."

Marvin shrugged his weary shoulders, "Yeah, Bo, it took a while. I couldn't just dump that stolen truck around the corner. I took it miles away, and then I had to walk back here."

Bo pointed to Bob and Clint sitting side by side on the couch. "Well, now it's your turn to babysit these old bastards. I'm going to bed."

"You could just let us get out of here, Bo," Bob whined.

"You shouldn't have come here in the first place," Bo replied.

"That ain't no shit," Clint nodded.

Bob turned an ugly look on Clint and opened his mouth to speak, but Bo moved in close. "Don't start that shit again. I'm tired of you two bickering. One more word, and I start breaking brittle old bones."

To Marvin's surprise, Bob heeded the threat. Bo turned and started toward his bedroom when Marvin called out to him.

"Did you come up with a place to take them, Bo?"

Bo stopped and turned to face Marvin. "No. I need to sleep on it."

"I think I might know of a damned good place."

Bo cocked his head, "How the hell would you know where to take them?"

Marvin took a second to steady his nerves and get it right. "You know my brother-in-law, Ryan Cornish?"

"Fuck yeah, I know him. You know I know him."

"Okay, well one day, when he was looking for a place to dump shingles, he took me out to the north side of town. We went way back on this piece of property, very isolated, and we came up on this huge old deserted barn. It's far away from anything, Bo, and I remember how to get back there."

"Shit, Marvin, that might be just the right place. About time you pulled some of your load around here."

"I want to do all I can to help," Marvin both lied and told the truth. He just didn't mention who he intended to help.

* * *

Sadie could not understand how she spent the last four days praying her heart out that he'd live, and now she felt like choking him to death.

"Damn, woman, I asked you to take my boots off, not my fucking legs, just my fucking boots," Gabe groaned.

Sadie stood upright to stare at Gabe laying back in his recliner. "I'm being as gentle as I can. Your feet are swollen. That's because you got up and walked out of the hospital, you Apache moron."

"This pillow behind my head still ain't right either."

"Maybe it'd feel better if I jerked it from beneath your head and placed it firmly over your mouth and nose." Sadie had been up all night tending to Gabe, and it was just barely four in the morning now. She desperately needed at least a nap.

"I thought you'd be glad to have me back home," Gabe said.

"Well, if you weren't such a pain in the ass, I would be," Sadie said as she bent once again to work the boots off his feet. "Fact is you weren't ready to leave the hospital. I should have shot Junior Pernell the minute he walked you through the door."

"Wasn't Junior's fault. Besides, you were damned rude to him anyway."

Sadie almost had the right boot off when the doorbell rang.

"I hope that's him coming back. I'll show him some real damn rudeness," she grumbled.

Gabe reached to take his pistol off the table next to him. "Won't be Junior. You stay away from that door, Sadie."

Had he said nothing, just the look in his eyes would have caused Sadie to feel alarmed. "Who do you think it is, Gabe? You think it's who shot you in the first place?"

His eyes remained glued on the front door. "I have a lot to tell you. None of it's good. So, don't go near that door. And be sure to stand out of my line of fire."

"Jesus Christ, Gabe, do I need to run and grab a gun?"

"Might be a good idea."

Sadie turned and started to bolt to the bedroom when a voice called from the front porch.

"Sadie, it's me, Kadie. Please open the door."

"Kadie? What the hell is she doing here at this time?" Sadie asked.

"That woman can't come in this damned house," Gabe thundered.

"Why the hell would you say that? They gave you too many strong drugs in that hospital," Sadie said as she walked toward the door.

"Don't let her in! Tell her to go away!"

Sadie unlocked the door and flung it open. Her sister stood sobbing. "Kadie, what's wrong honey?" Sadie wrapped her arms around her and pulled her into the house.

"You want to tell her what's wrong, Kadie, or do you want me to?" Gabe shouted.

"I thought he was still in the hospital," Kadie whimpered.

Sadie kept her arms around her twin, but turned to glare at Gabe. "Someone tell me what's going on, and tell me right now."

"Which one of us is it going to be, Kadie?" Gabe said angrily.

Kadie pulled out of Sadie's arms and thrust a small folded piece of paper in her hand. "I endorsed it to you." In the next instance she bolted out the door and ran to her car.

Sadie rushed out on the porch and watched as Kadie jumped into her running car and sped away.

* * *

Jerry Eastridge stared down at the videodisc in his hand. He studied if for long seconds before gently placing it beside the carefully stacked Polaroid pictures lying on his bed. He smoothed the bedspread around the shrine of tormenting memories. He straightened and walked as if in a trance to stare into the full-length mirror on his closet door. Eastridge made adjustments to the dress police uniform he now wore. He tugged the hem of the jacket to straighten it, and tightened the knot of his tie. He pulled a handkerchief from his back pocket to polish the medals over his right pocket, and then tucked the handkerchief back in place. Before turning from the mirror, he looked deeply into the image of his eyes, and saw nothing there worth looking at.

Eastridge turned and strolled back to the opposite side of the bed that supported the shrine. He slowly positioned himself on his back and lowered his head to the pillow. Staring at the ceiling, Eastridge pulled his service weapon from its holster and placed the barrel in his mouth to the back of his throat.

He hesitated for only a second, but it proved enough time to give him doubt.

Fuck this. It's crazy.

But he pulled the trigger anyway.

* * *

Gabe held his breath and painfully forced himself out of the recliner. "Come here, baby."

Sadie remained seated on the couch crying into tissues.

Gabe had seen her cry maybe twice in her life. He tried his best not to groan, but did so anyway as he took a step in her direction.

"I'm so sorry, baby, but it is what it is."

Sadie slumped to her side on the couch and heaved with every sob she emitted. Gabe slowly made his way to her, and lowered himself to sit next to her head. He reached and tenderly stroked her wet cheek.

"You know I've never been good with words. I didn't know any easier way to tell it."

Sadie placed her hand on his. "It's all so unbelievable. Kadie wanting Troy dead. Bo Conwoop wanting all of you dead, to include his own father. And Bob and Clint? How could they do such a shit thing after all the shit things they already pulled with your mother?"

"Don't know," Gabe sighed.

Sadie pushed herself upright and scooted next to Gabe. She took several deep breaths, and shook her head as if to bring back the typically strong Sadie. "Okay. You're right. It is what it is. What are we going to do about it?"

"We have a plan, but I ain't pulling you into that. The less you know, the better off you'll be."

Sadie turned her mean look on him. "Fuck that. I intend to do my part to make this all go away."

"Oh, you got a part to play."

"What is it?"

"I'm going to need you to take me to Red."

"Now? This early in the morning?"

"Yup."

"What for?"

"That three hundred-thousand-dollar check endorsed to you. I'll call him once you help me into the car."

* * *

Rheta walked down the stairs to find Woop sitting at the kitchen table drinking coffee. He looked up at her and offered a solemn nod.

"You came to bed later than usual, and now you're up two hours earlier than usual. Are you sick with something, Woop?"

"White Woman, truth is I'm feeling about as poorly as a man can feel."

Rheta smiled at his term of endearment, but worried over the look in his eyes and his hangdog demeanor.

"Why you feeling poorly, Red Man?"

"I made the coffee extra stout this morning. Pour yourself a big cup and take a seat, Rheta. You might even want to add a wallop of whiskey to it."

Rheta reached in a cabinet for a cup and filled it full with the strong black coffee. "Whatever you got must be horrible if I need whiskey to hear about it."

Woop nodded his head. "There's something going on that is just that horrible, but I feel even worse about telling you about it. So, you brace yourself, gal."

Rheta sat down next to Woop and hurriedly started sipping the coffee. "Okay. Let me hear it, Woop."

"Our son is paying four bikers from Colorado to kill me, Gabe, Troy, and Junior."

Rheta nearly spewed her last sip. "I'm truly right now hoping this is just another thing you've twisted in your mind about Bo." She assured herself as such before adding, "Besides, Bo is paying someone to kill you boys? What the hell could he pay them? Maybe fifty bucks?"

"No. Three hundred thousand bucks."

Rheta now knew for sure her husband was pulling her leg. "This is not a funny joke, Woop."

"You're right, sweetheart. Ain't a bit funny. And ain't no joke either."

"All right, I'll take the bait, big boy. And where is Bo getting three hundred thousand dollars?"

"From Kadie Rubottom. She first offered the money to Bo to kill just Troy. Then that fucking Junior, who ain't no junior in the first place, got his ass in a wringer with the four bikers. Now, Bo, is going to use the money he gets from Kadie to have them kill us all. Just that simple."

Rheta pushed up from the table and walked to the liquor cabinet. She pulled out a bottle of Jack Daniels and filled the empty space in her coffee cup. "I'm betting you didn't hear this bullshit from our Bo. Did you?"

"Nope. Comes from a kid named Marvin Purdy who's been living with our son."

"And, Woop, I'm betting you've not even discussed this bullshit with our son. Have you?"

"Don't need to. I know enough to know it's true."

Rheta wanted to throw the cup of coffee and whiskey across the room, but instead started pacing with it in her hand. Woop clearly had some wires crossed. He'd for so long been just too willing to think the worst of Bo. Some of it was justified, but her son wanting his own father dead? Total bullshit.

"Woop, you best get to talking to our son."

Woop emitted a bitter sounding chuckle. "Shit, woman, in the best of situations, he don't answer when I call, and seldom bothers to return my calls. But you, well, that's another matter. He's mama's boy and always has been. Grab your cell and give him a shout."

Rheta reached into the pocket of her robe and pulled out her phone. She made a real production of doing what Woop should have done in the first place, showing her husband just how simple it could be to talk to their only child.

Bo didn't pick up. The call went to his voicemail.

"Didn't answer, did he?" Woop grumbled.

"It's very early, Woop."

"It is for a full-grown man not used to getting up until noon. Dial it again. Dial it until he answers."

Rheta did just that. On the third attempt, Bo answered with a groggy voice.

"What the hell, mom?"

"Bo, I'm hearing just terrible things from your father. You tell me now that what I'm hearing is just . . ."

The line went dead.

Woop stood up and looked her hard in the eyes. "He hung up on you. Didn't he?"

"Might have been a bad connection," Rheta mumbled as a heavy feeling of intense dread set in.

"Now, I'll use the word . . . bullshit. That boy's never hung up on his mother. Let's see if he calls back."

Rheta fought off hysterics as she waited long moments for a return call.

"I'm sorry, Rheta," Woop said in a most sincere manner. "But he won't be calling back."

Rheta fell heavily back into her chair at the table. "What are you going to do, Woop?"

"We're going to try to pull those bikers into an ambush and kill them in self-defense. I'm hoping with all my heart that Bo has the sense not to be with them when it happens."

Rheta could no longer hold back the tears. "You'd kill our only child?"

Woop shook his head emphatically. "Hell, no. Not me. But I can't swear one of the others won't. I can only promise you, Rheta, that I will do my level best to get Bo free from this terrible mess that he put in motion."

Rheta slumped to lay her head on the table, and started crying like she'd never cried before.

Chapter Seventeen

"I don't know about this, Gabe. Sure think we should talk it over with the others."

"Not enough time to do so, Red," Gabe said from the back seat of Red's Cadillac. "The sun will be up in the next thirty minutes. We got to do this under the cover of darkness."

"We, Gabe?" Sadie grumbled from the front passenger seat. "No 'we' to it. I'm going to be the one to do it."

"Wish you'd reconsider, and let Red do it," Gabe grumbled back. He took note that Red did not object to allowing Sadie to do the dirty work.

"No. I want the pleasure of doing it. I'd just love to do more damage to the little fucker," Sadie declared.

"There's no prints on that envelope or the cash, Sadie. Be sure and wear those plastic gloves," Red said.

Gabe watched Sadie raise two gloved hands and wave them at Red. "Think I'm an idiot, Red?"

Red shook his head, "Just making sure, Sadie." He glanced over the seat at Gabe, "We're damned close. Where should I park?"

"Just right up front. Hell, ain't nobody in that house awake. Get as close as you can for Sadie."

Red moaned an objection as he turned the corner and drove straight for Bo Conwoop's house. He turned the car's lights off when they were one block away.

Gabe sucked in a deep breath as Red pulled to the curb and Sadie bailed out with a hammer in one gloved hand and a large and stuffed manila envelope in another. He held his breath as Sadie applied the hammer to the window of Bo's car and tossed the envelope on the driver's seat. The Camaro's lights started flashing and the horn blared as Sadie sprinted back to the car.

Gabe used the held breath to thunder, "Get the hell out of here, Red!"

* * *

Marvin ran into Bo's room with his gun in hand. "Bo! Wake up. Your car alarm is going off."

He'd never seen Bo move so quickly from bed without assistance from Woop or Scar. He scooped up his keys and grabbed the gun from Marvin's hand before rushing out the front door in his underwear. The ruckus didn't disturb Bob or Clint's sleep on the living room floor. Marvin fought off the urge to kick them both. He'd spent the night awake just watching the two old bastards.

The loud honking of the car's horn ceased, and a few seconds later Bo entered the house with a bulging envelope the size of a large handbag.

"Where did you get that, Bo?"

"Out of my fucking car."

Bo handed Marvin his gun before ripping into the envelope.

"Jesus Christ!" Bo blurted.

Marvin nodded his agreement. "Fuck, that's a lot of money."

Bo hurried into the kitchen and tossed the envelope on the table and pulled up a chair. He spilled the contents on the tabletop, and Marvin gasped at the huge amount of one hundred-dollar bills. He didn't even notice the single piece of paper until Bo picked it up.

Marvin leaned over Bo's shoulder and followed the typed words on the paper as Bo read aloud.

"Here is twenty-thousand in one hundred dollars bills. You get the rest when the job is done."

Marvin mumbled a "motherfucker" as Bo started to count and stack the bills. Minutes later he announced, "Damn sure is two hundred of them here."

"From Kadie Rubottom?" Marvin asked.

"I guess the fuck so, but don't know why she had to destroy my window to get them to me."

It didn't make sense to Marvin either, and he instinctively concluded that Kadie had not delivered the money. He knew better than to share that with Bo.

"What are you going to do with it, Bo?"

Bo looked over his shoulder and smiled at Marvin. "Going to give it to our Colorado friends as a down payment."

Marvin nodded his head. He knew Bo would take that as him agreeing, but he nodded to confirm that he thought it was the intended use of the planted money.

* * *

Troy took a seat with the others in the small cabin. Being with Gabe, Woop, Junior, and Red did nothing to improve his temperament.

"Why the fuck are we here?" he asked.

"There's been further developments," Red grumbled.

"I hope they are good fucking developments. I'm growing weary with this whole shit deal," Troy grumbled back.

Gabe leaned over the table to look Troy in the eyes. "You ain't going to like it at first, but I hope you'll give us the chance to explain."

Troy stared at Gabe for long seconds before saying, "You look like hell."

"Feel like I been there and only part of me came back."

"What do you have to explain, Gabe?"

Gabe reached into his shirt pocket and pulled out a folded check. He handed it to Troy.

Troy unfolded it, studied it, and said, "Why you giving me a check for two-hundred and eighty thousand dollars?"

"It's what's left of the three hundred thousand you gave Kadie."

Troy felt a volcano starting to erupt in his guts. "You best get to explaining real fast."

He endured tremors of rage as Gabe told about Kadie's early morning visit, and what they'd done with the remaining twenty thousand.

Troy looked from Gabe to Red and back to Gabe. "I ought to just shoot the both of you for not bringing me into this before doing it."

Red started to speak, but Woop beat him to it.

"I'm the one that ought to be doing the shooting, Troy. My son has now been set up for damn sure . . . but I see the silver lining in this dark fucking cloud."

Troy inhaled and exhaled bitter air as Woop explained to him and the others the information he'd received from Marvin Purdy on

Bob and Clint. He then imparted the guidance he'd given Purdy about a barn that set on land they all conjointly owned.

"The way I see it, boys," Woop concluded, "that twenty grand will help to insure we find those bikers in our old red barn."

"Along with Bob and Clint," Gabe growled.

"And probably your son as well, Woop," Junior added.

Troy paused to let it all sink in. His insides started to cool, and he voiced obvious questions. "Gabe, it's gotten around to this group that Bob and Clint shot you down. How do you intend to deal with them? And, Woop, if Bo's there, how you going to handle that?"

Gabe turned his eyes on Junior and spoke first. "You're not very good with secrets."

"Didn't know you meant to keep it a secret from this group. Haven't told anybody else."

Gabe shrugged his wide shoulders. "Don't really matter, Junior." Then he looked at Troy. "I don't intend to do them any harm, Troy, but wouldn't give a damn if each catch a stray bullet. Right now, I'm only hoping for a few days of healing before this all goes down."

Woop looked down at the table as he started to speak. "Rheta asked me nearly the same thing, Troy. I gave her a slightly different answer than I'll give you." Woop looked from the table to stare Troy in the eyes. "I do hope he's not in that barn, but if he is, and lends assistance to those bikers, I'm hoping one of you will put a bullet in him. If that's the kind of man he truly is, I'd just as soon see him dead."

Troy paused a moment before saying, "That's harsh, Woop."

"It's a harsh situation he's put us in," Woop responded.

Troy thought the comment over before starting to nod his head. "Yup. Him and my wife." At the moment, he wondered where she was, and although it made no sense whatsoever . . . he wanted her back.

* * *

Scar looked down upon the stacks of one hundred dollars bills and didn't fight back the urge to smile. "Okay. I consider that a healthy down payment. Now tell me about this barn."

"Well, Scar, Marvin here came up with it. I'll let him tell you," Bo grinned.

Scar preferred to deal with Marvin anyway. He didn't care for Bo. He considered him a slimy, unpredictable type. Marvin, on the other hand, seemed more dependable.

"Tell me about it, Marvin."

Scar listened as Marvin described the location and how he knew about it. He sensed uneasiness in the man, but Scar often invoked that in others.

"I want to see the place," Scar decided. "Bo, me and Marvin will take your car. Give him the keys." He knew Bo wouldn't like the idea, but his only objection showed in his eyes. He reluctantly retrieved them from a pocket and handed them to Marvin.

"Take care of my damned car," he hissed at Marvin.

Marvin nodded his head, but Scar added a jab at Bo. "Yeah, Marvin, don't bust out any windows or anything like that."

"Yeah, that's funny shit," Bo grumbled.

Scar thought it was and laughed to prove the point. He looked around the small house. "Where'd you put the two old men?"

"They're tied back to back and gagged in the back room. Got tired of listening to them argue," Bo said.

Scar nodded his head before saying, "Thumbs, Stoney, and Sarge are posted around the neighborhood. It's time we started taking every precaution. Can't afford any fuck ups. So, you stay here, Bo, and make sure neither of them two old men suffocate from being gagged."

Scar and Marvin were walking out the door when Bo hollered out, "Take care of my car, Marvin."

"Fuck your car," Scar growled over his shoulder.

* * *

Sheriff Preston moved from behind her desk to shake the extended hand of Anadarko's chief of police, Jay Sliger.

"Glad you were in, and thanks for seeing me on such short notice, Melody."

"Not a problem, Jay. Always glad to see you," Melody said as they shook hands. He'd been two years ahead of her in high school, and back then she'd had a crush on him. "You sounded upset over the phone, Jay, and worry's written all over your face."

"Yeah. It's bad. You best take a seat."

Melody moved to her desk, plopped into her chair and pulled in a deep breath. "Okay, what's happened?"

Chief Sliger selected one of the two chairs in front of her desk and lowered himself to sit in a weary manner. He looked her in the eyes, but appeared to have a difficult time doing so.

"Melody, Jerry Eastridge is dead. It looks to be an apparent suicide."

Melody ran a suddenly trembling hand through her red hair. "Oh, shit."

"Sorry. Told you it's bad, but not sure I haven't told the worst of it just yet."

241

She'd not lost her feelings for Eastridge, but had just put them aside for a life with Robert Morton. The news of his death affected her deeply and she couldn't imagine anything worse.

"It's the evidence he left behind, Melody. Uh, well, very explicit photographs and videos of you and Jerry. He wanted them to be seen."

"Oh, dear Jesus!" Melody had fought back tears of grief, but now ones of indignation started to flow freely. "I can't believe . . . My God, what a selfish and vengeful son of a bitch!"

"I'm sorry, Melody."

"You must be repulsed, Jay," Melody sobbed.

"No. Been at policing too long, and have seen it all. I don't judge you harshly, but do regret what you must be feeling."

Melody reached for tissues from a box on her desk and tried to regain her composure. "How many saw the *evidence*, Jay?"

"There were two uniforms on the scene and two detectives. I warned them about this getting out, but you know what it's like on a small department in a small town."

"It will be booked into your property room?"

"Afraid so. You know the procedure. Must be held until the autopsy is complete, and, of course, the DA will get involved. When he learns what was found at the scene, he'll want to see it."

Melody inhaled a deep and jagged breath. It'd been the DA's brother she'd run against and beaten to become the county sheriff. "He'll use that against me in the next election."

Chief Sliger sighed and nodded his head as he stood to leave. "Yeah, he'll find a way to let it be known."

Melody pushed to stand on wobbly legs as she extended her hand to Sliger. "I know you didn't have to let me know about this. I appreciate you doing so."

Sliger took her hand and offered a firm grip. "I know you'd do the same for me."

Melody struggled to smile. "Don't think I'd have to, Jay. I'd bet you don't have porno flicks floating around out there that you starred in."

"Well, truth be, Melody, I just never had the opportunity for such. Hang on to that sense of humor, Sheriff," Sliger smiled back.

Doubt the possibility of that, Chief.

* * *

Marvin carefully drove Bo's prized car back from the old barn as he listened to Scar organizing the next moves over his cell phone.

"The place is perfect, Thumbs. I need you to rent us a box van large enough to transport the bikes out to the barn. We'll then use it to move all of us and the two old fucks out there. Keep Stoney and Sarge on watch around the house while you're getting the van."

Surprisingly, Marvin felt more at ease around Scar than he did Bo. Enough so that he didn't mind asking a question once Scar disconnected.

"Aren't you worried that the van can be traced back to you?"

Scar chuckled before replying, "Thumbs always carries fake identification, and he'll pay in cash. He's a pro at this sort of thing."

Marvin didn't doubt it. "Glad you're keeping a watch on the house. There's a big mean-assed city cop that keeps tabs on me and Bo." The last thing he needed was Eastridge fowling things up before he could make a clean break and get the hell out of Anadarko for the rest of his life.

"A big cop you say? Would his name be Eastridge by any chance?"

As concerned as he was about the car, he couldn't keep from taking his eyes off the road to glance at Scar. "You know him?"

"Intimately," Scar grinned. "And I'll tell you this and nothing more. He's the reason we're on alert, but I seriously doubt he'll interfere again."

Again?

Marvin damned sure wanted to ask, but thought it best that he just keep his mouth shut.

* * *

"Now you know why I can't stay with Sadie, and I have no place else to go, Margaret," Kadie said to her older sister.

Margaret Stinney took a long drag off her cigarette before dropping it in an ashtray. She exhaled a plume of smoke as she spoke. "Jesus, child, didn't think you had that kind of spunk."

"I've never been as strong as you and Sadie."

"I would have agreed with you, baby sister, before hearing you hired someone to kill your old man."

"You must think I'm awful."

"Well, don't think it was the smartest thing to do, but someone should have killed all four of those bastards long before now."

Kadie took a moment before asking, "So, will you let me stay with you until I sort things out, Margaret?"

"Did you know that my Melody is going to marry Dr. Robert Morton?"

The sudden topic change took Kadie by surprise. "Uh, no, I had no idea."

"She sure is. She called last week to tell me. Melody doesn't call often. Can't blame her. We don't see eye to eye on most things, and I was a terrible mother. However, she has me to thank for her good fortune. It was me that insisted to Morton that he make the move and pop the question."

"Well, uh, that was good of you to do so. I'm happy for Melody," Kadie said, wondering what this had to do with her asking to stay with Margaret.

"So, anyhow, Kadie, I have Melody taken care of now. Guess I can turn my efforts on you. Yes, you can stay with me. Straightening your life out will be my new project. I seem to have a knack for such."

She thanked her older sister, but doubted she had a chance in hell of undoing the terrible knot Kadie had tied.

* * *

They were within a half a block from Bo's house when Scar growled, "There's a truck in the drive. Do you know who it belongs to?"

Marvin sure did. "That's Cassie Pernell's pickup."

"Pernell? Is she kin to junior?"

Marvin emitted a sigh. "Yeah. It's his daughter. Her and Bo kind of got a thing going on."

Scar grumbled something Marvin couldn't make out, but didn't ask him to repeat it. He pulled in next to the pickup, and Scar bailed out. He made it to the front porch before Marvin could put the transmission in park and kill the engine. Marvin had one foot out of the car when Scar applied his fist to the door, nearly taking it off the hinges. Marvin broke into a run and made it in the house just in time to see Bo and Cassie scurrying for cover.

"What the fuck is she doing here?" Scar bellowed.

Bob and Clint sat tied back to back in the living room floor, but no longer gagged.

"They're sweet on each other," Bob said, "She's Junior's baby girl, and that ain't no good for you, biker trash."

"Shut the fuck up, Bob," Bo hollered.

"Close the door, Marvin," Scar ordered.

Marvin had to make adjustments to get it back in the frame.

"I know you're not just real smart, Bo, but I didn't figure you for a fucking idiot," Scar hissed.

"She just dropped in, Scar. She's my woman. What was I supposed to do?" Bo replied.

"I'm not exactly his woman," Cassie inserted, "and I think I'll go now."

Scar blocked her path to the door. "I think you'll stay until I sort this out."

Cassie made an attempt to get around him. Scar grabbed her by the throat and gave her a mighty shove, sending her nearly flying to the far end of the living room."

"Hey, motherfucker!" Bo screamed.

Scar used the same hand to grab Bo by the throat, but he didn't toss him. He pulled him in close. "You want to make a stand for your woman, Bo?"

Marvin watched as Bo wilted in Scar's grasp.

"Oh, man, she ain't no threat to us," Bo whimpered.

At that moment, Marvin finally realized he had no reason to fear Bo. A man that wouldn't fight for his girl wouldn't fight for anything. Scar released the grip on Bo's throat.

"I do believe you're right, Bo. At this point, all she can do is help us," Scar grinned.

"Like, uh, how?" Bo asked.

"Like giving those four just another reason to come to that old barn," Scar answered.

"I don't understand, Scar."

"Ain't all that complicated, Bo. But let me break it down for you. Now we have four reasons those dudes will show up. We have Bob and Clint, and now we have your little lady."

Cassie sat upright on the floor and rubbed at her throat. "Kick his ass, Bo!"

Bo turned his head to stare at Cassie, and Marvin almost felt pity for the helpless look in his eyes. Bo made no move to kick Scar's ass.

Instead, he surmised, "Uh, but that's only three reasons. What's the fourth?"

Marvin let go with a chuckle, and it felt damned good.

"What the fuck you find so funny, Marvin?" Bo said with a hateful glare.

Marvin didn't let it faze him. "You're the fourth reason . . . dumb fuck."

Bo turned a startled look on Scar.

Scar grinned at him. "Looks like you have been usurped . . . dumb fuck."

Chapter Eighteen

Melody Preston didn't bother calling. She'd spent the night stewing on it, and decided to catch Robert Morton before he left for his clinic. She used her key to open the front door, but called out upon stepping into the entryway.

"Robert! It's me, Melody."

Seconds later he appeared on the second-floor landing fully dressed for work. "Well, this is certainly a nice morning surprise," he said with a smile.

She certainly dreaded bursting his bubble. "We need to talk, Robert."

His smile faded. "Pour yourself a cup of coffee. I'll be down in just a few minutes."

Melody walked through the house to the kitchen, poured two cups of coffee, and sat down at the table. She took the few minutes to rehearse what she'd say.

"So, I'm assuming you're having second thoughts?" Robert said as he entered the kitchen.

The dread in his voice poked a sharp finger at Melody's heart. "No. Not at all. I think it will be you with the second thoughts."

Robert sat down beside her and wrapped a hand around his cup of coffee. "Please explain."

Melody took a sip from her cup, and then sat it aside. "It will be all over the news today, and I wanted you to hear it from me. Jerry Eastridge committed suicide."

Robert stared down at his coffee for a few seconds before picking it up and bringing it to his lips. After a few sips, he turned his eyes back on Melody. "Although I only knew the man through you, I am shocked. It's always saddening when someone takes his or her own life. How are you dealing with it?"

"I'm angry, Robert, but not for reasons you can even imagine. That's why I dropped in unannounced. It won't immediately make the news, but I'm implicated in his death."

Robert sat upright as if preparing for a blow. "How could that be?"

"He left videos and photographs for the investigators to find."

Robert exhaled a moan. "And what do they portray?"

"By the expression on your face, I think you know. How detailed do you want my answer to be?"

Robert's shoulders slumped and he dropped his head to stare at the table. "Pornography?"

"Yes, Robert. A man and a woman doing what men and women do."

And then some.

For long seconds Robert clearly struggled with his thoughts. "Melody, you know I'm no prude, but why would you make a record of the things you did, and then leave him with the record?"

"I was dating him exclusively at the time, Robert, and he wanted the videos and the pictures." Melody paused to consider a follow-on, and chose the stark truth. "You of all people know how accommodating I can be."

"So now it's evidence being held by the police?"

"It is."

"Who all will end up seeing it?"

"An assistant DA, and then the DA. You know my history with him. He won't be able to show it around, but he'll get the word out of its existence." Melody drew a deep breath before continuing, "I expect the news will travel county wide by the next election."

"You do realize, Melody, that portions of it could find its way to the Internet."

"Not legally it can't. I'll be filing law suits if it does."

The look in Robert's eyes revealed pain. "I guess you can turn to your other lover Brad Smith to help with that."

"That's an ugly thing for you to say."

"Does he have photos and videos as well?"

Melody's first response was insult, but she swallowed it back. Considering the circumstances, a fiancé had the right to ask. "No, Robert. He does not."

Robert took a final gulp of coffee before pushing to his feet. "I have to get to the clinic."

Melody stood as well. "I understand your pain and anger. I certainly don't blame you, but I'd just ask . . ."

Robert displayed palms to hush her. "Please, Melody, don't ask for anything right now. I don't want to give a rushed or rash response."

Robert started for the door to the garage as Melody removed the engagement ring from her finger. "Robert!"

He turned to look back.

She held the ring toward him. "Would you prefer that I just leave this here on the table?"

He paused for a second before wearily nodding his head. "That might be best for right now."

* * *

The van's first trip took the four bikes and Scar's three men out to the secluded red barn. Marvin rode along now on the final trip to the destination. Scar ordered him to take the passenger seat, while Bo, Cassie, Bob, and Clint were relegated to sit on the bare floor behind the driver and passenger's seat. Marvin's gun was tucked down the front of his jeans. Scar had stripped Bo of his gun the night before. All was quiet in the van except for the low drone of a local disc jockey talking on the van's radio.

Marvin's mind spun with thoughts of how it would all go down at the barn, but a word spoken on the radio caught his attention.

"Mind if I turn that up, Scar?"

"Go ahead."

"*. . . the eighteen-year veteran of the Anadarko Police Department died of apparent suicide. No arrangements have been made for Officer Jerry Eastridge's services . . .*"

"Did I fucking hear that right?" Bo bellowed from the back of the van.

"Eastridge is dead," Marvin partially questioned and partially confirmed for Bo.

"Did they say suicide?" Bo asked.

Marvin cut his eyes at Scar. "That's what they said, Bo."

"Motherfucker!" Bo said gleefully.

Scar turned his head to meet Marvin's eyes. He winked and grinned. "Must have been one depressed son of a bitch."

Marvin nodded his head. Now there was one less obstacle to keep him from getting out of Oklahoma, but the news evoked more dread than jubilation. The man sitting next to him had something to do with the suicide, and clearly intended to see four more dead. Thankfully, Scar had turned his eyes back on the road and didn't see Marvin tremble from the icy sensation that tickled his spine.

* * *

"Are you serious, Woop? Don't you read a paper or listen to news?" Red asked.

"I told you, I ain't heard whatever news you asked if I've heard. Now you going to tell me or just pick at me, asshole?"

Red sat across a booth from Woop in the Dixie Diner. "Jerry Eastridge shot himself in the head." He watched as the big Indian scrunched his face.

"No shit? On purpose?"

"Why, I guess so, dumb ass. I never heard of someone accidently putting a gun in their mouth and pulling the trigger."

"You didn't tell me that part. Is he dead?"

"Oh, Jesus Christ," Red mumbled before taking a sip of coffee.

"Hell, Red, not everyone who shoots themselves in the head dies."

"He's very dead, all right, Woop?"

Red watched as Woop processed the information. The look in his dark brown eyes and the sudden clenching of his strong jaw line gave no indication of satisfaction.

"Could have told me that outright and saved a bunch of useless talk," Woop grumbled.

"Woop, three days ago, at the cabin, Purdy said you saved him from Eastridge. You said it was a long story. Tell me about it."

Woop took a couple of hits from his coffee cup before granting the request. "He was trying to use Marvin as a snitch to get at Bo. Do you know that hairdresser here in town, Cindy Wade?"

"This is Red you're talking to. I know everybody in this damned town."

"Well, I knew she had some shit on Eastridge. So, I went to see her. Turns out that ol' Jerry enjoyed having his ass spanked by pretty young women. She had a video of such, and I used that to get Eastridge off Marvin's ass."

Red could not keep his mouth from falling open, but got control of it to ask, "Are you shitting me?"

"Not a damn bit."

Red gave the revelation a few seconds of consideration. "Why, hell, Woop, that could be the reason he killed himself."

"I do hope that's not the case, Red. I mean, the guy was a total asshole above and beyond being a cop. Still, I hope that's not the reason he sent himself to hell."

"Boy, this is one messed up world," Red deduced.

"You know what's been on my mind since getting that from Cindy Wade?"

"What's that, Woop?" Red sighed.

"Gabe and Troy's niece, and our county sheriff, Melody Preston, she dated Eastridge for quite some time."

Red summed up a couple of seconds of thought with, "Hmmm, now that does tickle the imagination for damned sure, Woop."

Woop started to respond, but Red's cell phone started ringing. Red didn't recognize the number, but the phone identified it as a Colorado caller. "Oh, shit, best answer this, Woop."

"Mr. Winfield?" a gruff voice responded.

"This is Red Winfield. Who is this?"

"You can call me Scar . . ."

Red listened, and had no questions to ask. "I know the old red barn you're talking about." He thought he did a good job of acting surprised about the particulars he already knew. Those he didn't know truly surprised him. "I'll pass that to the others," he said before pushing the end button.

"Woop, we need to get to the cabin. I'll call the others to meet us there."

"From what I heard, that's the call we've been expecting."

"It was, but now's there's more." Red scooted out of the booth to hurry to the register.

"You ain't telling me more than that?" Woop called after him.

"I don't care to repeat it but once and to all concerned," Red said over his shoulder.

* * *

Bo sat on his ass on the dirt floor and looked around the vast interior of the big barn. He'd come here as a kid with his dad. The years had not been kind to the once grand structure. Cassie sat next to him, and Bob and Clint a few feet away. Marvin stood looking down on them all.

"Considering all I did for you, Purdy, this is some fucked up shit," Bo hissed.

"I agree, Bo. I wish it didn't come to this. But if you want, you call Scar over here and tell him you don't want me keeping an eye on you four."

"Fuck you."

"Fuck you back, Bo. If not for you, none of us would be here."

"Fuck you both," Cassie chimed in. "Wish I'd stayed clear of you two losers."

Bob mumbled something, but his mouth was gagged again.

"Think they'll feed us something?" Clint asked.

Bo, along with Marvin and Cassie, ignored Clint.

"Well, you just know this, Marvin," Bo said, forcing a fake grin, "This place, and all the other land those fuckers have, will soon be mine. I just regret not being able to do my part in the killing."

"Why the hell would you want to kill anyone Bo? And what about your dad?" Marvin asked in his whiney voice.

"You want to hear the first memory I have of my dear old dad, motherfucker?"

Marvin shrugged his bony shoulders, "I've got nothing but time."

"He put me on a green-broke horse when I was five, maybe six. I didn't want to be on it. He called me a pussy. Didn't even know what that was then, but knew it was no compliment. Before putting me in the saddle, he slapped me hard on the back of the head, 'You going to ride this horse, *pussy*. Ain't no son of mine going to be a *pussy*.'

"We were in a round pen, and that young horse just walked at first. Not good enough for the famed rodeo cowboy Johnny Conwoop. He popped the horse on the ass with a training whip, and that horse tore off in full gallop. I made it about halfway around the round pen before coming out of the saddle. I hit hard, and started to cry. He ran over and jerked me off my feet and slapped my face. 'Don't you dare cry, *pussy.* Conwoop men don't cry.'

"Then he spun me in the direction of the house and said, 'That's where you need to be. Inside with your mama, so you can do women kinds of things.' All the way from that round pen to the house, he kept kicking me in the ass. I fell down several times, and each time he'd jerk me to my feet and kick me just a little further toward the house. After that, he wouldn't even look at me for several days. That's when I began to hate him."

Bo watched Marvin turn his eyes to the earthen floor at his feet. "That's a terrible story, Bo."

"Yeah, it is, Marvin, and I got many more to tell. So don't you ask me why I'd want to kill my own dad."

Marvin bent down close and lowered his voice. "Bo, think about this, he might just make up for all that horrible shit. It might fall directly on him to save your life."

"What the fuck you talking about?"

Bo watched as Marvin scanned his head and eyes to look at Scar and his men.

"Bo, you honestly believe them to be the types to leave witnesses?"

Bo took his turn to look at the four bikers as Cassie scooted in close to him. He'd not considered the possibility. Doing so made something deep inside to suddenly ache.

* * *

"This will probably be our last time to meet here before all gets ugly," Red said to the four gathered around the table inside the cabin.

Gabe felt a bit stronger than the last time he'd sat the table. Still far from one hundred percent, he wondered if he could move well enough to be more than a simple target. His thoughts turned to the two who'd reduced him to this.

"So they have Bob and Clint at the barn?" Gabe asked.

Red nodded his head, "They do, but seems they don't consider just those two enough hostages to lure us out there."

"What the hell you talking about?" Troy blurted.

"They don't have Kadie, if that's what you fear," Red answered.

Gabe observed what he thought was relief in Troy's eyes. He turned to look back at Red, "Well then, who do they have?"

Red moved his eyes to stare at Junior. "They have Cassie."

Junior shot out of his chair, "Goddamn! How did they get Cassie?"

Red displayed his palms, "Don't have a clue, Junior. Just know that the one called Scar told me they have her."

"I will cut his guts out and feed them to him," Junior bellowed.

Red let Junior rant and turned his chair to face Woop. "Scar told me Bo's been demoted to a hostage as well."

Gabe watched Woop think on the development. He didn't take the news the same way Junior had.

"Well," Woop said with a shrug of his broad shoulders, "Guess that can be considered a good thing. Now one of you boys might not have to kill him. If he survives this . . . hell, if I survive it, I'll be making sure he leaves Caddo County and will never return as long as I'm living."

Gabe thought Troy might claim bids on Bo, seeing how Bo agreed to kill him in the first place, but Troy remained silent. Gabe asked, "What else did he say, Red?"

"Only that you four have twenty-four hours to show up at the barn. Guess we better get to our planning. Is that the only road into that place?"

"Yeah. It's the only road," Gabe answered.

"But there's another way in," Woop said, "We'd just need a special type of transportation, and I got a suggestion on the type."

Gabe listened as Woop laid out his plan. Once he finished, Gabe smiled and started nodding his head.

"I damn sure like that idea," Troy said.

Gabe chuckled before saying, "Just the kind of tactics I'd expect from a Comanche warrior."

* * *

He thought about the question, and brought a hand up to rub the side of his face that did not bear scars. "Well fuck me, Sarge. That's one hell of a question."

"Ain't trying to make you feel stupid, Scar," Sarge quickly pointed out.

"I damn sure feel stupid, but don't blame you. It's something I should have come up with on my own. Glad you asked it." If physically possible, Scar would kick his own ass. How could he have possibly made such an amateurish mistake?

Ain't never made plans to kill numerous people.

Scar moved around Sarge and walked over to where Purdy watched the four hostages. "Bo, what plans did you make for getting the rest of the money from Troy's wife?"

"Uh, well fuck, Scar, I haven't talked to her about that. Hell, she bashed in my window and put that . . ."

"We didn't take your phone from you," Scar interrupted. "Call her now."

Bo pulled his phone from a back pocket and started thumbing at it. Scar struggled with anxiety as Bo moved the phone to his ear.

"Oh fuck," Bo moaned.

"What?" Scar barked.

"Got a recording," Bo quaked. "No longer a working number."

"Motherfucker," Scar hissed before turning to Purdy. "Take the damned phone from him, Marvin."

Scar stomped away to a corner of the barn far away from the others. After no small amount of thinking, only one conclusion came to mind.

* * *

Red sat alone in his office trying to take care of a few tasks that did not involve the Four Horsemen. He struggled to keep his mind on the documents in front of him even before his cell started to ring. Red grumbled expletives as he grabbed the phone. It once again displayed the Colorado number, and Red's guts clinched.

"What do you want, Scar?"

"A little love and understanding would be nice, Red. Oh, and, uh, two hundred and eighty thousand bucks."

Red made his living counting money, and didn't have to do the math. "I wondered why that didn't come up in our last conversation."

"Well, Red, truth is, I am a very dangerous man, but I do fuck up from time to time."

Red smiled as he pointed out, "It's up to Kadie Rubottom to get the rest of the money to you. You made the deal with Bo, who acted as her agent."

"Now that is some complicated shit Mr. Banker Man, and you know it ain't going to happen. So, let's simplify this situation. When those four show up, if they show up, just make sure they have the money with them."

Red laughed at the response and a realization. "Scar, you're just not real bright, are you?"

It took a few seconds, but Scar replied, "You don't want to fucking piss me off, Red."

"No, I really don't, but I do want to point something out to you. See, Scar, your logic is eschewed. Here's what you're saying, 'You four ol' boys come out here so we can kill you. And by the way, you bring the money to pay us for killing you.' You following me here, Scar?"

Silence reigned on the other end of the call. "You still there, Scar?"

"I'm still here," Scar grumbled.

"Okay, you wanted to simplify the situation. Would you be willing to simplify it even further while applying sound logic and a little common sense?"

"I'm listening."

"You have four hostages. This is no longer about killing for hire. We're past that. Now you are simply demanding a ransom. So, I could come there with the money you want, give it to you, and you let the hostages go, and haul your asses back to Colorado."

Long seconds ticked by before Scar replied, "When will you be here?"

"Tomorrow at noon."

"Just you?"

"Just me . . . and the money."

Scar hung up without a goodbye, and Red pushed back into his high-backed leather chair and chuckled. If the others didn't agree with this new plan, it would work hand in hand with what Woop proposed and the others accepted.

Chapter Nineteen

Troy breathed a sigh of relief upon finding Kadie's car parked in front of her older sister's house. Margaret Stinney met him at the front door with the look of disgust she'd always shed on Troy.

"I'd like to talk to my wife, Margaret."

"I just bet you would, Troy Rubottom. You should have thought about that before you kicked her out of her own home."

"I really don't care to discuss my business with you, but I'm sure you already know she offered money to have me killed."

"And you blame her for that?"

Troy swallowed back his pride and allowed his shoulders to drop in defeat. "No. Not really. Not anymore. That's why I'm here."

"You know, I just might call my daughter and have you arrested for trespassing."

"Melody wouldn't arrest me and you know that, Margaret. Now I've eaten just about as much shit as my stomach can tolerate. Please send Kadie to the door."

Margaret opened her mouth to snarl something ugly when Kadie popped into view.

"Sis, I need to handle this," Kadie said softly.

Margaret glared nothing short of hate at Troy before turning to Kadie. "Don't you dare take no bullshit off him."

Troy exhaled a sigh of relief as Margaret stomped back into the interior of her home.

"Why'd you take the time to find me, Troy?"

"Well, Kadie, you are my wife."

"And I made arrangements to have you killed."

"Yeah, and I still don't fully understand that. I know I'm a hard man, but didn't realize I'd treated you so badly as to be killed for it."

Kadie leaned against the door jam and looked past Troy's face to stare into the distance. "I've come to believe, Troy, that I just might be emotionally unstable."

Troy allowed himself a chuckle that caused Kadie to turn her eyes back on him. "Hell, Kadie, you point out just one person in this county that isn't."

Kadie stared down at her bare feet. "So, what do we do now?"

"I don't really know. I just wanted to bring you up to date on a lot of things you don't know, and tell you what's about to happen."

Troy told her the whereabouts and particulars of Bo, the bikers, and the others. He explained the plan they'd adopted from Woop. Through it all, he watched her face display a wide range of sorrowful emotions. When he finished talking, Kadie stepped out of the doorway and moved within a foot of him.

"Sounds like you could end up dead after all, Troy."

The tone in her voice depicted sincere concern, but Troy needed confirmation. "I damn sure don't intend to, but need to know, Kadie . . . is that truly what you'd want to happen?"

Tears filled her eyes. "I don't know what I want Troy, but I know now what I don't want. I don't want you dead. That would not make me . . . *happy.*"

Troy started picking at the calluses of his right hand with the index finger of his left. "What changed your mind?"

"Two nights ago, when you kicked me out, I heard you crying in the living room."

Troy pulled off his cowboy hat, closed his eyes, and rubbed at his forehead. "Yeah, well, uh . . . don't know what to say about that."

"Don't have to say nothing at all. What do you want me to do, Troy?"

Troy remained standing with his hat literally in his hand. "If I make it back home when all is said and done, I'd like to find you there waiting for me."

"I'll be there, Troy."

Troy nodded his head and stepped off the porch. He turned back after a few feet and put his hat back on his head. "When I see you again, I'll do my very damned best to help you find happiness."

* * *

Woop looked at the number displayed on his ringing phone and quickly pulled his truck to the side of the road. "Damn, Marvin, about time you called," he huffed into the phone.

"Sorry, Mr. Conwoop, couldn't afford to take chances. Scar has had me watching the others. They took Bo's gun, but let me keep mine."

"We know all about that, Marvin. Is there anything else I need to know?"

"This is just a gut feeling, sir, but I expect if they can kill you all, then they'll kill us too."

"Speaking of which, how are they armed?"

"All four of them have handguns A couple of them have two each."

"Okay, listen to me, Marvin, some things have changed. There's a number of ways this can go down. I'm going to tell you what to expect and what to do."

Woop explained the possibilities and Marvin's role for each. He then questioned Marvin to make sure he understood. When he felt assured Marvin understood, he wished him luck and started to tell him goodbye.

Marvin interrupted, "Mr. Conwoop, I didn't have a chance to charge this phone before we left and we have no electricity here. I don't know that I have enough battery to make another call."

"Damn," Woop hissed, but then added, "Marvin, just do as I said, and after that, follow your instincts. I got faith in you, boy."

"I'll do my best not to let you down, Mr. Conwoop, but I ain't got no faith in my . . ."

The line went dead, and Woop chose to do something he'd not done in years. He said a prayer.

* * *

"I've come up with a whole new plan, boys. I hope you think it's a good one," Scar said to Thumbs, Stoney, and Sarge. "I made a second call to that banker, Red, and an obvious opportunity hit me like a brick." That was not entirely a lie.

Scar took what Red suggested, and twisted it to make it his own as he explained it to his crew. "That's it, guys. What do you think?" he concluded.

"Damn, Scar, makes perfect sense to me," Stoney grinned.

"We get the money and don't have to get our hands dirty," Thumbs said. "I'm damned sure down with it."

Scar turned to Sarge, and fought back from wincing at the doubtful look on his face. "Go ahead, Sarge, speak your mind, brother."

Sarge shook his head, "Damn sure sounds good, but also sounds just too easy to me, Scar. I have a hard time believing, from what we know about them, that they're just going to let us ride out of here with three hundred thousand of their dollars."

Scar grinned. He'd not failed to prepare for surprises. "I've made plans. We'll be ready for any possibility. We start by setting out perimeter guards tonight. Two of us at a time starting at sundown for four-hour shifts."

* * *

"This is about another stupid-assed thing to do, girl," Melody Preston said out loud to herself.

As stupid as letting Jerry film your twisted love-making?

Yeah. Much more stupid. Borders on insanity.

However, if she could pull this off, it would go a long was in countering the political tactics that would be used against her. She knew county voters would be most impressed with her law enforcement skills.

Just an hour earlier she'd sat and had coffee with her mother and Aunt Kadie in her childhood home. The story they told utterly amazed her. Mind boggling kind of shit like she'd never encountered.

"I don't really care what happens to your two asshole uncles and their other two asshole buddies," Margret Stinney said. "I just thought that you and your deputies should be aware of it."

No shit!

Now Melody was preparing to do just exactly what her mother hoped she would. Although not in a fashion of which dear old mom would approve. Melody didn't bother informing her deputies, and intended to handle it all by her lonesome.

She'd pulled up with lights out and stopped when she could just barely see the hulking outline of the old barn. As an adolescent she'd ridden horses here with her Uncle Troy. She'd spent enough time here to know well the layout of the property. That alone could give her an upper hand against four armed men.

Melody killed the engine and crawled out into the darkness. An overcast sky blocked out the light from the stars and quarter moon. The stark black of night would also work to her advantage. She walked to the back of her cruiser and chose an assault rifle over a pump shotgun stored in the trunk. With a round in the chamber and the safety off, Sheriff Preston took off in a tactical crouch.

* * *

Junior hoped Jolene would be asleep when he came in, but she wasn't. She sat on the couch just smoking and waiting.

"With those men in town, I worry so badly when you come in late, Junior."

"You should have stayed another week with your family."

"My place is here with you."

Junior had considered leaving the house the next day without even telling her what might happen. But if he didn't return, he feared he'd live with it on his afterlife conscious for eternity. Still, he really didn't want to discuss it tonight.

"Jolene, you haven't cracked a single joke since returning home."

"Oh, hell, you never laugh when I do."

Junior forced a grin. "Say something funny, and I'll laugh this time."

Jolene took a deep drag off her cigarette and exhaled it with a sigh. "Truth is, Junior, I don't feel like being funny anymore."

Junior took a seat beside her on the couch and emitted his own sigh. "Honey, I have something to tell you, and it ain't good."

His wife stiffened next to him. "Oh, Lord, Junior, you killed those men?"

"Hell no, that would be a good thing. Brace yourself, it's much worse than that. Do you remember that piece of land we own north of here with the big red barn on it?"

Jolene pushed off the couch and stared down at him. "I do," she said with worry building in her eyes like a spring storm on the horizon.

Junior got up as well to stand face to face with her. "The bikers are holed up there. We made that happen as part of a plan to get them. Of course, Bo's with them . . . and so is Cassie."

Jolene looked at first as if she might collapse, but spun and started darting around the room. "Why is she there? Is she a part of them too, like Bo?"

"No, Jolene. They are holding her as a hostage."

This time she did collapse, landing on her knees in the middle of the living room floor. Junior rushed to her side, bent to one knee and used both hands to steady her.

"Sweetheart, me and the boys are going to get her out of this mess. I promise you that."

She began to sob and rock back and forth, but Junior maintained a steady grip on her shoulders.

Between gasps for air she said, "I can't help but believe it was you and the boys that got her in this mess."

Junior used all the words he could think of to comfort Jolene before deciding she might feel somewhat relieved if she heard Woop's plan. Junior explained all, and Jolene's response proved he should have followed his instincts and left without offering details.

"So, what you're telling me, Junior," Jolene sobbed and gasped, "is that by this time tomorrow my husband and only child . . . could both be dead."

* * *

"Damnit to hell, Saupitty, "You don't have a dog in this fight."

"How in the hell can you say that, woman?" Gabe growled back at Sadie. She'd not taken well to hearing of the upcoming events at the red barn.

"Ain't your goddamned son or daughter there."

"Yeah, okay, but what about Clint and Bob?"

"You said you don't intend to do them any harm."

"And I don't intend to let those scum bikers to do them harm either. But I do intend to kick their wrinkly old asses around a bit when all is said and done."

Sadie stomped over to Gabe's recliner. "When it's all said and done, you could be dead, you stupid-assed Apache."

"Now why you always have to bring my heritage in on our stupid fucking fights? I don't constantly prod you for being a member of a 'civilized' tribe whose members are more white than Indian. Besides, I don't plan on being dead."

Sadie hissed through gritted teeth as she kicked at Gabe's legs hanging off the footrest of his extended recliner.

"Damn!" he groaned as the force of the kick shot up his legs to tear at his tender guts.

"See that?" Sadie shouted. "You ain't up for a fight, Saupitty. You can't even take a kick from a white looking Cherokee squaw. You move around like a man twice your age. You don't stand a snowballs' chance in hell of carrying out that asshole Comanche Woop's plan."

Gabe waited until he could speak without showing physical pain. "Don't kick me again, woman. Or I'll show you just how fast I can move."

Sadie spun around and started pacing angrily about the living room. "You ain't going, and that's that. I'm calling our niece. We'll let her and her deputies handle those men in the barn."

Gabe jerked on the handle to lower the footrest. "Bullshit! I ain't putting Melody in the middle of this fray. Hell, she could end up getting her ass blown away."

Sadie stopped and turned to face Gabe. "So, you're telling me that trained officers might not be able to handle those men, but you four old farts can?"

Gabe slumped in his chair and sighed heavily. "Please have some faith in me, Sadie. I can still hold my own."

Sadie moved up close again, but not in an aggressive manner. "I'm your own, Gabe. Take me upstairs and hold me. Show me you can take care of your woman. If you can, I'll believe you're well enough to stand against those bastards."

Gabe watched as tears formed in her eyes and trickled down her cheeks. He pushed out of the recliner and pointed to the staircase. In the most tender way he knew how, Gabe said, "You lead the way, my Cherokee princess."

* * *

Melody made her way close enough to the barn to see that dim lights glowed from within. Most likely lanterns, because she'd not seen any tall poles that could provide electricity. From this distance, she could hear no sounds coming from the barn. With her assault rifle at the ready, she continued to creep closer. She made it to within yards from the barn when a strong beam of light struck her in the face.

"Move another inch, and you're dead where you stand," a voice warned from less than ten feet away.

The bright light ruined her night vision. Melody closed her eyes and turned her head away. She could spray bullets, but the man with the light held the upper hand. Even if she proved lucky enough to get this one, three more still remained.

"Drop the fucking rifle!" the man bellowed.

Die here quickly, or God only knows what happens in the barn.

Melody swung her rifle toward the light, but her moments of hesitation had been moments wasted. Hard medal landed on her forehead. She crumbled to the ground, and felt her own handcuffs being applied to her wrists behind her back. The man standing over her didn't bother helping her to her feet. Instead, he used a grip on the handcuffs to drag her toward the barn.

"Lady cop bitch, you just fucked up big time."

* * *

Woop scratched at his thick head of short cropped and graying hair. "I thought you'd throw a fit. I kind of expected screaming and you tossing shit at me."

Instead, Rheta sat at the kitchen table eerily calm. But she did turn sad eyes up to stare at him. "Oh, it's not a good thing . . . our son now being held hostage. And I do have fears that this plan you came up with has a good chance of getting you and Bo both killed."

Woop pulled up a chair next to her and slumped his weary ass down on it. He placed one of his hands on both of hers. "Then why aren't you slinging snot and tears?"

Rheta shrugged her narrow shoulders. "Because it ain't what it was. Now, instead of you going to kill our son, you're going there to save him. It just makes a terrible situation a little easier to stomach. I want to cry, but what good would that do, Woop?"

"Don't guess it would do any good, love of my life."

Rheta looked to nearly smile. "That's a sweet term of endearment, and you've always been the love of my life as well. You know, all these years together, I always took some pride and enjoyed the excitement of being married to one of Caddo County's famed Four Horseman. But, at the very moment, I'm wishing I'd married a simple farmer, or even a store clerk."

Woop nodded his head a couple of times before responding. "I can understand why'd you feel this way."

"You were always hard on him, Woop. From the time he could crawl to the day he walked out of here."

Woop wanted to disagree, but knew she was right. "It's how my old man treated me. I didn't know any better. But, if I could go back now, I'd be a much different father."

"Well, you can't do that, Woop, but if you get a chance tomorrow . . . try to show him in some way that you love him."

Woop stood up and walked to the bar. He pulled a bottle of whiskey from the cabinet, uncorked the bottle and put it directly to his lips. He took several strong swigs before turning back to his wife. "Just for you, Rheta, I'll give my life for his if it comes down to it."

Rheta motioned for him to pass the bottle to her. He handed it over, and she took a gulp.

"Woop, you need to know that if either of you die, I'll hate you for it for the rest of my life."

He walked past his wife and out the back door. His Comanche ancestors prized one possession over all the rest. If given as a gift, it often proved as powerful medicine to protect a warrior in battle. Woop stepped into the darkness of night to ready his gift. His Comanche blood and soul warned that he needed all the powerful medicine he could get.

* * *

"Look what the fuck we have here, boys," Scar beamed.

Stoney and Thumbs rushed to meet him. Sarge had remained on perimeter watch. Scar used his grip on the handcuffs to jerk the female cop to a standing position. He then shoved her so she'd land at his soldier's feet.

"Motherfucker," Stoney exclaimed, "are there more out there, Scar?"

Scar laughed his response. "Apparently not. Sarge is searching now, but I think she came alone."

He used the toe of his engineer style boot to flip the woman from her stomach to her back. She still looked dazed from the blow he'd landed to her head, but conscious enough to be questioned. He bent low to put his face close to hers.

"What the fuck is it with you local cops? Have you never heard of bringing a back-up?"

It took a few seconds, but the woman did reply, "I have help on the way."

"Maybe. Maybe not," Scar grinned. "I'm thinking maybe not. The last *officer of the law* we dealt with had no help whatsoever."

The female cop clearly struggled to clear her damaged mind. "Who? What officer?"

"Great big dude. Came alone just like you. His name was Eastridge."

The name seemed to strike the woman like lightening. Scar threw back his head and laughed heartily before saying, "You knew him, didn't you? Guess you would, It's an awfully small fucking town."

He reached down and tugged at the collar of her uniform shirt. "Four gold stars? Does that make you a general?"

"I'm the sheriff of Caddo County," the cop mumbled.

Scar bellowed laughter again as he realized he'd struck gold. He let go of the collar, wrapped his hand around her throat, and jerked her to her feet. He pulled her close to put his face barely an inch from hers.

"Did the big fucker work for you?"

"No. Anadarko city cop."

Scar reached to the back of the Sheriff's head and fumbled until he removed the pins holding her hair in a tight bun. Lovely thick and red hair relaxed and fell to her shoulders.

"Lady Sheriff, first I'm going to tell you what we did with the big cop. After that, me and these two other romantic bastards . . . are going to do worse to you."

Chapter Twenty

It all went to hell in a blink of an eye. He was no stranger to the powerful impact and the searing pain of torn flesh that quickly followed. Only ten days had passed since he'd first experienced bullets piercing his body. One of the others screamed out in pain as gunshots rang out from seemingly all directions. Junior Pernell already lay withering on the ground, clawing at what remained of his face.

Forgive me, dear Sadie. You were right. I was in no condition to take this on.

He fell from nearly five feet above the ground to land face down. Blood filled his mouth as the mayhem suddenly fell silent.

Except for the sound of distant ringing.

"Gabe? Gabe? Answer your damn phone!"

Gabe shot upright in bed, soaked in sweat, he tried to clear his vision. "What time is it?"

"Just after midnight. Hell, I finally fell asleep and now someone is calling. Please answer your damn phone."

Gabe grabbed his cell from the nightstand. "Hello," he responded gruffly.

"Gabe, it's Red. Hate to bother you at this hour, but I'm calling each of you. I think there might be a different way of dealing with those assholes."

Gabe listened, and might have objected to the proposition, had he not moments earlier felt the sting of death.

* * *

Melody forced herself to stare into the terribly maimed face with the dead eyeball. How could she have been so terribly stupid? Her emotions raged and stark fear fought to overtake all, but she summoned what little gumption remained to ward off hysterics.

"Now, you are going to like this part," said the one she'd heard aptly called Scar. "Keep in mind, we couldn't have the big fuck coming back . . ."

He jerked her even closer. His lips nearly touched her nose and his hot breath seemed to emit the decay of the dead eyeball.

". . . So, he's sitting there naked, and we rubbed our dicks all over his face."

Scar bellowed laughter as realization struck Melody like a closed fist. "So, that's why he committed suicide."

"Well, I like to think so," Scar grinned.

Fear turned momentarily into utter rage. Standing before Melody was the catalyst of her ruined career and marriage. She ducked her head and didn't bother considering the repercussions before driving the top of her head into the grotesque face.

Scar screamed out in pain as he fell back a few steps away from her. It felt as if she'd crashed her head into a brick wall. The blow stunned her as much as it did Scar, and with her hands bound behind her back, Melody could not advance the attack. A sharp blow to the back of her head sent her face down on the dirt floor. One heavy boot landed in her ribs, knocking the breath from her lungs. She tensed for additional strikes, but then . . .

"Stop! I don't want this bitch passing out," Scar thundered. "I want her wide awake for what happens next."

The other two men each grabbed an arm and jerked Melody to her feet. Scar moved up close again. Blood gushed from a busted nose and a split lip. She only had a moment to revel in the damage she'd inflicted before Scar reached with both hands.

He used them to rip her uniform shirt wide open. He dropped his right hand to his side and brought it back up to display a hunting knife. Melody could not choke back a scream. It sounded like a siren and went on and on while he used the knife to cut the small strip of elastic between the cups of her bra. Her suddenly exposed breasts prompted Melody to scream even louder.

She struggled against the arms that held her in place. She kicked out at Scar with first her left leg and then her right before one of the men placed a leg in front of hers to block her attempts at landing a kick. Scar clamped a hand over her mouth, and then put his lips against her right ear.

"I'm sure you've been told this before . . . you certainly have beautiful tits."

He kept his hand in place to muffle her screams as he started to lower his bleeding face. When the skin of his face made contact with her exposed flesh, Melody's knees buckled. Scar's men held her upright as he . . .

Groped.

Licked.

Nuzzled.

Sucked.

Nibbled.

When Scar raised back up, Melody dropped her head to look down at his blood smeared all over her breasts. She did not hear a snapping sound, but something came apart deep within her. Whatever it was apparently released a fog that worked its way up to her mind to provide a numbing effect.

Scar nodded his head to the right as he slowly started undoing his belt and jeans. "Take her into one of those horse stalls, and strip her down naked."

Melody thanked God for the fog.

* * *

"Aren't you going to do a goddamned thing?" Clint shouted.

Marvin could not see into the horse stall, but felt unable to remove his eyes from that spot. Stoney had tied Bob's hands and feet some hours earlier after the old cowboy tried to bolt for an exit. Still gagged, Bob now rolled around on the floor trying to break free from the ropes around his wrists and ankles, screaming muffled objections Marvin could not make out. Stoney had also thought it wise to tie the hands and feet of both Bo and Cassie, but didn't bother doing so to the mild-mannered Clint.

"Yeah, big man," Bo grinned up at him. "You got a gun, but no balls to use it."

Cassie sat with her head between her knees sobbing.

Clint struggled to his feet and moved up close to Marvin. "Damn you, that's little Melody Preston. You do something or, by God, I will."

Marvin took too long turning his eyes from the stall to look at Clint. With a quickness and agility Marvin would have thought impossible, Clint reached and grabbed the automatic from Marvin's waistband. Marvin reached to get it back, and Clint struck him in the face with it. Marvin stumbled backwards, but didn't fall. It took him only a second or two to shake it off, but in those mere moments, he saw Scar step out of the stall and Clint hobbling toward him with the gun raised. Marvin took off in a run to stop Clint, but Bo extended his legs and tripped him. Marvin stumbled and fell face forward. From that position he heard the single shot ring out.

He jumped up and observed Scar still holding a pointed gun, and Clint lying on the floor. He rushed to Clint and dropped to a knee. The bullet had struck him in the chest, and Clint gasped for air.

"That kind of shit just ain't right," Clint mumbled, turning glazy eyes up at Marvin. "I had to at least try." Clint stopped breathing, but his eyes remained locked on Marvin.

"You can't handle just one fucking old man!"

Marvin pushed to his feet to stand face to face with Scar. He wanted to respond, but words failed to find the way to his lips.

Scar reached down and scooped up the gun Clint dropped. He thrust the barrel to Marvin's forehead. "Now everything is fucked up. Tell me why I shouldn't blow your brains out the back of your worthless head?"

Marvin stared into the one eyeball glaring hate, and words suddenly came to mind. "Fuck. Just do it."

Scar held the gun to his head for several seconds before dropping it down to his side. "Now, because I have a dead hostage, I might need you for more than I intended, but you fuck up again, and I'll make your last moments on this earth a living nightmare."

Scar thrust the gun into Marvin's hand and turned toward his two fellow bikers. "Thumbs, it's your turn to have at the bitch."

Marvin watched as Thumbs enthusiastically moved toward the stall. He turned and walked back to those in his charge. Bob now sat upright, staring at Clint's body. He no longer struggled, but tears trickled down his creased and leathery face. Melody had rolled into a ball on her side, and Bo grinned up at him.

Marvin took seconds to stare at the grinning face before launching a vicious kick. It landed squarely in Bo's face and he fell backwards unconscious.

"Grin now, motherfucker," Marvin whispered.

* * *

Melody lay on her back with her legs spread as the last of the four finished with her. With her hands still cuffed behind her back, she'd lost all feelings in her arms, but the vicious thrusts and poundings had caused the hardened steel to saw at the bare flesh in the small of her back. Still, she did not move to alleviate the pain. Hurting in that spot helped keep her mind off a more sensitive region that surely would be ripped and torn.

She'd not screamed out once during the ordeal, knowing that would just add to their pleasure. Now she struggled to keep from crying for the same reason. She tried to block all from replaying in her mind, but it didn't work and culminated in a flash flood of nausea. Melody quickly turned her head to keep from choking on the vomit that gushed from her mouth.

"Oh, damn," Scar's voice sounded from the opening of the stall. "I hope it wasn't our love making that sickened you."

Melody clamped her knees together and closed her eyes. Maybe he'd come this time to kill her. She refused to listen to the voice within that hoped he did. Dying would release her from physical and emotional torment. But being dead would rob her of any chance for revenge.

She didn't open her eyes even when she felt a hand grasping her hair. She gritted her teeth and fought back from crying out as the handful of hair was used to jerk her to her feet. She did open her eyes when Scar used the grip to move her toward the opening. Only one other biker stood outside the stall. He grinned and winked at her. Melody spit at him but missed. She then concentrated on moving her aching legs and watching the ground to keep from tripping as Scar moved her briskly forward by the hair of her head.

Then she eyed the still form lying on the ground.

Oh, Dear Jesus . . . Clint Avants.

Scar stopped and held her in place next to the body. "You being here caused this to happen."

"Fuck you," Melody hissed.

Scar jerked her around in place like a rag doll, but didn't say another word as he then moved her toward a tight grouping of four people. Melody knew all but one in the group. Bob Nettle sat tied and gagged with puffy red eyes. He paid her the courtesy of turning his head at the sight of her naked body. The thug Bo Conwoop and Junior Pernell's daughter, Cassie, were restrained as well. Bo's face looked swollen and the flesh around his eyes was starting to blacken. Cassie never looked up, but Bo leered at her, scanning his bloodshot eyes up and down her body. Melody didn't know the slender young man standing over the others. A gun protruded from the waist of his jeans, but he surely didn't look to be a biker, and he didn't leer at her either. If anything, he seemed embarrassed.

Scar tossed her on the ground in the middle of the others, and stomped away. Him and the other biker then walked out of the barn.

"Well, *how do you do,* Sheriff Preston?" Bo snickered.

The young man with the gun in his jeans quickly moved alongside Bo. "Take your eyes off her and shut your mouth, Bo, or I'll kick you harder this time."

"Eat shit, Purdy," Bo growled.

Melody assumed it to be a last name, and didn't know anyone of that name in the county. Purdy jerked the gun from his jeans and put it to Bo's head.

"I'm going to untie you, Bo. You try anything, and I swear to God I will shoot you in both legs."

"You ain't got the balls to use that gun, asshole," Bo snickered.

But Purdy did use it. He raised it up and then brought it down on the top of Bo's head. It looked to Melody as if he intended only to get Bo's attention, not knock him out. Bo screamed out in pain.

"You want more, Bo?"

Bo winced from the pain and shook his head.

Purdy untied the ropes from Bo's hands and feet before ordering, "Take off your shirt and jeans, Bo."

"What the fuck?" Bo moaned.

Purdy raised the gun a second time.

"Okay, motherfucker!" Bo blurted as he started to strip.

Purdy took the jeans and denim shirt and laid them aside. After he bound Bo again, he picked up the clothing and stepped over to Melody.

"Ma'am, do you mind if I put these on you?"

The kind gesture brought tears to Melody's eyes. "I would appreciate that."

Purdy worked gently to get her into the jeans. He then helped her into a sitting position and draped the shirt around her shoulders and buttoned it in place.

"Who are you?" Melody asked.

"Ma'am, my name is Marvin Purdy. Believe me, I'm here on accident."

Melody nodded her head before closing her eyes again. "Mr. Purdy, I wish I could say the same."

* * *

Junior heard the sound of an engine and walked out of his office to the main barn door. Johnny Conwoop had pulled up in his truck and pulling a horse trailer. Junior strolled to meet him, and peered between the aluminum slats of the trailer while waiting for Woop to get out of the truck. A single horse stood inside the two-horse trailer, and not just any horse. It was the mare Junior had wanted for so long now.

He turned as Woop came around the front of his truck. "With all we have going on, Woop, why would you bring this horse here to just rub in my face?"

"Ain't what I'm doing, Junior. If you still want her, the horse is yours."

Junior had known Woop most of his life and now expected the punch line of a cruel joke. "For what price?"

"Best damn price you'll ever be offered. She's yours for the taking."

Junior shook his head to clear it. "What do you mean?"

"I mean she's free. I'm giving her to you as a gift."

Junior stared hard into Woop's eyes and saw no sign of joking. "Why, hell, I can't take her for free. I'll give you the last offer I made."

"Can't let you do that, Junior. It'd fuck up my medicine."

Junior's face scrunched involuntarily. "Some kind of Indian thing?"

"Yup. Comanche tradition, and don't you say a damn thing ugly about it."

Junior was far from doing so. "Woop, is this your way of telling me that you think that one of us is going to die today?"

"Nope. But figure both our chances are pretty good of doing so."

"You haven't talked to Red, have you, Woop?"

"Nope. Haven't answered my phone today. Part of the way of preparing myself for traditional Comanche warfare."

Junior took the time to update Woop on Red's new suggestion.

"You think that can work?" Woop asked.

"Well, I agreed with it, and I know Gabe and Troy did too. I'd just assumed you had as well."

Junior watched as Woop considered the proposal. Seconds later, he nodded his head. "Much safer for our two kids."

"Yes sir, that's what sold me on it too."

Woop settled back against his horse trailer and inhaled a deep breath of the fresh morning air. "Junior, what have we come to be? There was a time, and I don't know when it went away, that we wouldn't think about letting any ten men rob us of not even a dollar. Now, we intend to let four walk away with three hundred thousand."

Junior chewed on the question a long moment before responding, "We each only have one child, Woop, but much more than three hundred thousand bucks to our names."

Woop shrugged his shoulders. "Guess that's about right. Well, get to unloading your horse, Junior."

Junior cocked his head and grinned, "After what I just told you, you're still giving me this horse?"

"Yup. See, my people have lived through a couple of centuries now of white man fucking things up. Ain't willing to bet we won't have to revert back to my plan."

* * *

Marvin paced back and forth between his small group. Bo and Cassie had fallen asleep. Bob lay on his side with his eyes open but looked to be in a catatonic state. The lady sheriff sat with her legs tucked beneath her, swaying to and fro. She'd kept her eyes on the comings and goings of the four bikers, but now looked up at Marvin. She motioned with her head for him to come closer.

"Yes, ma'am?" Marvin asked as he lowered to a knee in front of her.

She spoke in a whisper. "Could you please untie and take the gag off poor old Bob? I've known him all my life. I promise you, he'll behave for me."

"Well, Sheriff, they haven't told me that I can't." He walked over to Bob and released first his ankles and then his wrists. Before removing the gag, he bent to whisper in the old man's ear.

"Bob, Sheriff Preston says you'll be good for her. If you don't, they might harm her even more."

Bob nodded his understanding. Once free from all restraints, he crawled awkwardly on his hands and knees to plop down beside the sheriff. Marvin moved to stand close by them.

"He killed Clint, Melody," Bob sniffled.

"I know, Bob, and I'm so sorry it happened."

"Hell, I'm the only reason he was here. All these long, long years, we both feared I'd sooner or later end up getting him killed. Now that's what I've up and done."

Tears once again trickled down his cheeks.

"Bob, it wasn't your fault. He made the decision to try and save me. He died honorably. You need to take pride in that fact."

"I do, I certainly do, Melody. I hope you know, I was trying to get free to do the same."

"I have no doubt about that. You've always been one of my heroes, Bob."

Bob raised an arthritic hand to gently stroke her face. "How bad did they hurt you, sweet Melody?"

"They hurt me really bad."

Marvin winced at the declaration, and now so regretted not doing more to help.

"They tied me up yesterday. Thought I was trying to escape. But I was going for that over there."

Marvin and Melody looked in the direction of the pointed finger. Marvin couldn't tell what he was pointing at, but Melody did.

"You were going for that pitchfork, Bob?"

Only then did Marvin see the tool propped against the far wall next to a door.

"I sure was, honey, and if given a proper chance, I'll go for it again."

"I didn't even know it was there," Marvin mumbled.

"Hell, son, you don't need a pitchfork, you got a gun, but as that shit lying right over there said, you ain't got the balls to use it. You might have saved Melody from them if only you tried."

Marvin allowed his head to slump forward. "I know that, and I'm damned sorry, Ma'am, that I didn't try to stop them."

"Don't be sorry, Marvin. Me above all people now know that one going against four is a stupid idea. They'd killed you, for sure."

Marvin couldn't bear now to even look at her.

"Marvin, what accident brought you here?"

Marvin stepped over to insure Bo was actually sleeping before moving even closer to the battered lady. "Ma'am," he whispered, "I've been working for Mr. Conwoop. I kept in touch with him until my phone went dead. No one here knew I had it. He gave me a plan for getting these people out of danger, but I don't think it's going to work now."

"Marvin, when everything goes to shit, and it will, please promise me you'll try to grab up my clothing over there. Hopefully, my hand-cuff key is still attached to my belt."

Marvin made himself look her in the eyes. "I'll do it, Ma'am, or I'll die trying."

Chapter Twenty-One

Red turned his Cadillac Escalade off the graveled county road and onto the dirt road that would take him to the red barn. He glanced at the SUV's clock. One minute until . . .

High noon?

Red moved his tongue around inside a very dry mouth before mumbling, "Dear Lord, I know you don't hear much from me, but please don't let this play out like a western movie."

He idled the Cadillac down the very rough old road, working the steering wheel to miss the deepest of holes and washed out areas. He hoped that very soon the suitcase in the passenger seat beside him would insure him driving back the other way with a car full of passengers.

* * *

Scar anxiously brought his cell up and pushed the answer button, thankful he and his men had been able to keep their batteries charged by using the plug in the van.

"He's here, Sarge?"

"Damn sure is. Right on time."

"Is he alone?"

"Couldn't see anybody in there with him, but they could be lying on the seats or floorboards. No other cars in sight."

"Okay, you stay put just long enough to make sure none show up, and then get on back here. I'll call Stoney and Thumbs."

After making the two calls that pulled his men in closer to the barn, Scar turned toward the center of the barn and shouted out, "Marvin, he's here. You better keep your shit together, boy!"

"Don't worry, Scar, I'm good to go," Marvin hollered back.

Scar wouldn't bet his life on it, and hoped to hell it didn't come down to that. He didn't know how the bagman would take the news about the one old cowboy, but figured he'd consider the female cop a suitable replacement.

* * *

Red pulled to a stop about fifty yards from the barn. He put the SUV in park, but didn't kill the engine. He glanced around the clearing and didn't see anyone. The two big doors at the front of the barn were closed, so Red turned his attention on the regular sized door a few feet away from the big ones. Within seconds, the door opened. A large and rough looking man stepped out of the barn, but just a few feet. From his driver seat, Red could just barely see the scarring he'd heard tale of. He tried to control his breathing as he pushed the door open and eased out of the car.

"Guess you're Scar?" Red called out.

"Come closer, and there'd be no guessing to it," Scar shouted.

"I'm close enough, thank you. The money is in the front passenger seat."

Scar turned his head to the left, cupped a hand around his mouth and shouted, "Thumbs! Check on the money."

Red turned his head in the direction Scar shouted and watched a man step from behind a huge tree at the edge of the clearing. He carried an assault rifle at the ready. A distinct sound of a boot crunching ground sounded from behind Red. He spun around to find another biker standing not twenty-feet away. This one pointed a pump shotgun at him.

"Don't be worried, Red," Scar called out. "Not unless you got something to be worried about. They're out there just as a precaution. That's Sarge with the shotgun, be nice. He has no sense of humor."

Red had plenty to worry about, even before seeing the unexpected firepower. Marvin Purdy had told Woop the bikers were armed only with handguns. Red worked his fingers over sweaty palms as the biker with the rifle crossed in front of him and walked around to the passenger door. This man wore long and stringy blonde hair and a full beard. Every piece of skin Red could see on him bore ink. He slung the rifle over his shoulder, pulled out the suitcase and placed it on the hood of the engine. After opening it and examining the contents, he turned toward Scar.

"Shit load of money here, Scar," he shouted.

Scar left his position beside the door and walked up to Thumbs and the money. Red watched as he took the time to count each and every one of the large bills. Once he finished, he closed the suitcase and walked around the hood to stand face to face with Red.

"It's damned sure all there," he grinned.

It was difficult for Red to look the man in his one good eye without wincing, but he managed to do so. "Of course it is. I make my living counting money, and I'm no damned idiot."

The grin remained on Scar's hideous face as he said, "You've proved that. But, how understanding are you?"

Something ugly started tap dancing on Red's guts. "What do you mean?"

"I have good news and I have bad news. Are you the type of man that prefers the good before the bad or visa versa?"

Red took a second to insure his voice would not quiver. "Just give it to me straight up."

"Okay. We still have five hostages that I'm willing to turn over right here and right now, only the names have changed. See, uh, one of the old cowboys, the one named Clint, he got hold of a gun and intended to shoot me with it. It didn't work out that way. I had no choice but to shoot him dead."

Red choked back a groan. "Then how do you still have five hostages?"

"Someone decided to stick her nose where she shouldn't have stuck it. We now have Sheriff Melody Preston to throw into the deal."

Red suddenly felt incapable of not showing real emotion. "Oh, Dear Jesus."

Scar threw back his head and laughed, "No. He hasn't showed up yet. Now, are you going to accept her in place of the stupid-assed old bastard, or are we just going to have to kill you, and take the money and leave?"

Red didn't have to think real hard or long to reach a decision. "Of course I'll take her." It'd be up to Gabe, Junior, Woop, and Troy to decide what would be done about Clint's death.

Scar took a few steps and reached to grab the suitcase, before starting back for the barn he nodded his head at Red. "Then you have a deal. I'll go get the goods all this money paid for."

* * *

Marvin was positioned where he could see Scar when he stood just outside the door. When Scar started walking away from the barn, Marvin had turned his eyes on the sheriff.

"He's walking away, Ma'am.

"Hurry, go grab my uniform."

He'd run to where the uniform lay crumpled on the gun and grabbed the shirt, trousers, boots, and a gun belt that no longer held a gun in the holster. He'd been out of breath by the time he got the items back to Melody.

"Check the front right pocket of my pants," She'd ordered anxiously.

Marvin found the key and helped her to her feet, released the cuffs, and turned his back as she stripped out of Bo's clothes and scrambled to get dressed in her own.

"Can I have your gun, Marvin?"

He'd passed it off to her without hesitation.

"Hey, Marvin!" Scar's voice now called from the doorway.

"Yeah, Scar?"

"Start bringing them out two at a time."

Marvin so wished the sheriff would have said more before disappearing in the deep and dark recesses of the barn. She'd left him with no instructions and without sharing what she planned to do. Now it fell squarely on him to explain her absence. He helped Bob to his feet, and then Cassie. He would take them first while buying time to think. He passed them off at the door to Scar.

"Go get the other two, and hurry it up. I'll be back in a flash," Scar ordered.

Marvin hurried back to Bo, his mind racing faster than his feet.

"Looks to me like you're fucked, Marvin," Bo grinned up at him.

Marvin worked quickly to untie his hands and feet, and scooped up his shirt and jeans. "Hurry and get dressed, Bo."

"I don't have to be in no hurry, asshole."

"Bo, please listen to me, no one has to die here. We can make this work if you do your part."

Bo pulled on his jeans and slipped into his shirt. "Oh, I'm going to do my part." He then turned and sprinted toward the door.

"Scar!" he shouted as he bolted, "Marvin gave Melody his gun!"

Marvin didn't give chase. Instead, he ran back in the direction where Sheriff Preston had disappeared into the darkness. He'd not gotten far before he heard Scar bellowing an order.

"Thumbs! Stoney! Sarge! Get the fuck into the barn!"

* * *

Junior turned his head to look at Woop. "Damn. Gabe's new look sends chills even down my spine."

"Yeah," Woop grunted. "I'm a member of the native peoples, and he's making my preparations for battle feel inadequate."

"Hey!" Troy hollered, "There's a car in that thicket over there."

The four of them converged on the abandoned car at the same time.

"Oh, fuck," Gabe blurted, "That's Melody's cruiser."

Junior didn't have time to draw conclusions before Troy whipped out his cell.

"I'm going to try and call her. See what the fuck is going on," Troy said.

Junior took the initiative to search inside the car. "The keys are still in the ignition."

"She ain't answering her damned phone," Troy advised.

"I'm calling the Sheriff's Department," Gabe said as he too produced a cell.

Junior used the keys to open the trunk. He knew about the hardware that county officers kept stored there. "Her shotgun and AR-15 are gone," he informed the others.

All turned to look at Gabe as he talked into his phone, and then paused to listen. Moments later, he tucked the phone back into a front pocket of his jeans.

"Ain't good news, boys. Dispatch says they've being trying to contact her for hours. Can't get her to answer her cell or home phone. Deputies are out searching for her now."

Junior's already profound fear for his daughter's life suddenly spiked to near panic state that he couldn't keep from sounding in his voice. "If all went well, we should have heard from Red by now."

Woop pulled in close to the others. "It's back to my plan now, fellers. I suggest we get to it."

Junior damn sure felt no need for further persuasion.

* * *

Marvin crouched in the corner of a feed bin behind a partially closed door that hung only on one hinge. Most of the planks of the door had long ago rotted away. Both hands clutched the pitchfork Bob had pointed out hours earlier. Because of the door's poor condition, he could more clearly hear Scar barking commands.

"We need more fucking light in here. Rip those things off the windows."

Up to now, the dark had offered Marvin what little hope he had. The old barn had lots of windows. Upon first entering the structure, and looking for possible avenues of escape, he'd noted how inside shutters had been nailed closed with strips of lumber. He cringed and listened at the creaking and moaning of old wood as Scar and his men pounded to dislodge the boards.

And still, he had no idea where the Sheriff might be. Parts of him hoped she'd made it safely out. The remaining parts longed to hear a sudden firing of the gun he'd provided.

"Motherfucker!"

Marvin had been around them long enough to distinguish their voices. It was Stoney who bellowed out in apparent surprise. Marvin then heard the pounding of running boots.

"Son of a bitch!" Scar cried out.

"Scar!" Sarge shouted, sounding extremely excited. "I bet I'm seeing the same thing out this window!"

"Fuck! They must have us surrounded!"

Scar's summation caused Marvin to drop his head, close his eyes, and thank God.

* * *

Scar slumped below the window and tried to clear his thinking. "Never seen nothing like that," he grumbled to Stoney.

"Looks like shit out of a western movie," Stoney agreed. "What do we do?"

"Only thing we can do," Scar said. "When they start shooting, we shoot back."

Suddenly, a loud and guttural chanting sounded from outside the window. Scar turned his head to look at Bo Conwoop as he paced back and forth by the door. "Get your ass over here, Bo, and look out this window. Tell me who the hell that is on that horse."

Bo trotted over and carefully peaked through the window. "Fuck, Scar, ain't never seen him painted up like that, but that long hair down on his shoulders, he normally wears in a braid. That has to be Gabe Saupitty."

"What's that shit on his face, man?" Scar asked.

Bo dropped to a knee beside Scar. "Fucking war paint, and that noise he's making is a war cry. Scar, you give me a gun, and I'll fight with you. My ass is fucked either way it goes."

If Bo had not earlier sounded the alarm, Scar would most likely been ambushed by the sheriff. "Thumbs!" Scar shouted, "You got the rifle. Bo's coming to get one of your handguns."

Bo started to move, but Scar grabbed him by the arm. "I have a special assignment for you. I want you to search this barn. If they're still here, I expect you to take care of that bitch sheriff, and that other bitch Marvin."

"Bo grinned. "My pleasure, Scar."

"Scar," Sarge shouted, "Best I can determine all four are here on horseback. They've got us surrounded, and all four have Winchesters."

Scar nodded his head, and forced a chuckle. "Okay, boys, they want to play cowboys and Indians. They're fucked. They're out in the open, and we're behind cover."

To prove his point, Scar jumped to his feet and took aim at the wailing savage.

* * *

Red crouched behind the Escalade with Cassie and Bob. Before the biker with the shotgun headed into the barn, he'd stuck the barrel of the gun to Red's forehead and demanded that Red give him his cell phone. Red had no choice but to comply. Then the man had reached in and killed the engine and removed the keys. At the moment all he could do was take cover and wait.

"I want to do my part in this fray, Red. I know you didn't come here without a gun. Where is it?" Bob piped up.

"It's in the small of my back, Bob, and for now, that's where it's staying."

Red could hear near frantic shouting from inside the barn, and certainly understood why. He'd moved around at the back of the SUV peeking from different points, and saw the boys come thundering in on fast moving horses. With cowboy hats pulled low, Winchesters held high in one hand, and black dusters fanned out behind them like long capes, three of the four made one hell of an impression of impending doom for the bikers. The fourth, Gabe, didn't have a hat or long coat, but with his white-washed painted face embellished with black lightning bolts down both cheeks, and his long black hair whipping in the wind, he surely struck a chord of terror for the intended victims. Although Red's guts felt tied in knots, he could not help but grin when Gabe let go with his war cry.

Gabe still chanted, hooped and hollered, but two gunshots rang out, and his ancient ritual of preparation fell silent. His horse wheeled about and reared up. Gabe dropped his rifle to grab the right side of his torso. Red simultaneously observed the blood that spouted from the horse's neck and Gabe's side. The horse fell, pinning Gabe beneath it.

"NOOOOOO!" Red bellowed as he reached to the small of his back to retrieve the semiautomatic Smith and Wesson. He started bringing the gun out and up, when it was jerked from his hand.

Bob took off toward Gabe in the only form of running he could manage. He aimed and fired several times in the direction of the barn as he moved. In unison, Junior, Troy, and Woop let go with their Winchesters.

Red shouted both curses and encouragement at Bob as he continued foreword in a half limping and half stumbling kind of jog. Chunks of wood splintered from the old barn as sheets of lead tore and ripped. Red could see muzzle flashes from the windows that gave evidence of the men inside shooting back.

"Can you see my dad?" Carrie screamed.

"He must be on the far end of the barn . . ." Red shouted back to be heard over the reverberating sound of manmade thunder, ". . . but I can assure you, he's giving them hell!"

* * *

Gabe's side felt like it'd been dipped in hellfire, but he quickly determined it to be a glancing blow. His greatest concern was having his left leg pinned beneath the horse. His surely dead companion seemed to be coming apart in bloody chunks as gunfire pounded the carcass, but it served to block the rounds trying to do the same to him. Gabe's rifle lay just out of reach, so he pulled one of the two single-action Ruger Vaqueros he packed, raised it above the horse's body, thumbed back the hammer and started returning fire. Then he heard additional gunfire coming from his right side, and it seemed to serve in slowing down the bullets hitting his horse.

Moments later, Bob Nettle plopped down beside him, taking cover behind the dead horse. He sucked in great and wheezing breaths of air before displaying the gun in his hand.

"How many rounds does this son of a bitch hold?" he gasped.

"I think fifteen, Bob."

"Thank God, got plenty left."

"Damn, Bob, you shouldn't have . . ." Gabe started.

"Bullshit," Bob huffed. "Gabe, I'm so very sorry for all I've done to you. Now, I plan to get you out of here and back there to that tree line."

Bob put a shoulder into the carcass and started tugging to remove Gabe's pinned leg. Gabe used his free leg to push on the saddle, and applied all of his might to pulling the left one free. Surprisingly, all the effort paid off, and Gabe flexed his leg to determine it was not broken.

"Give me a minute to catch my breath, Gabe, and then we'll head backwards to cover."

"Bob, you just lay here next to this horse. I think I can manage on my own."

"Bullshit again. I've done you evil more than once, and I ain't doing it no more. Let's go."

Gabe felt himself being hoisted to his feet with a strength he didn't think an old man could muster. The gunfire from the barn kicked back up with a fury. Both men moved backwards. Bob shot back with the Smith and Wesson, and Gabe aimed and fired what few rounds he had left in the six-shooter. He could hear what sounded like super bees buzzing past his ears. Somehow, they made it into the tree line.

Bob assisted Gabe to the ground, and knelt over him. "Gabe, can you find it in your heart to forgive me? I loved you when you were a kid, and still love you now. Don't know how I ended up dealing you so much misery. Can you forgive me?"

Gabe stared up into age-yellowed eyes filling with tears. "You saved my life, Bob. All is forgiven. You were like a father to me, and I love . . ."

Then Bob's head seemed to simply disintegrate into mush as a bullet found its mark, sending the body slumping to the side. Gabe lay on his back and slowly started to reload the spent Ruger. Then he reached to fill his free hand with the other. With his eyes turned to the heavens, he blinked back tears and quietly said, "And I love you too, Bob."

He rolled to his stomach, pulled in several deep breaths and pushed to his feet. He staggered forward from the tree line taking careful aim with one revolver and then the other, following the bullets with a shouted promise.

"I will kill you now, motherfucker! Then I will kill you again in fucking hell!"

* * *

"Thumbs! Get over here with that rifle," Scar shouted to be heard over the gunfire. "I need to reload. The fucking painted Indian is charging. Drop his ass!"

Stoney had left Scar seconds earlier to return fire from another window. Scar felt certain he'd hit the old man, which apparently pissed off the Indian that Scar wounded with one of two lucky shots. The other had killed the man's horse. Thumbs ran toward Scar as he fumbled to put shells in the magazine of his semiautomatic.

"Fuck! I'm running short on ammo," Scar said.

"We all are, Scar. Need to finish this quickly," Thumbs said as he stepped to the window and raised the assault rifle to take a shot.

Scar, on his knees below the window, just happened to look up at the exact moment a bullet struck Thumbs right between the eyeballs, causing him to collapse in a heap at Scar's feet.

Scar stared momentarily at Thumb's dead face before grabbing up the assault rifle. He raised it above his head and thrust the barrel out the window. Without aiming, he jerked the trigger until all rounds were expended. He then placed the useless rifle across Thumb's chest and before scampering away mumbled the only words that came to mind.

"Hope the fuck for better luck than you had, Thumbs."

CHAPTER TWENTY-TWO

Marvin remained in place even after all hell broke loose. Some of the zipping and zinging bullets tore into the walls that surrounded him, but none so far had penetrated. For terribly long minutes now, Bo had been calling his name. From the sound of his voice, he grew nearer to where Marvin crouched.

Please, Sheriff Preston, get to him before he gets to me.

He'd honestly lost any hope of that happening. If she were still in the barn, Preston would have by now taken action. The best he could hope for was a stray bullet finding Bo before Bo found him.

The rickety door to the feed bin dropped free from its one remaining hinge. Marvin jerked his head up to stare into Bo's grinning face as he thrust the barrel of a handgun to his forehead.

"Any last words you fucking traitor?"

"Bo, please, it's not too late to help the others take out Scar."

"You just don't get it, do you, you stupid son of a bitch? If Scar doesn't win, I don't end up a very rich man. Marvin, you should have chosen better dying words."

Marvin wanted to close his eyes, but couldn't. He watched as Bo's finger pulled the trigger.

And he felt no pain.

Because nothing happened.

"Fuck!" Bo shouted.

Like Marvin, he probably just realized that the hammer had to be cocked first. Bo's thumb landed on the hammer, but then he screamed out in pain.

It seemed to Marvin that he'd not consciously thrust the tines of the pitchfork deep into Bo's guts. Marvin let go of the handle, and Bo fell backwards. His hands replaced Marvin's on the handle. Both of his legs kicked as Bo squirmed on the ground. Marvin didn't care to do anything else but watch until Bo stopped twitching.

"Poor fucking, Bo. You ain't so good with dying words either."

* * *

Junior stopped his new horse behind a clump of trees to reload the Winchester for a second time, and with the last ten rounds he had. The sweat soaked horse heaved beneath him. The mare was all he thought she would be and then some.

"Just rest a minute girl," Junior said as he reloaded. "You've done a fine job, but we've got to go at it again. We got to get that son of a bitch with the shotgun."

With his gun again ready for action, he rested the barrel across the pummel of his saddle holding it by the small of the stock with his right hand. He reached back with his left and pulled the back of his duster up for observation. Just as he expected, he found it to be tattered by a volley of the double-ought buckshot fired from the shotgun.

"Damn if that wasn't a close one, girl," he sighed as he paused to catch his breath. "Hate to just keep calling you girl, but a fine horse like you needs a fine name. I'll come up with one as soon as we get out of this shit."

If we get out of this shit.

Junior readied the rifle in his hands, and gave the horse her verbal cues. She obeyed and bolted from the tree line like a bullet. He reined her toward the far south window on the east side. He closed the distance quickly at a break-neck gallop, and saw the man take aim from the window with Melody Preston's shotgun. Junior dropped the reins, and used the pressure of his legs and spurs to guide the horse.

The shotgun fired, and missed. Junior held his fire, wanting as close as he could get. He saw the man work the pump to eject the shell and chamber another. Junior took his first shot, and missed, but it hit close enough to make the man duck for cover. Junior had already levered another round and cocked the hammer when the man stood to place another shot. Junior took careful aim, but hesitated one moment too long before pulling the trigger.

Junior had been kicked by horses and ran over by bulls, but he never felt anything with such force as that which now collided with his chest. His arms fell limp and his boots came out of the stirrups, he felt himself going backward and over the cantle of his saddle, knowing his impact with the ground would be horrendous.

But after that point, Junior never felt a thing. The deep darkness had already consumed him.

* * *

Woop saw Junior take the blast square in the chest, and gritted his teeth as Junior tumbled from the back of his galloping horse.

When Junior hit the ground and didn't move another inch, Woop shouted at the man with the shotgun, "You killed Junior! Now, it's your turn, motherfucker!"

He wheeled his horse, applied his spurs, and galloped straight toward the window harboring Junior's murderer. He got off one round and then another, making the man with the shotgun move away from the window. At that very moment he pulled back hard on the reins. Woop jumped from the saddle and fell to one knee to take careful aim.

When the man showed his face again. Woop put a bullet in it.

* * *

"SARGE!" Scar screamed as he saw his most competent man hit the ground. Scar ran to him and stared down at what remained of his head. He spun in desperation.

"Stoney! Where the fuck are you?"

"Over here, Scar," Stoney called from the far side of the barn. "Taking on two of them now. Only have a few rounds left."

Scar scooped up the shotgun and searched Sarge's leather vest to find what few shells still remained. He then ran over to Stoney.

"You take this shotgun and run out the front door. Go to the left and draw them to you. I'll shoot them from the closest window."

Stoney turned wide eyes upon him. "Fuck that, Scar. You run out there and I'll shoot from the window."

It'd been such a long day, and all had gone to shit. Stoney's refusal to obey a command proved to be just the last straw. Scar raised the Colt .45 he held in his left hand, and put two rounds in Stoney's chest.

"Fuck that? No, fuck you Stoney."

The sudden sound of Marvin Purdy's shouting voice brought Scar back to what little senses he held intact.

"Only one still standing!" Marvin bellowed out a window. "All dead but Scar!"

Marvin stood not thirty yards from Scar. Scar raised the Colt and took aim, but immediately realized Marvin could do him more good alive than dead.

* * *

"Scar is the only one still alive!" Marvin shouted again out the window, before grabbing the sill of the head-high window with both hands. He hoisted himself high enough to get his upper torso through the window. Then he felt the set of hands grab his legs.

"Get your fucking ass back in here!" Scar thundered.

Marvin kicked and squirmed and managed to twist enough to one side to pull Bo's gun from his waistband. He cocked it with his thumb, but Scar was winning in the tug-of-war game. Marvin threw both hands out to brace his arms to the outside walls. Suddenly he caught a glimpse to his right of a cowboy hat and a long coat. At that moment, Scar gave a tremendous tug, and Marvin's right index finger accidently pulled the trigger.

Marvin's right ear ringed from the blast, but as he fell back through the window, he heard a man bellow in pain.

I just shot one of the Four Horsemen.

Nothing else mattered at that point. He didn't even care to raise a hand to block the heavy gun that came crashing down on his forehead.

* * *

Red heard Troy's voice calling for the others to hold their fire. He stepped around the back of the SUV to see Troy starting to circle the barn at a gallop holding his rifle in one hand over his head.

"Hold your fire! Stop shooting!"

He rode up to Red and reined his horse to a halt. Troy swung out of the saddle and handed the reins to Red.

"Marvin Purdy is shouting that they're all dead except Scar. Hold my horse, Red. I'm going to walk alongside the barn up to the window he's shouting from."

Troy leaned his rifle against Red's Cadillac and pulled a handgun from its holster before starting off in a run toward the barn. Red watched him disappear around the corner just as Woop rode up.

"What the fuck's happening, Red?"

"Red said he heard Purdy shouting all were dead except Scar."

Woop's facial expression darkened. "What about Bo?"

Red shook his head. "Don't know, Woop."

Then a single shot rang out from the far side of the barn.

* * *

Troy lay on his back staring up at the blue skies. He could feel the blood gushing through his fingers that gripped the entry wound in his upper abdomen. He didn't know how long he lay there before realizing Woop was kneeling at his side.

"Want to get you to cover, Troy, but don't know that I should move you."

Troy tried to focus on Woop's face, but couldn't. "Don't matter, old pard. Ain't got but a minute or two left in me either way it goes."

"You don't seem to be in much pain. So, just hang in here with me, Troy."

"Hurt like holy hell at first, but don't feel a thing now. Must have severed my spine. How are the others?"

"Gabe is still on his feet, but hit. Junior's dead. I saw him take a shotgun blast to the chest."

Just pulling in air started becoming difficult. "Ironic isn't it, Woop?" Troy gasped.

"What's that?"

"It was an accident, but Purdy ended up doing what was planned in the first place."

"Troy, why don't you try and save . . ."

"Woop . . . tell Kadie I love her."

Troy heard a sniffle.

"I'll do that, Troy."

"Woop . . ."

"Yeah, Troy?"

". . . Don't see no angels coming down to get me . . ."

* * *

When they heard the gun shot, Woop took off on his horse in the direction Troy had walked. Several long minutes now had passed and it both relieved and worried Red that he'd not heard additional shots being fired. Another few minutes drug past when Red saw Woop coming back around the corner of the barn leading his horse. A still form was draped across his saddle.

"He's dead," Woop called out as he grew closer.

Red wanted to run and meet him, but his legs seemed unwilling to obey. "Oh, fuck, Troy," he moaned.

When Woop grew closer, Red could see the tracks that tears had made down Woop's dust covered face. Of course, he didn't comment on it. Red fully understood.

Red could not take his eyes off Troy's body until he heard the sound of approaching hoof beats. He glanced up to see Gabe riding in, struggling to stay in the saddle.

"That's the horse I gave Junior," Woop said with a sad tone.

"Yeah," Gabe moaned, "I caught her."

"Did you see Junior?" Woop asked.

Gabe turned nearly glazed eyes on Red. "Where's his daughter?"

"She's on the ground back behind my car. She's near comatose from fear."

Gabe turned back to Woop, and said just above a whisper, "Nope. Didn't care just yet to see him dead."

"I saw him from afar," Woop nodded, "Don't care to see another of our dead up close either."

Gabe nodded at the body draped across Woop's saddle. "Guessing that can't be no one else but my brother-in-law."

Woop dropped weary looking eyes to stare at the ground. "Afraid so, Gabe."

"HEY!" a voice called from within the barn. "Can you hear me out there?"

Red recognized the voice and responded, "We can hear you, motherfucker!"

"I'm going to open this door," Scar's voice sounded again. "If you shoot, you'll first hit Marvin Purdy."

"We'll hold our fire," Woop hollered.

The door flew open, and Red looked upon a barely conscious Marvin Purdy with Scar peeking over his shoulder, holding him upright with one hand, and pressing a gun to Purdy's bleeding head with the other.

"Here's the only deal I'll make," Scar shouted. "Whoever is still alive out there, best jump in that high-dollar Cadillac and get the fuck out of here. If you don't, I'll kill this piece of shit right here and right now."

"Where's my son?" Woop shouted back.

"And where's my niece, Melody Preston?" Gabe asked in like fashion.

"If I have to shoot this one, then I'm darting back to do the same to Bo. He's tied and gagged right now. That sheriff? She made her way out the backside. I'm sure she's looking for her car to call in on the radio, but it's been destroyed, and the car's been disabled."

"What the fuck do we do now?" Gabe mumbled as he swayed in the saddle.

Red watched Woop turn his attention to Troy's body. All remained silent until he replied, "Let's load up and get the fuck out of here."

"That idiot probably don't remember at this point," Red grumbled, "but he took my keys."

* * *

Marvin struggled to remain conscious, but he did realize that both the gun to his head and the one holding him upright suddenly fell away. Marvin stumbled but did not fall. The voice that sounded behind him provided a shot of adrenaline.

"Now the gun's to your head, asshole," Melody Preston's voice said calmly. "Marvin, get on out that door."

"Go ahead and shoot me, bitch," Scar hissed.

Marvin took an unsteady step forward when he heard the same noise he'd heard when Scar struck him hard with the gun. A louder thud followed. Marvin grabbed the doorjamb for support and turned his head to see Scar lying on the floor, cradling the back of his head with both hands.

"Get out of here, Marvin," she ordered.

Marvin turned back to look outside and saw Woop and Red running in his direction.

Melody called out to them, "Boys, you can step up to help Marvin, but you won't be coming in here."

Marvin stumbled forward and would have hit the ground if Woop had not caught him. From what seemed a great distance away, he recognized Gabe's voice.

"Melody! What are you going to do?"

"Don't worry about me, Uncle Gabe. You best just get off that horse before you fall off it."

"You intend to arrest him, Melody?" Red asked.

"No, Red, don't at all have that in mind."

Woop was helping Marvin to the ground when he heard the barn door slam shut behind them.

* * *

Woop asked Red to help him get Marvin off the ground and back to the Cadillac. Once they'd laid him back down, Woop kneeled beside him.

"Marvin, what happened in there? What's Melody up to?"

"It was just terrible, Mr. Conwoop," Marvin said sounding critically weakened by the deep gash to his head. "Scar, and the other three, sir . . . they took turns raping her."

Woop heard Gabe let out a tortured groan.

"Sorry sons of bitches," Red growled. "Whatever Melody decides to do, can't be bad enough.

Gabe responded, "I wish I'd been there for her . . ."

Woop looked up at Gabe teetering on the mare. Tears were streaking the black lightning bolts on his painted face.

" . . . and wish I could be in there now," he continued before turning his tearful eyes on Red. "But you're wrong about saying she can't do bad enough things to him. She's half Cherokee. You got to live with a Cherokee woman to understand that."

"Mr. Conwoop," Marvin moaned.

Woop turned his attention back to the bleeding kid. "Yeah, Marvin?"

"Scar lied to you. Bo is dead."

Woop heard, but didn't want to believe. "Are you damn sure about that?"

"Yes, sir . . . I killed him."

Woop slowly rose to his feet and stared down at Marvin as tears started spilling from the young man's eyes.

Yet my eyes remain dry.

Woop did feel pain, but he felt it for Rheta. As for himself, all he could muster was guilt. He should have raised the boy to be a better man.

"What happened, Marvin?"

Marvin had begun sobbing, but now showed signs of fighting it off. "He wanted to help them. He put a gun to my head and pulled the trigger, but it didn't go off. I had a pitchfork in my hand. I stuck it in him before I even thought to do it."

Woop took several deep breaths before the right words came to mind. "Sounds like it came down to you or him. I do believe the best man won . . . *son.*"

"*Jesus Christ Good Lord in Heaven!*" Red let out in a near scream.

Startled, Woop jumped to his feet and looked in the direction Red faced.

Junior Pernell had just rounded the corner of the barn and was walking slowly toward them rubbing his chest with both hands.

"Are you man or are you spirit!" Gabe called out.

"Thanks for checking on me, motherfuckers!" Junior returned the call.

"Spirits don't use foul language," Gabe summed.

Woop ran out to meet him. "Damn, Junior, I saw you take a full shot of double-ought right to the chest."

Junior grabbed what remained of the front of his shirt, and ripped it wide open.

"A fucking bullet-proof vest?" Woop gasped. "Where the hell did you get that?"

Junior gave him a weary grin. "A gift from Craig Johns. He left it in my office the night he stayed to watch over Jolene."

"Well, that's damned sure a gift from the grave," Woop said.

"Still knocked the shit out of me, Woop. Just came to a few minutes ago."

Woop stood and watched as Junior walked on past him and right up to Gabe.

"What are you doing up there on Craigetta?" Junior asked.

"Craigetta? What kind of name is that for a horse?" Gabe asked.

"It was either that or Caigalena. Craigetta just feels better on the tongue. I named her after the man that saved my life, you awful looking painted motherfucker. Now get off my horse."

"Help me down, Junior, and when I get all healed up, going to kick your ass for mocking my heritage."

It seemed perverted that Woop almost grinned at the exchange of words and the sight of one hurting man helping another from a horse. But, Rheta still had to be told about Bo, and there was still Melody in the barn alone with the monster Scar.

"Oh, Dear Lord," Junior exclaimed. "Troy's draped over your horse, Woop."

And there was that as well.

* * *

Scar bolted wide-awake. He pulled with his arms and tried to kick with his legs, but his body did not bulge an inch. It only took seconds for him to realize he was bent and stretched over a heavy wooden workbench. His hands were tied tightly to the front legs of the bench and his ankles to the back.

"Get me the fuck off this!" He said through gritted teeth.

No response was returned. He craned his head to the left and to the right but could not see the female cop. He wanted to, but knew better than to believe she'd simply bound him only to leave.

"Where the fuck are you, bitch!"

"I'm in here, Scar," a voice calmly responded.

He jerked his head upwards to look straight forward, and observed the stall in which he and the others did all they cared to do with her. He fell into a frenzy of jerking at his restraints, but to no avail. Giving up, he clenched tightly to keep from shitting his pants.

"Earlier you said, 'Go ahead and shoot me, bitch.' Did you really think it would be that easy, Scar?"

"Fuck you!" Scar shouted. He heard in his own words a bravado that he certainly did not feel.

"No, afraid not, Scar. You already did that. Now, it's my turn."

Scar looked back up at the opening of the stall just as Melody Preston stepped out. She held a gory pitchfork in one hand, and his knife in the other. He forced his single eye to remain open as she took slow steps toward him.

She brought his knife up and placed the sharp tip to his forehead. He tried to lower his head, but she applied enough pressure to keep it upright.

"You ruined my life, Scar, and then you defiled me. I do want you dead, but a bullet just gives you a fast track to hell. I want you to go slowly."

She pulled the knife back. Scar dropped his head and started pulling in quick and shallow breaths as she moved to stand behind him. When he first felt the blade being applied to the back of his waistband, he bit his tongue to keep from screaming out. When he felt her tugging his jeans and underwear down toward his knees, he could not help but let his tongue free.

"Please, please, listen to me, Sheriff. Please just let me . . ."

"So, now I'm Sheriff? Not bitch?"

He felt a hand land sharply on the exposed cheeks of his ass before Preston stepped back in front of him.

She brought up the blunted end of the pitchfork's handle. He opened his mouth to plead.

Want me to beg for mercy? Okay, I'll beg and beg and beg . . .

Before he could, she crammed the end of it into his mouth so far that he could do nothing but gag.

"There you go, mighty Scar, get it good and wet. Only lubricant you can hope to get. I know you want mercy, but this is the best I'm willing to offer. You, and those other dead fucks, you didn't show me the same courtesy."

She jerked the handle from his mouth, and he gasped for air. As she moved back behind him, Scar started to sob.

"No, please . . . No! Don't do this . . . NOOOOOOOOOOOO!"

* * *

The louder the bastard screamed, the harder Melody thrust the handle. She did her best to rip and tear and destroy the deep inner parts of the man who did the same to her. Melody only stopped when the final scream fell silent. She left the pitchfork in place and walked around in front of the man to watch him taking his final breaths. Scar's one good eye remained open, and appeared as if it was staring into the hell that awaited him.

Melody removed the badge from her shirt and straightened the pin that had held it in place. She bent forward to look into his face and said, "You fucked me. I fucked you. Now, fuck this job."

She jabbed the pin into Scar's dying eye as far as it would go. He released his final breath with a mournful grown. Melody left the badge that now covered his eye and walked toward the door with thoughts of picking up the pieces and forming them into new beginnings.

Chapter Twenty-Three

Rheta lay on her stomach across their bed. She cried so hard that her body seemed to be convulsing. Woop sat on the bed next to her and gently rubbed her back. He'd told it all, and now wished he could find words to help take away Rheta's pain. He knew he would spend the rest of his life searching for such words, and he knew he'd trudge through the remaining years dealing with the guilt of not feeling the same pain.

He remained at her side until she finally rolled over on her back. He helped her adjust the pillows beneath her head, and reached to grab a box of tissues from her nightstand. It surprised him when she turned puffy and blood-shot eyes to look him directly in the face. He expected it would be quite some time before she could manage such.

"You know I will never get over this," her voice quaked.

Woop nodded his head.

"A large chunk of me died today along with my son."

"I know, Rheta," he said softly.

"What will I do with what remains of me, Woop?"

Woop closed his eyes, shrugged his shoulders, and slowly shook his head.

She remained silent for several minutes, and Woop didn't open his eyes again until she spoke.

"Is it true the man that killed Bo turned down the offer you made him?"

Woop forced himself to look her again in the eyes. "Why would I lie about that?"

"To make me somehow feel better."

"No. Don't expect anything would make you feel better, Rheta. But, if I knew of any such thing, I'd make it happen."

"I want to meet him, Woop."

"Oh, baby, I don't think . . ."

"I want to meet the man that killed my son," she reiterated forcibly.

"Okay. I'll make that happen."

* * *

Sadie was getting out of the car when Kadie opened her front door and stepped out on the porch. It was nearly a thirty-minute drive from the Saupitty ranch to the Rubottom ranch, and Sadie had yet to determine how she'd deliver the terrible news.

"It's over?" Kadie called from her porch.

Sadie waited until she was up on the porch with her twin before saying, "Yeah, Sis, it's over. I wish I . . ."

"And how is your Gabe?"

"Well, a bullet grazed his side. He's refusing to go to the doctor. Says all he needs is rest. Kadie, you need . . ."

"That's awfully good to hear, Sadie. I mean, not that he got shot, but that he made it home to you."

Sadie cocked her head to study her sister. "You already know, don't you?"

Kadie raised a hand to brush away tears starting to trickle down her face. "Knew the minute you drove up instead of him."

"I'm so sorry, sweetheart. I don't have the words that . . ."

"Ain't no words. I cursed his luck. I knew all along he'd not make it back here, but didn't tell him that. He said he wanted me here waiting for him. Said he would help me find happiness, but I knew he'd die there at that old barn."

Sadie reached to touch her sister, but Kadie backed away. "Do you know who killed him, Sadie?"

"Yes. It was Marvin Purdy, but his gun went off accidently. Honey, in his last words, he told Woop to tell you that he loved you."

Kadie nodded her head as the tears streamed. "Sadie, get on back to your man. He needs you, and you can't do me any good."

Kadie stood and watched helplessly as her sister went back in the house and shut the door behind her.

* * *

Brad Smith sprung from his chair when Melody walked unannounced into his office.

"Melody! What a pleasant surprise . . . Why are you not in uniform?"

"You'll never see me wearing a uniform again, Brad."

Smith moved around his desk and offered Melody a seat.

"No, thanks. Best say what I have to say standing up. But, please, sit back down at your desk. I'd feel better you hearing it at a distance."

Smith took his seat without questioning the request, but worry and curiosity clearly struggled to control his expression.

"You surely know by now about Eastridge killing himself."

"Of course. It's all over town. I'm sorry for you that it happened."

"He left behind videos of us having kinky and what I now consider disgusting sex."

"Oh my," Smith exhaled.

"That too will soon be all over town. To add to that, overnight, I was raped by four men."

Smith shot out of his chair a second time. "Dear God, Melody, what the hell . . ."

"They're all dead now, Brad. I only got to personally kill one of them. I ass fucked him to death with the handle of a pitchfork."

Smith fell back into his chair and brought fingers up to rub his forehead. "Damn, Melody, I'm like in shock. I just don't have words . . ."

"I do. I'm all packed, and I'm leaving here today for Tulsa. Brad, if you'd still have me, I'd ask that you be there in one month's time. You can reach me on my personal cell phone."

Smith's mouth fell open, but only for a second. "Melody, as soon as you walk out of here, I'll start closing or transferring every case I've got. I'll see you in Tulsa in two weeks' time."

Melody nodded her head before turning and taking the first steps of her new life.

* * *

Junior had asked Red to stay and have a drink out in the barn office once he helped get Cassie back with her mother. One drink turned into three.

"I guess, Red, I'm just trying to make sense of it all," Junior added to what had already been discussed about the day's events. "Troy one time used the word 'virtue.' I'd heard the word but didn't know the true meaning. He explained it to me. What I'm saying now is I can't find the virtue in what all has taken place."

"I'm not sure you should even try, Junior," Red replied before taking a swig of bourbon.

"Might be old Troy's spirit working through me, doing all this philosophy bullshit, but I need to sort it out. See, I did a horrible wrong long ago, and I wanted to right that wrong, but my efforts just brought death and destruction.

"If I'd never sent Craig Johns looking, he'd not brought those four back here, and he wouldn't be dead now. On the matter with Kadie wanting Troy dead, why hell, that Purdy kid never intended to pitch in and help Bo. So, Bo might have been stupid enough to take Troy on by his lonesome, and he would have just ended up dead. Now, both Bo and Troy are dead, and Melody Preston, I'm betting that poor woman is scarred for life. As for Bob and Clint, I don't think Gabe would have ended up killing them, but now they're dead as well. Ain't no virtue in any of that shit, Red."

Junior kept his seat as Red stood to leave. "Maybe there's no such thing as virtue, Junior. There's probably one man I ever knew deep thinking enough to probably make sense of all this, but now he's no use to us."

"Yeah," Junior nodded before pouring himself another round. "Because he's dead."

Red made it nearly out the door before turning back to Junior. "You know, it just occurred to me, that initially, all four of you were going to be dead. Now, three of you are still alive."

"By God, Red, that's a damned fine way of thinking. But it's going to take the rest of this bottle, and another bottle every night of my life, to help me see that as making up for all who did die."

* * *

Marvin sat in the passenger seat of Woop's truck as it pulled into the drive of the Conwoop home. The sun struggled to keep from dropping beyond the horizon, and Marvin didn't want to be here.

"Mr. Conwoop, I still don't think this is a good idea."

"Maybe not, Marvin, but some day, hopefully, you'll have a good woman. If so, eventually, you'll learn to give in to her wants and wishes. God willing, sooner than I ever did. That's Rheta waiting up on the porch for you. Go on and get it over with."

"You're not going with me?"

"Hell, no. Going to stay right where I am. And look the other direction."

Marvin forced himself from the truck and walked up close to the porch not daring to look directly at the grieving mother.

"So, you're the one who killed my son?"

Marvin dropped his head to stare at his shoes. "Yes, ma'am, but if I had it do all over again, I'd let him go ahead and kill me first."

"Why would you do that?"

"Because I'm thinking that how I feel right now will never go away, and I'd just as soon be dead. And, if he'd killed me, I wouldn't have been able to accidently kill Mr. Rubottom."

Rheta remained silent for so long that Marvin almost looked up at her.

"Woop tells me that him and the others promised to pay you three hundred thousand dollars, and that now you're refusing to take it."

"Yes ma'am."

"Look up at me, Mr. Purdy."

Marvin reluctantly obeyed the command. The intense look of pain on Rheta's face hit him like a fist to the stomach.

"Why would you turn down such a great amount of money?"

Marvin had decided the second this woman's son took his last breath that he'd never accept it. "It's blood money. No matter what I used it on, it'd never amount to anything good."

Rheta looked hard into Marvin's eyes as if to probe his soul. He could not fight back the tears he felt filling his eyes.

"Do you have family here?"

"I have a sister, Mrs. Conwoop, but her husband doesn't want me around. Both of my parents are dead, and I have an older brother I've not seen in fifteen years."

"What will you do with yourself?"

"I'm going back to California."

Rheta stood up from the porch swing she'd been sitting in and walked to the edge of the porch to stare down at Marvin. "Marvin, this is so hard for a mother to say, but I know in my heart, that had Bo killed you . . . he wouldn't be feeling the way you are now, and he'd had no qualms with taking the money. Even if that meant his own daddy being dead."

"I don't know, ma'am."

"I do. Don't like admitting it now, but Bo . . . he badly lacked something you seem to have in abundance."

"I'm so very sorry, Mrs. Conwoop. I just hope one day you can forgive me."

"Well, if you go to California, you'll never know if I do or don't."

"Maybe someday, a long time from now, I'll come back."

"No, Marvin. Once a man starts running from his past, he never finds the finish line. There's a little house out back. We'd always hoped Bo would live it in, and help Woop out with all he has to do. It wasn't in Bo to do so. If you want a chance to get your life back on track, you're welcome to stay there and work for Woop."

Marvin looked for words, but gave in first to sobbing.

* * *

Gabe walked gingerly to the back bedroom of his home. He knocked softly on the door before opening it. His mother lay on her back in bed moving her lips as if talking to herself.

"How you doing, Mom?"

Nancy turned her head to look at him. "Who are you?"

Gabe moved to the side of her bed. "I'm your only son, Mom. It's me, Gabe."

"You playing hooky from school again, Gabe?"

"No. Come to tell you some bad news. Bob and Clint are dead."

"Bob Nettle and Clint Avants?"

"Yes, Mom."

"Dirty no accounts, the both of them. Should have been dead long ago."

Gabe expected as much, and wouldn't have shared the news if he thought it would cause her pain. He also knew she wouldn't remember him telling her.

"Don't care about them. Where's Seymour?"

Gabe anticipated the question, and chuckled before delivering a pre-planned lie. "Don't you remember, Mom? He's over fighting the Germans. I'm sure he'll be the one to find and kill Hitler."

Nancy smiled fondly. "Now, there's a man, son, that you should have tried to be more like."

Gabe pulled in a deep and haggard breath, and let it out slowly through lips formed into a sad excuse for a smile. "Hell, Mom, I did okay for myself. Climbed to be one of the highest of the no accounts in this county. Yup, established myself as an aristocrat of the low-lifes."

And, by God, I rode as one of the Four Horsemen.

ᴀCKNOWLEDGMENTS

Because these contributors are all so very dear to me and equally important to the outcome of this novel, I've listed them in alphabetical order.

To Sheriff Craig Countryman, retired Oklahoma Sheriff, I can't thank you enough for telling me the story that morphed in my imagination to result in this novel.

To Henry P. (Pat) Scully of Scully Associates, thank you for producing yet another cover design that I consider a work of art.

To David Shupe, thank you for once again applying your amazing editing skills to another of my novels. Only you know how much I desperately need your services.

To Jennifer Sims, sincere thanks for your photography skills that lead to the production of the cover design.

About the Author

Keith Remer is a retired Army colonel. After thirty-two years of service in the Army, he taught various courses as an adjunct professor before buying a horse ranch. He has to date written twelve novels and is the recipient of the *International Indy Book Award for Best in Fiction* for his thriller, *The Hiding Place of Thunder*. Keith lives on his ranch in rural Oklahoma City where he writes his novels and tends his horses.

To connect with Keith, visit his Facebook page @KeithRemerAuthor, or his webpage: keithremer.com

www.ingramcontent.com/pod-product-compliance
Lightning Source LLC
Chambersburg PA
CBHW031935110726
47902CB00001B/186